CAPTURED SOUL

By the Author

Forsaken

Bitter Root

Buried Heart

Captured Soul

CAPTURED SOUL

by
Laydin Michaels

2017

CAPTURED SOUL
© 2017 BY LAYDIN MICHAELS. ALL RIGHTS RESERVED.

ISBN 13: 978-1-62639-915-0

THIS TRADE PAPERBACK ORIGINAL IS PUBLISHED BY
BOLD STROKES BOOKS, INC.
P.O. BOX 249
VALLEY FALLS, NY 12185

FIRST EDITION: OCTOBER 2017

CREDITS
EDITORS: VICTORIA VILLASENOR AND CINDY CRESAP
PRODUCTION DESIGN: SUSAN RAMUNDO
COVER DESIGN BY SHERI (GRAPHICARTIST2020@HOTMAIL.COM)

Acknowledgments

Many thanks to the great team at Bold Strokes Books for your dedication and hard work. You make this job so much easier. Thank you to Monique Mouton, my abstractionist, for your help with technical details and for your amazing artwork. As always, thanks to my heart, MJ.

Dedication

For MJ, forever.

PROLOGUE

I'm so excited about the lecture tonight. I can't wait to meet Sheva. Her work is surreal," Carlyle said.

"Huh?"

"Come on, Kadence. Her bronze abstracts are amazing. I can't even imagine how she comes up with her ideas. Just imagine how strong she must be. They say she designed her forge to allow her to work without help. It took three of us in my sculpture class to get one medium sized aluminum sand sculpture done, and her stuff is way bigger than what we created."

"Carlyle, you know you didn't take that class seriously. Tara and I did ours without help. If you weren't so stuck on fashion design, you'd be more connected to the other disciplines."

"You're probably right. I like making wearable art, nothing wrong with that. Sculpting intimidates me, but I still find it amazing. You'll come with me tonight, right?"

"I don't know. I have to finish my piece for the spring exhibition."

"Cop out. You can finish that painting tomorrow. Please? Come with me."

"Okay, on one condition."

"Yeah?"

"You come back to my dorm after. We haven't had a night together in weeks, and Tara went home for the weekend."

Carlyle sighed. "Okay, I guess."

Kadence's heart dropped when she heard the resignation in Carlyle's voice. They'd been seeing each other since March of their second year, but after the summer break, Carlyle hadn't had much time for her. She'd been fearing that a breakup was looming, and now she was almost certain.

She didn't understand why. She still felt as excited and emotionally charged when she thought about Carlyle as she had when they'd met, but she knew Carlyle didn't feel the same. It was an open circuit. The energy wasn't coming full circle. What was it about her that Carlyle found lacking? She'd have to be the one to broach the subject and it killed her. Maybe she'd ask her tonight.

Nahl Hall was jam-packed, not an open seat to be found, but Carlyle stayed positive and worked them around the room to the right. They found some leaning space against the wall just in time. The hall erupted in applause as the year's official visiting artist took the stage.

Sheva was dynamic, even from this distance. Her long, flowing black hair hung halfway down her back. She wore a black leather vest and cuffs, worn, baggy jeans rolled above her ankles, and leather slides with turquoise adornments. Her skin was alabaster, much like freshly carved marble, and her smile was a beacon in the crowded space.

She lifted both hands in a humble wave at her audience and waited as everyone settled back into their seats. She walked to the lectern and Kadence realized how tall she was. At probably five nine or ten, her height added to her over-the-top persona. The podium only went up to her waist, allowing the crowd a full view of her muscled upper body. *She's hot. Damn, she's hot.*

Kadence slid a sideways glance at Carlyle and noticed the flush of heat on her neck and cheeks. *I'm not the only one who thinks so, either.*

The lecture was interesting, all about lost wax casting and why the ancient style of sculpting was what drew Sheva to her craft. It was inspiring. Clearly, Sheva was devoted to the medium, archaic as it was.

The whole process was exhaustive. The sculptor started with an idea that they then built in clay on a small scale, called a maquette, then they created the same piece on the scale they wanted for the final sculpture using a wire frame. After making a rubber mold from the frame, using alginate, they poured in hot wax and rotated it to get an even shell, usually a quarter of an inch thick. Then the wax model had to be unmolded and wax sprues added so the melted wax had a place to go during firing.

The next step involved covering the wax model in a ceramic slurry and fine silica. Once completely dry, it was fired in the kiln to melt the wax and harden the ceramic. Finally, the molten bronze was poured into the negative molds and allowed to cool. When the ceramic was chipped away, the bronze piece was revealed and was ready for chasing—grinding off the sprues and rough spots.

It was way too complicated for Kadence, but it was a process that had endured since the Bronze Age, making it specialized and highly durable. And the more Sheva talked of her passion for sculpting, the more Kadence could see her words affecting Carlyle. She was charged with emotion. This could be a good thing for their plans later on, or it could be disaster. It all depended on how Carlyle felt about her. She hoped it would lead to a renewal of their own private desires, but she had to prepare for the opposite outcome. She didn't want to lose Carlyle. It would hurt. She'd had enough losses in her life to know that. But maybe it would make her work deeper. *A brooding artist is an expressive artist. Great.*

Suddenly, the hall erupted a second time and everyone flew to their feet. Carlyle was cheering along with the crowd.

"What did I miss?" Kadence clapped and whistled.

"Huh? Woo-hoo!"

"Why are we screaming?"

"You're kidding, right? Did you not listen? She's starting a whole new period with her work, right here at CAA. She's going to start sculpting figures. I can't wait to see them. And she's asking for models. I'm totally going to volunteer."

"What? But her abstracts are so amazing, why go to figures at this stage?"

"Who cares? She's ready for a change and she's making it happen while she's with us. That means we get to benefit from the experience. I'm so flipping jazzed by this."

The crowd noise slowly died down, and Sheva went on to talk in depth about her goals for her new pieces. It certainly sounded exciting. The thought of watching her work evolve was a charge. If sculpting were Kadence's thing she'd be beyond happy, but as it was, it would make for an interesting last year.

She'd graduate in June and step out into the art world to make her own name. That was daunting to think about, but it was happening. Carlyle would graduate, too, but she already had an apprenticeship in New York at a big design house. Kadence had secretly hoped they'd go together and share a place. Now, who knew? *Whatever. It is what it is.* She'd deal.

When they got back to Kadence's room, it was clear the night was going to be a good one. The energy from the lecture had Carlyle all wound up, and she threw herself into Kadence's arms as soon as the door closed.

The kiss was deep and full of promise. Kadence considered halting the moment, but it felt too good. She went with her feelings and gave herself fully to it. Maybe she'd been wrong, maybe they were still okay. She devoted the night to pleasing Carlyle in every way she could, to impress upon her, through her lovemaking, how much this relationship meant to her. How much she needed her.

When the sun rose, she felt satisfied and loved. She was where she was supposed to be and with the person she belonged with. This was right and good. Nothing could change that. She wouldn't let it. She slipped out of bed and pulled on some sweats and a hoodie to run down to the coffee shop and grab some bagels and coffee. She passed a flower stall on the way and picked up a single red rose.

She booted the door open and flicked it shut behind her, arms full of breakfast and the rose between her teeth. When she turned to the bed, it was empty. She deposited her goods on the table and went to tap on the bathroom door.

"Car?"

Silence answered her, too deep to be good. "Carlyle?"

She turned the knob and eased the door open. Empty. She was gone. Kadence felt the absence like a blow to her gut. She dropped onto her bed. It was still warm from Carlyle's body. No note, no nothing. Where had she gone?

Her phone buzzed on the table, where the bagels had covered it. She slipped it out and saw the text.

"Thanks for the night. Got a full day today, so I'll catch you later. Want to be first on Sheva's volunteer list!"

She tossed the phone away, not wanting to think about how quickly the day turned sour. She needed to finish her painting. *Suck it up, Buttercup.* Let Carlyle fawn over Sheva and she'd plod along, channeling her disappointment into her art. Ever since the new term started, things between them had been different. When they parted for the summer, Carlyle had been sweet and kind to a fault. Everything had been easy and they'd been inseparable, but now, there was always some tension. Kadence had put it down to this being their final year. She'd been busy with her portfolio, and Carlyle had been resentful of the time apart. She'd become snappish and irritable. *It's not like it used to be.*

She threw the bagels out, appetite gone, but she drank the coffee, needing its caffeine embrace. She'd think about what to say to Carlyle later. Right now she needed to move on, to produce something uniquely hers. That was something she'd always been able to do.

When her father left them when she was six, her grandma had given her a box of watercolors and a sketch pad. "Paint yourself happy," she'd said. Kadence had done just that. She'd spent hours painting that book. Color filled the empty spaces in her heart. She could ignore her mom's crying while she painted. Later, she could ignore the drinking, the yelling. She started using brown grocery bags as canvases as she ignored the men who filtered in and out of their lives. She painted. When her grandma died and things got really tight, she ignored her hunger by painting. When the bullying started at school, she painted. She could always paint.

Today's twelve-by-six canvas had a blue-toned field. She'd used gesso and watercolors to achieve a balance of tone and texture that sung to her. She slipped her earbuds in and hit play. The hard edge of the music meshed perfectly with the sharp planes of her heart. She let the music guide her strokes as she described her pain to the canvas and plied it with her disappointment.

Soon her fear of losing Carlyle washed into the canvas and out of her head. She was one with the work and it flowed effortlessly. She worked until her shoulders ached and her stomach demanded attention. She fought through it, feeling the burning sensation slip to the back of her mind. When she finally stopped, it was finished. Complete. She named it *Moonlight*, and walked away wiping the paint from her hands. As was her custom, she didn't look back at the canvas until she was as far from it as the room allowed. She turned and slid down the wall to take it in.

Washed in shades of cerulean and cobalt, the hint of blue white peeked out in an off-balanced circle in the upper right quadrant. The cobalt fell into phthalo blue in increasingly large wheels of color, highlighting the starkness of the center. It was powerful. She could feel the emotions she'd imbued the painting with wash over her. Yes. This one was good.

Satisfied, Kadence washed her brushes and cleaned her station. She felt the comfortable numbness that was as much a part of her as her painting, surround her. It didn't matter. Whatever happened, she'd be okay.

As the weeks went by, things became more unstable. Carlyle was selected as a model for Sheva and scheduled to begin sitting in mid-November. Kadence was busy with her senior exhibition work, creating more pieces than she had in the past three years.

The night of Carlyle's first sitting Kadence was working on her final piece for the show. It was a four-by-four canvas coated in layers of the palest magenta, fading to a cool white in the center. The upper left quadrant held a cross-hatching of black and cobalt lines set in angles. She called this one *Confusion*. It was how she felt about the whole situation with Carlyle. Confused.

Her heart ached with the weight of turmoil. She couldn't help the anger that flared inside. Carlyle had to know how this was affecting her. If she wasn't such a wimp she'd break things off herself, but the rejected child that lived in her heart couldn't do it. *Damn*. She grabbed the tub of gel medium and threw it against the wall. The plastic cracked and a splotch of gel splattered the wall. She watched as it slowly dripped toward the floor.

She spun on her stool and stood, heaviness falling around her like a dark wash of paint. Tremors started in her legs and worked their way through her body as flashes of her childhood came back. Things battering the walls, thrown near or at her…the yelling, rushing to her paint box to avoid an angry hand. She had to get a grip. Her

mother had always resorted to violence, and she wasn't going to let that happen to her. Her phone buzzed on the table. She bent to wipe her hands on her cloth and picked it up. Carlyle.
Meet me at Sprout now. We need to talk.
Sprout? Kadence liked the juice bar, but they'd made plans to have dinner at Armstrong's Pub with some friends. Why did Carlyle want to meet at Sprout?
She texted back that she'd need a shower first, but could be there in forty.
Not okay. I'll come to your studio.
What was this about? Not okay that she needed half an hour to clean up? Really? Kadence pushed away the thoughts of her mother and made herself go on with cleaning her brushes and ordering the place. At least she'd be ready to leave when Carlyle got there.
She'd just finished when Carlyle pushed through the door.
"Hey, sorry I couldn't head straight over. I'm kind of a mess."
"I see. No problem. I wanted to do this in a public place, but this will have to do."
Kadence watched Carlyle's body for clues. She was tense, her posture defensive. "Do what in a public place?"
"I don't know how else to say it, but this…thing between us? It's done."
Kadence reacted as if she'd been struck. She wrapped her arms around her middle, and tried to keep the fragments of their eighteen-month relationship from exploding outward. "What? Carlyle, what are you talking about?"
"You, Kadence. You and me. We're quits, get it? I thought you were going to be some big artist, you know? Someone who could balance my love of design with their flare of creativity. But you're not. These"—she gestured to the paintings lining the studio—"aren't special. They don't *live*. They're pictures of nothing. You know what I mean? You can't really expect to make it big with this kind of empty work. I'm going to be big. Mark my words, my name is going to be in the closets of the most fashionable people around the world, and I can't be tied to a might-have-been painter of rectangles. I'm sorry. I know that's harsh, but it's true."

LAYDIN MICHAELS

Kadence rocked back onto her stool. She felt like she'd been hit by a truck. What was Carlyle saying? Her work wasn't good enough for her to love Kadence back? The dig at her work hurt more than anything. Every emotion Kadence felt went directly into her paintings. Carlyle calling them pictures of nothing was a knife to her soul. Her paintings were full of her. Carlyle dismissing them like this cut deep. When they'd gotten together, she'd been so supportive, so complimentary. Her legs turned to jelly and her stomach threatened to bail on her.

"I don't understand. Where is this coming from?"

"I'm through. Sheva's work is alive. It breathes energy into the room. When I was with her I felt my whole world roll into place. She's who I'm meant to be with. She's my future. What we had, well…I enjoyed it, but it was dying. It's dead. Let's just bury it and move on, okay? I know you have to have felt it too. Right?"

Kadence forced herself to deny what she'd felt, not wanting to give an inch of ground in what she knew was a hopeless fight. "No. Not really. I've felt distance and I've been confused, but no. I didn't see this coming."

Carlyle's whole body straightened and then relaxed into what Kadence called her "brattitude," all elbows and hips, and to hell with the rest. She'd seen it a million times, but had never been on the receiving end before.

"I'm sorry then, but it is what it is. I've got to go. I'm meeting Sheva for dinner. Good-bye, Kadence."

"Carlyle, wait."

"No, it's easier this way. Process and move on, Kadence."

"But—"

Carlyle shook her head and pushed back out through the swinging door.

Kadence sat in stunned silence. It was for the best, really. They'd been drifting apart all semester, but it still hurt. It wasn't fair for her to dump this on Kadence and leave without giving her a chance to speak.

Carlyle's words echoed in her head. *Pictures of nothing, painter of rectangles.* The words were like a searing hot knife through her soul. *Empty work.* She had to get out before she took her pain out on her canvases. She shot out the door and ran back to her room.

She felt her anger rise like a flame on dry tinder, flaring through her. How could Carlyle say those things? And what did that say about their history? Had she been the only one emotionally invested? That stung, too, knowing Carlyle only considered her for the possibility of notoriety, and had never seen her as a person. But she hadn't seemed that way when they'd gotten together. Was it really all just a farce? Just a way to use her? *Just like Mom.*

She wasn't going to cry. She'd wasted enough tears in her life on heartless people. She stripped out of her paint covered clothes and flung them at the hamper. *Damn you, Carlyle.* She went into the bathroom and turned the water to its hottest setting. The water nearly scalded her back as she slipped into its flow, but it felt good. It made her body feel, washed the numbness away, and finally, allowed her tears to breach her heart.

CHAPTER ONE

K adence wiped her sweaty hands on her jeans as she walked into the ARA NYC Gallery, and tried to appear at ease and where she belonged. *What a joke. I'm in way over my head.* She ignored the butterflies battering her stomach and swallowed against the dryness in her throat. The galleries she'd been in before had been small storefronts. The place was massive. The scope of the place was daunting. The walls were as white as blank canvas. Big, bold paintings arched across the expanse, reinforcing her intimidation. *Why did I agree to this? My paintings will look like orphans in a place like this.*

When the call came that they wanted to produce her show, she'd been completely floored. She'd hoped to get some exposure, and the move to New York had been a step in the right direction. Her abstract paintings were her life, but she had yet to develop a following. She'd piggybacked on a couple of smaller shows, warehouse artists mostly, but this was going to be her first solo showing. She had no idea what to expect.

She walked around the first wall and into a larger, open area of the gallery. The space contained six full-sized bronze figures. One was a torso and the bottom half of a face, its features lost in folds of bronze, one slender arm upraised. Stunned by the impact of the piece, Kadence walked closer. Everything was in perfect proportion, absolutely beautiful. *It's almost like she's alive, like if I held out a hand to her, she'd take it. How did they do that?* The others were of the same quality, but different in what they depicted. One form was captured as it burst from water, the face missing above the chin. One was a faceless head resting on delicate arms, the lines of the body so lifelike that Kadence was enraptured.

The one that most captivated her was a hollow form, the front of a woman's torso, her chin and lips showing her pleasure as other female-looking hands cupped her breasts. It was so real that Kadence found her heart pounding, and without thought, she ran her hands down the smooth surface of the figure's hips. The bronze was cool, but warmed quickly under her hand. *So real.*

She snatched her hand back and stuffed it into her jeans pocket. *You don't lay hands on art unless you're invited to.* She knew that. She looked around, hoping no one had noticed her faux pas. There were only one or two people in the space, and they were engrossed in the paintings. *Thank goodness. Keep it together, Munroe. You may be a novice, but you don't have to act like one.*

Natural light filtered onto the seductive bronzes, and she glanced up at the large skylight. Two of the walls behind the sculptures were a bold turquoise, perfectly highlighting the bronzes. *Whoever set this place up knew what they were doing.* The color and lighting of a space could totally change the way a work was perceived. The color gave the statues a quality of movement that was understated. *I feel like they'll get up and move any minute. These are amazing. Whoever did these pieces is gifted.*

Kadence found a placard with the artist's information and her blood ran cold. *Sheva.* This was Sheva's work. Kadence drew a breath as the hair on the back of her neck stiffened. She was transported back to art school and the first time she heard of the sculptress as bile flooded her mouth. She'd tried to forget the pain and bitter feelings about what had happened. Her confidence in her work had been shaken after Carlyle's vitriolic breakup speech, and it was still a struggle to believe her work held meaning for others. Seeing Sheva's work again brought all of those insecurities to the forefront.

Why does she have to be showing in this gallery? It wasn't fair that Sheva would cast a shadow on her first big show.

"Ms. Munroe?"

Kadence turned and saw a woman in a tailored business suit, her blond hair streaked with waves of sunlight, her smile wide and welcoming. Her brown eyes were bright behind her thick black-framed glasses, and Kadence felt the warmth of her smile go right through her.

"Yes, that's me."

The woman held out her hand and walked toward her. "I'm Mallory Tucker. It's a pleasure to meet you."

"Ms. Tucker, the pleasure is all mine," Kadence said.

"Let's go back to my office and talk about your show."

"Great, thanks."

Kadence followed her to the back of the gallery where stairs led up to the office suite. The place had such clean bare lines that the stairs appeared to float unsupported. The suite contained a small reception area and two tall mahogany doors on either side of it. When Mallory opened the door, Kadence sucked in a breath. The office reflected the clean lines of the outer space, but its walls were alive with color.

Two long, narrow watercolors hung stair-stepped behind a glass and steel desk. Kadence knew those pieces. Those were Sanford Tucker's, the most renowned watercolorist alive today. *Tucker? Could Mallory be a relative? Or did she just like the work?*

"You like the paintings? Yes, they're the real thing. My mother, you know."

"I didn't, but WOW! They're amazing. Do you mind if I take a closer look?"

"Not a bit. Help yourself."

Kadence walked to the paintings. The long panel on the right was alive with orange and red mesas, a lone, white-clad figure in the foreground. The left panel was a perfect complement, where similar reds and oranges described coastal cliffs and deep turquoise and white were the crashing waves at their feet. *Absolutely powerful.* Kadence let herself be immersed in the feelings the pieces drew out of her. She must have been quite engrossed, as Mallory finally called her back to their task.

"Ms. Munroe? Come, sit down. Let's chat."

"Oh, I'm sorry. Amazing work, truly," she said.

She returned to the chair she'd been shown. Butterflies fluttered in her stomach making her queasy and uncomfortable.

"I can't tell you how lucky we feel at ARA to be hosting your first showing. You have some amazing pieces yourself."

"Thank you." Kadence was humbled by the praise. She wasn't used to people actually getting her work.

"I'm sure it's a bit overwhelming, but I want to go over our contract before we talk details." She pushed the form across the desk.

"This is a standard contract. We split sales fifty/fifty. There's a ninety-day cancelation clause, meaning you can't withdraw from the show, nor can we cancel during that time period. If the show goes well, we have the option to extend the contract, though the percentage will be up for negotiation at that point. How does that sound?"

Kadence thought it was more than fair, but she needed to know what costs she might have.

"That sounds good, but I have a few questions."

"Shoot."

"Who pays for advertisement, and what will that entail? What about notices and such? Can I invite people?"

"We'll handle the commercial advertising, papers, and websites. As far as notices and invitations, we'll send out a certain number to collectors we know might be interested. I can spare…say, twelve of the opening night invitations? Does that seem fair?"

"More than fair. I only need five."

"Great, then let's make it six and I'll reserve six additional in case you need them."

"And about opening night?"

"Yes?"

"Um…will there be alcohol and appetizers?"

"Of course. Nothing too messy, but mini quiche, wrapped figs and such. Red and white, flat and sparkling."

Kadence felt her gut cramp. She didn't have much in the way of disposable income. If she had to pay half of the cost of opening night, she didn't think there'd be one.

"How much do you think that will run?"

"Oh, heavens, you don't have to worry about those sorts of incidentals. ARA has contracts with local caterers. Cost of doing business. Relax, Kadence. May I call you Kadence?"

"Sure."

"The ARA is excited to give you a proper introduction. This is a business arrangement. I feel strongly that your work has a voice that's missing in today's art scene. I've confidence in my ability to pick winners. No worries, okay?"

The relief that washed over her nearly made her dizzy. She'd dreaded finding out how much the show would cost. She'd been prepared to walk out tonight a starving artist, but Mallory believed in her work. *She thinks I'm a winner.* Kadence signed the contract and slid it back across the desk. A grateful smile pulled at the corners of her mouth. She couldn't help it. This was more than she could've imagined.

"That smile looks good on you." Mallory gave her a wink. "Nice to see it there. Let's be sure you keep it until after opening night. Now, come with me and we'll talk about where your show will be."

She led the way out into the gallery space. Kadence looked down at the sculptures. They were captivating, even from above. So perfectly symmetrical. She turned to walk down the stairs when Mallory gently touched her forearm.

"Not there, you're going to be in the loft room. Come on." She walked in the opposite direction and rounded the office suite. A floating staircase ascended four steps and opened to an airy open space. The walls were a mid-dark gray. This would be perfect for her work. *I really hope I don't wake up.*

"Now I'll want two of your best pieces to photograph for advertising and then to place in the front foyer. Make people bite as they walk past. Great way to bring in new patrons."

"Okay, when do you need them? I can get a cab and bring—"

"Oh, no, that won't be necessary. I need them by next Friday. If you give me a time, I'll send the gallery van and our movers. They're fully bonded and insured."

"Even better. How about next Wednesday between nine and eleven?"

"Perfect. I'll set it up."

"Great." *It can't be this easy.* She needed to keep herself from believing this was real. She was waiting for the catch, for Mallory to tell her it was all a mistake, and it was some other artist she meant to contract. Her stomach was a ball of tension.

"Thank you. If you don't have any more questions, I think we're done here."

Relief like a strong wind rushed through her. It was real; this was happening. Now she was disappointed the meeting was over. She liked Mallory Tucker. "Oh, okay. Thanks for your time."

"Kadence, wait. Would you like to grab a bite to eat? It's on the gallery. I'd like to get to know you a bit on personal terms. I think it really makes those occasional bumps during a show easier to smooth out if we both have a sense of who we are."

Personal terms? All Kadence's defenses went up. This was a professional engagement, and she didn't do personal. Her mouth tasted sour. No way was she going to open herself up for this gallery director. "Uh, sure. As long as it's a place suited to my outfit, not yours."

Mallory laughed. It was a lilting, musical laugh that warmed Kadence and made her more at ease than she'd felt since walking in the door.

"Tiger Cry? That work for you?"

Tiger Cry was an eastside legend, the place all hopeful artists and musicians went for food and companionship. The owner happily accepted artwork or labor as forms of payment when you were really on the downs. Tiger Cry had opened at the peak of the Pop art movement, and the owner had wisely managed her early success to allow for her generous giving back to the community who built her business.

"That would be awesome. I love that place."

"Yeah, I figured. I love it, too. Come on."

They walked over, and Mallory talked about how she came to be where she was. Kadence was fascinated by the fact that Mallory had grown up in an artist's colony. She had a million questions about her experiences. The sheer number of artists who influenced Mallory's early life and her breaking into the gallery scene was astounding. She was blown away. When their food was served, she couldn't wait to ask questions.

"So, you lived with Frances Kornbluth? That's unreal! What was that like? I mean, living so close to so many amazing artists, and with your mother? I can't imagine what life was like."

"It was pretty isolating. I mean, there weren't a lot of other children around. My mom and her friends took my education in hand, but they couldn't give me friends, you know? I spent much of my childhood as my mom's accessory." Mallory's smile was slightly melancholy and she picked at her food.

"Oh, that's sad. I'm sorry. What about your father?" Kadence caught the subtle tightening in Mallory's face and wished she'd not asked.

"He was busy most of the time. His office was in Boston, so I only saw him on weekends. He died the week I graduated from high school. Don't get me wrong, there were good times. Mom's friend Jamie taught me to sail, and his wife, Phyllis, taught me patience. I loved living on Monhegan, but I was glad to go away to school in my teens. I needed to be with people my own age."

"That must have been culture shock."

"You think? That's an understatement. I spent the first year keeping my head down and learning the rules. It was the best thing that ever happened to me, really. I learned who I was, what I wanted, and how to stand up for myself. What about you, Kadence? What was your childhood like?"

Kadence sucked in a breath. Her childhood. It wasn't pretty, but it was hers. Would Mallory understand how her painting had rescued her from the nightmare of her reality? It felt too personal, too raw to reveal that part of her to someone she'd just met.

"Um, it was pretty uneventful. You know, public school, no famous people, just plain and ordinary."

"Where did you grow up? Do you have any siblings? What did your parents do?"

There it was. The question she dreaded above all others. There was no easy way to say your dad had left you and your mom was basically a call girl. What impression would that give? *Stick to the safe story.*

"I grew up in Houston, and no, no siblings. My grandma was the biggest influence on my life. She helped raise me, until I was thirteen. She gave me my first set of paints."

"I'm so glad she did. Your paintings are fantastic."

"You think?"

"Yes. The show is going to be a hit. I bet you sell out."

Kadence felt a wash of warmth at the encouraging words. It'd been hard to recover her confidence after Carlyle's words. She hadn't quite trusted that she was as good as her heart told her she was. With her words and her faith in Kadence's talent, Mallory had done more to help her confidence than anyone else in the past two years.

"So, tell me your feelings about the gallery and your show."

What were her feelings? Did fear count? "I love that gallery space. It's so expansive. I think the loft is the perfect place for my work. The gray walls will make the subtle play in light and color pop."

"I agree. I knew it would be the right place for you."

"Will the other artists showing be at my opening? I mean, is that the procedure?"

"Typically, we invite all artists in house to openings, in case someone attending wants to speak to them. We do a lot of cross sales at new shows."

Kadence's heart sank. She would be fine if she never had to see Sheva again.

"Why so glum? You should be excited."

"It's nothing. I'm just nervous." She wasn't about to let on she had personal issues with another artist. It could wreck her chances, and she wouldn't let Sheva do that to her again.

"No need to be. This is going to be good for you. I promise. Listen, I have to run back to the gallery. You stay as long as you like. Here's my business card, call me if you have any questions. I'll grab the bill on my way out."

"Okay, thanks for lunch."

"My pleasure. Let's do this again, okay?"

"Sure."

Mallory rose and held her hand out. For some god-awful reason, instead of shaking it, Kadence pulled it to her mouth and kissed it. She wanted to kick herself. *Why did I do that?* She looked up at Mallory as she let her hand go. The look on her face was hard to interpret. She didn't look disgusted, just puzzled, surprised, maybe.

"Okay, then. I'll have the drivers call when they arrive next week. Take care." Mallory turned and moved through the restaurant with an easy pace.

Damn, I hope I haven't screwed this up. Artists are supposed to be unconventional, right? The fast beat of her heart and the sweat that popped out all over didn't comfort her. *Why did I do that? I've never done something like that in my life.*

She finished her meal and walked back to the train, which she rode back to her place in Brooklyn. She'd managed to sublet a room from a fellow CAA grad who was spending a year in Vancouver. The fourplex had been created from a single-family residence in a choppy, haphazard fashion. The other tenants were nice enough, but they had very little in common beyond the shared bathroom and kitchen. The room itself was exactly what she needed right now. It was big, with a picture window and plenty of room to store her canvases. It had a mini fridge and a small counter with a microwave, which was just about all she needed. Best she could figure, it had been the living room of the home at some point, though no one had to walk through her room to get to their own now, thankfully. She'd made it her own and she liked the energy of the place. She was usually the only one home on weekends, and she could kick on her music and paint.

She unlocked her door and dropped onto her small bed. Why had she kissed Mallory's hand? She hadn't picked up on any attraction from her, she was just nice. Really nice. *And she cared about me. She wanted to know more than how many pieces I had for the show.* Maybe the kiss could be forgotten. She could just ignore that she'd done it and go on like they had been. Why not? Mallory wouldn't know how out of character that had been for her. She might just think she was a harmless weirdo. Maybe she'd kiss everyone's hand she met, then it would just seem part of who she was. No, that wouldn't work. Kissing hands wasn't natural. She'd just have to forget it happened.

Easier said than done. She kicked open the trunk that held her paints and pulled out her mixing board. She was in the mood to paint reds. Fiery reds and yellows, maybe orange. Deep, passionate colors that would hold her angst over her stupid kiss and her hope that the show would be as big a success as Mallory forecast. She chose a four-by-four canvas she had previously layered with subtly tinted gesso. She'd built the layers to give real depth and texture to the blank canvas. It was ready to receive color, to be transformed into the place that was burning inside her right now. In moving from her internal place to the canvas, her emotions would be likewise transformed. She could let go of her dread about her next interaction with Mallory and get back to herself. Kadence had used her art as a therapeutic tool her entire life.

The center of the canvas became her open heart, red and burning with embarrassment, shaken with insecurity. It was engulfed in yellow and orange flames of purifying fire, burning with release instead of shame. The outer edges of the piece held the promise of renewal and she reached out for them with her brush. Before she knew it, she felt herself righted. The discomfort with what had happened was gone, and it had only taken three hours of painting.

She cleaned her brushes and walked to the far end of the room. She slid down the wall and gave her full attention to the painting. Her shoulders loosened as she saw what she had created. She leaned back against the wall and clasped her hands behind her head. It was perfect, capturing all she had felt in the hour before she lost herself in its creation. This was what made her work real. Carlyle had never seen it. She'd never *tried* to see it. Kadence let the hot tears come. She needed to find a way to release that disappointment. The hurt she'd experienced when Carlyle dismissed her love and her work had been the hardest thing she'd ever had to get over. It didn't make sense that she could transfer so many painful emotions to canvas, but hadn't succeeded in losing that particular pain. Seeing Sheva's figures had brought it right back to the surface. *I wish I'd had the chance to truly have closure with Carlyle. If she'd only come back to school. Maybe I could find her. Talk to her now. It's been two years; maybe she'll talk to me.*

Kadence pushed up off the floor and went to her worn leather messenger bag. She'd carried that thing all over for years, rarely going through it to take things out. She dumped the contents out on her bed, searching through the debris of her school years for the small notebook she'd used for the important stuff. It was tattered and stained, but she leafed through it and found Carlyle's old home address and her parents' phone number. Her calls to Carlyle's number in the months after their breakup had led to Carlyle changing the number. She'd never gotten the new one, so her parents were the only connection she had. *Should I do this? Her folks probably won't even remember me.* It was worth it, if she could talk to her again. Just to have a chance to say the things she should have said back then, so she could get the closure she needed. In part, she wanted to stand up for herself and take back some of the power Carlyle had taken from her that day. Kadence slid her phone out of her pocket and thumbed it open. It was after ten, too late to be calling anyone's parents. *I'll call in the morning.*

She showered and dropped into bed, relieved to have made the decision to reach out. It wouldn't matter what Carlyle's reaction was. She was at a good place in her life, more mature. Carlyle was probably in a similar place. They should be able to talk about what happened. Kadence would be able to say the things she hadn't been able to before. She'd get some closure and maybe she could start trusting her heart again. She slipped into sleep without difficulty and slept dreamlessly.

CHAPTER TWO

Mallory walked out of the restaurant smiling. She liked Kadence Munroe. She was so different from what she'd expected. She knew Kadence was a fresh voice in the somewhat stale local art scene. She'd caught a warehouse showing with a few of her pieces and had been struck by the emotion in her work. It was usually challenging to connect with the message of abstract art, but not with these pieces. Each of the three she'd seen called to different places in her. Sorrow, ecstasy, pain, all loud and clear in the play of color. She knew from the minute she saw them that the artist would have a deep emotional life. When she'd seen her in the gallery, snatching her hand back from the bronze figures, she'd felt a connection. She'd been unable to keep from caressing the beautiful sculptures herself.

She'd called her name and Kadence had turned, and she'd been surprised at how young she was. Her work spoke of so much life experience, it had been a shock. She'd expected someone in their mid to late forties, and here was this twenty-something. She was tall and slim, to the point of being too thin. Dark curly hair, worn long, highlighted sharp cheekbones. *To hide her features?* Maybe. She was somewhat shy, but Mallory liked that, too. So many of the artists she'd contracted were positive they were God's gift to the world, it was refreshing to meet one so unsullied.

Then there's the kiss. She chuckled, remembering the look of surprise on Kadence's face afterward. *She hadn't planned that, I'm sure.* It had been sweet and honest, the best kind of surprise. *We're going to be good friends.* She checked the time. *Damn.* She had to get back and finish her report for the board then contact the movers for

Kadence's pieces. She was going to be cutting it close, but she had to get that done before she met Sheva for dinner.

Sheva was the opposite of Kadence. She was full of confidence and had a generous helping of self-appreciation. That had been a bit of a turnoff for Mallory when they'd met, but Sheva was nothing if not persistent. She'd made sure Mallory knew she was interested and pursued her doggedly. Mallory had finally said yes to a date, only to make certain Sheva understood they were incompatible, but she'd been wrong. Sheva was sure of herself, but she was also interesting and caring, an attentive date, and unbelievably generous in bed. They'd been seeing each other since the second week of Sheva's three-month contract, and two months later, things were still good.

She felt the heat speed through her at the thought of Sheva's touches, her passionate lovemaking. That was definitely on the agenda for later tonight. Mallory let herself drift in the dream of the life she wanted. Definitely kids. She'd be a great parent, not like her own. She'd make sure her kids knew they were always her priority. She'd support their dreams, believe in them. They'd never wonder if they mattered. Nothing was going to stop her. She just had to find the right person to build the dream with her. She doubted Sheva was that person, but for now, she was fun and exciting. She made Mallory feel sexy and desirable, and she liked that.

Mallory left her third lunch meeting with Kadence, laughing. They always seemed to have such a good time together. She'd been going over little details about advertising the show when she looked up and saw chopsticks hanging out of Kadence's mouth. She looked like a cartoon vampire. Mallory knew it was a delaying tactic, trying to break her focus on the tedious paperwork, so she just looked down as if nothing was amiss. Kadence opened her mouth so wide the chopsticks fell onto her plate with a god-awful clatter.

"How can that not make you laugh?" she said.

Mallory finished reading the passage, pushed her glasses up, and looked at Kadence like a mother at her errant two-year-old. "This is a business meeting, Ms. Munroe."

Kadence fell off her chair and Mallory couldn't hold it together any longer. She tried, but her efforts ended in a bark of laughter. Kadence jumped up and pointed at her.

"You are human! I was worried."

Mallory laughed until her sides ached, then gave Kadence a long look. "Have you always been so silly?" She knew she was asking Kadence to open up a bit, but something made her want to know.

Kadence's smile faded and her shoulders drew in. "No, not always. Sometimes being a clown helps me forget things, you know?"

"Okay, what kind of things do you want to forget? I mean, I spend a lot of time trying to forget my dad. I was never good enough for him. Every time I achieved something, no matter what it was, it was always the wrong thing." She sat back, curling her arms around her middle. *I shouldn't have said that. It was too personal.*

Kadence surprised her, sitting forward and moving her arms away from her sides. She wasn't shutting down, she was opening up.

"That's a shame. No kid should have a parent shut them down like that."

Right? "The worst part was that I never had the chance to talk to him about it. He died too soon."

Kadence stiffened, letting Mallory know she was back to uncomfortable.

"Sometimes it's better that way. My mom is still alive, but so wasted all the time, she probably doesn't remember she has a kid."

Mallory hurt for her, she could hear the bitterness in Kadence's voice.

"I'm sorry, Kadence."

Her whole body slumped, and when she spoke, her voice was full of resignation. "That's okay. At least she's not beating me and trying to pimp me out anymore, right?"

The image of a young Kadence, beaten and abused, filled her mind and she flinched. Kadence saw the reaction and lowered her gaze.

"I'm okay now. That's all in the past," Kadence said. She didn't look up.

Idiot, you're making it worse. She grabbed her chopsticks and slid them under her lips, crossed her eyes, and said Kadence's name.

Like a balloon pricked with a pin, the tension and discomfort burst, allowing them both to laugh. *Sometimes, less is more. Laughter is underrated.*

They finished their work and shared a Vietnamese coffee before going their separate ways.

She walked into the gallery, expecting to find it quiet, but her assistant, Tarin, met her at the door with a frantic look on his face.

"What?"

"It's your mother. She's upstairs."

"My mother? What's she doing here?"

"I've no idea, but she's waiting in your office."

"How does she seem?"

"Serene."

"Damn. Okay, I'll deal with her. Call me in ten minutes, okay? I might need an out."

"Okay. She scares me."

"Me too."

Mallory climbed the stairs with dread growing like a poison mushroom in her gut. If her mother was serene, she had an agenda. What would it be this time?

She pushed open her door and saw Sanford lounging in her desk chair, arms draped casually over the sides.

"Darling. Where have you been? I've been waiting for hours."

"Hello, Mother. It hasn't been hours. I've only been at lunch up the street."

"Well, it feels like hours. You should pack a lunch, you know. Or call out for food. Send that what's his name for something. The gallery requires your full attention."

"Believe me, the gallery is in good hands with Tarin when I'm indisposed. I was lunching with a new client. It was work."

"Really? Lunch with a starving artist is work now? I wish someone would have told me."

"Is there something I can help you with, Mother?"

"Why, yes, dear, of course there is. I want you to come home for the long weekend and have brunch with me on Sunday. I won't take no for an answer, Mallory. I simply won't."

"So, I can't leave for lunch, but you expect me to leave for days? You know how busy the gallery is this time of year, Mother. I don't see how I can do that."

"Sunday brunch is only an early lunch, after all. You can do it with clients, you can do it with your mother."

As usual, her mother's logic was both flawed and working only toward her own goals. "But it's not that simple. Going to Monhegan takes more than an hour. We've talked about this before."

"This time, I want you to make time. I want you to be home with me. Please, Mallory?"

Mallory thought about the last time she'd gone home for a holiday. It'd been several years. She probably should plan a trip. Her mother meant well, she knew that. Her life was so completely different from Mallory's. She wasn't getting any younger, and Mallory might not have many more chances to spend time with her. She'd regret it if she didn't make time for her, exasperating as she could be.

"Okay, Mother. I'll come to the island on Saturday and stay through Monday. That's really as long as I can be away."

"Thank you, darling. You don't know how happy this makes me."

"I know, Mother."

"Good. I'll be on my way, then."

She rose and headed to the door, pausing before leaving. "By the way, who is the sculptor of the exquisite figures? They're remarkable."

"That's Sheva's work."

"The Goth hippie woman from California?"

Mallory choked down a laugh at her mother's accurate but somewhat unkind description. "Yes, Mother, that's her."

"Ah. Well, then, good-bye."

"Good-bye."

And without another glance back, her mother was gone. *She takes all the air in the room. Why can't she see how she affects me?* Mallory shook out her hair and breathed. A month until the long weekend, not nearly long enough to build up her reserves. She wondered if any of the others would be there. It would be great to see Jamie and Phyllis again.

She looked up as Tarin entered the room.

"You okay, boss?"

"I survived. Would you get me the sales figures for last week? I need to get this report done."

"I'm on it."

She relaxed into her routine, letting the feelings that seeing her mother brought up flow away. It wasn't her mother's fault. *I know she loves me, but she doesn't see me. She doesn't get that my goals are valid and real. Maybe one day she'll understand that my love of art is genuine, that I don't have to produce art to appreciate and understand it.*

She finished her report for the board and sent it off. Thank God for Tarin and his help holding things together. The whole day could have ended differently if not for him. She made arrangements for Kadence's paintings to be moved the following week and left her a voice mail with the details. This was going to be a good show. She could feel it in her bones.

Finally free, she grabbed her bag and met Tarin on the landing.

"Let's lock things up and get out of here. I need a drink after that visit. Care to join me?"

"I'd love to, but I have dinner plans tonight. Some other time?" She was glad he didn't look too disappointed. She depended on him and wanted to make sure he felt appreciated, but tonight wasn't the night.

"Sure."

As she set the alarm and waved good-bye, Mallory felt her body warm to the thought of this evening and Sheva. She was such a dynamic person. When she was with her, she felt alive in a way she hadn't before. *It's like her body is charged with electricity that pulses out and engulfs me. I can't get enough of being with her. But sometimes in that moment of pure electricity, it's like I vanish as a person and I'm only an extension of her power.* She wondered, not for the first time, if Sheva saw her as a person or as a conquest of some sort. *Does she see us as a couple or am I an accessory? Am I re-creating the relationship with my mother?* The little hard knots of anxiety pressed against her stomach and brought that uncomfortable feeling of uncertainty.

Not finding an answer, she headed home.

She was just putting the finishing touches on her makeup when Sheva's distinctive knock sounded. She was glad she'd had time for a shower, and the only thing she had yet to do was to pull on her shoes. When she opened the door, she was surprised to see Sheva's choice in outfits. She was wearing ripped jeans and her engineer boots with an oversized white button-down shirt.

"I thought we were going to Annisa." Mallory knew they had a strict dress code and Sheva must have changed their plans without letting her know, something she did occasionally.

"Yeah, that's not going to happen."

"Why? I was looking forward to dinner."

"That place is so pretentious. I don't want to get that vibe all over me, so I figured we could eat in."

"And you decided to wait until now to tell me because…"

Mallory could see Sheva stiffen. She didn't like being called on things.

"Jesus. If you insist, we can go out, just not there. I don't even know why I'm bothering with this."

"With what?"

"With this. You and me. Why should I try when all you do is question me?"

"Oh, come on. We made plans for dinner a week ago. I had to call in some big favors to get us a table on such short notice, and suddenly the restaurant is too pretentious? Seriously, Sheva."

"Nag, nag, nag. If I wanted a wife, I'd marry one. Look, I've been in the studio all day and I'm tired. I want to be relaxed and comfortable. Is that too much to ask?"

"Of course it isn't, if you'd bother to ask. That's not what happened. You decided we were going to stay in, then announced it to me when I thought you were here to pick me up. Don't I deserve a little respect? Couldn't you have called to let me know how you were feeling?"

"You know, you're right. You deserve better than me. I'll let myself out. Good luck with finding someone better."

And without another word, Sheva walked out. Mallory was shocked, not just by her sudden departure, but by the whole encounter. *What the hell?* It made no sense. They'd planned the evening out,

Sheva choosing one of the most difficult places to get a table, and Mallory had made it happen. Then she just flipped the tables and walked out? There had to be more to it than appeared.

Mallory crossed to the liquor cabinet and pulled out a bottle of Macallan. Wine wouldn't do tonight. She needed the smooth smoky taste of scotch to calm her nerves. She didn't like arguing, and hated the fact that Sheva thought it was okay to blow up their plans. She poured herself a drink and took it to her couch.

Sheva had always been a little unpredictable, but this was new. This had been hostile. What happened between last night and today that could have brought this on? She scrolled through her text messages, reviewing their communication from the day. Sheva seemed to be fine all day. Why had she gone off the rails? *I don't know her that well. Maybe there's something she hasn't shared with me.*

Mallory decided she would let it go for now and see what, if anything, Sheva had to say tomorrow. What they'd shared had been hot and intense, but this new tone wasn't something she would put up with. It was too much like her father. She'd tried so hard to do everything he expected, to be the perfect daughter. Then, when she knew she'd found a way to make him proud, when he'd have to acknowledge her accomplishments, he'd pull the rug out from under her by making her success seem unimportant. *You won the Humanities competition? Well, you should focus your attentions on improving your accounting skills. You're not going to impress potential employers with a piece of shiny plastic on a marble base. Apply yourself, Mallory.*

Her impudent rage against him flared brighter than a mushroom cloud, but she couldn't change the past. She'd never been able to confront him about it. He'd died before she was self-aware enough to stand up to him. Never again. She wouldn't let Sheva do the same thing to her. She deserved better than that. She tossed back the Macallan, let its smooth rich heat counteract her futile anger, and set the glass carefully on the table.

There was no reason she couldn't enjoy the evening. She had the reservation at Anissa. She could go solo, or maybe find someone who could join her on short notice. Tarin would probably go, or she could call one of her friends. Kadence's quick smile and the mass of curls that tumbled down around her heart-shaped face came to mind.

Mallory tingled all over at the thought. *Maybe she'd like to go to dinner?* It was worth asking. They'd had several nice lunches, and the time they'd spent together had been easy and fun. She could even make it a working dinner, since there were more things they could discuss regarding the show. Mallory could deftly turn a spoiled date into a nice evening, provided Kadence was available. All it took was a phone call.

❖

Sheva looked up at Mallory's window as she walked away from the apartment. That had gone better than she expected. It was almost time. The tension was building nicely. She had her exactly where she'd hoped to. Soon she'd be at the perfect place. Her soul would be in turmoil, her head and heart confused. It would be the right time to move, to capture her in bronze. She would be an exquisite addition to her collection. She had to make sure all her preparations at the foundry were complete before she executed the breakup and created that perfect moment. The timing was crucial. If she missed the moment and Mallory moved past confusion and anger into acceptance and recovery, her soul wouldn't be ripe for harvest. She had to act while she could.

❖

Half an hour later, Mallory was in a cab, waiting for Kadence to come down from her apartment. When the door opened, she felt a shock of arousal. Kadence was dressed in a charcoal gray suit, a black shirt, and an emerald green tie that matched her eyes. The suit accentuated her tall, slim figure. She either had excellent taste or a friend with a good eye. However it had come about, Kadence rocked the look and Mallory found her damn sexy. *She'll be the eye candy tonight, not me.* She tamped out the spark and reminded herself this was business. One irascible artist lover was more than enough.

"Over here, Kadence," she called.

Kadence turned her way and smiled as she walked to the cab. As she slid into the seat, her shoulder brushed against the exposed skin of Mallory's upper arm. *God, she smells good, too. Business, it's business.*

"I'm so glad you could join me on such short notice."

"Oh, no problem. I hope this suit is okay. It's from my graduation, so it's a couple of years old."

"It's stunning. You look great."

Mallory felt herself heat as Kadence gave her outfit an appraising look.

"You look stunning yourself, Ms. Tucker. So, why did you decide to invite me to dinner tonight? I thought we covered everything at lunch today."

"Oh, well, yes, but I thought it would be nice to talk about the specifics of your opening. It's your first show, so I'm sure you have questions that have come up, even though we've discussed lots of other things. I'm all about being available to my artists."

"Okay. So, you do this for all your artists?"

"Um, no. Truthfully? I had reservations and my dining companion had to cancel. I didn't want to lose the table, and, well, you came to mind."

"That makes more sense. I was just going to watch a movie and order pizza, so this works out for me, too."

"Good. So tell me about your process. How do you decide what to create? Your work is so incredibly evocative."

Mallory watched as Kadence shifted uncomfortably in her seat. She wasn't used to talking about her motivations, obviously. Mallory needed to help her get past that. She predicted that Kadence Munroe was going to make a splash in the art world. She hadn't been wrong yet when it came to those kinds of predictions. As such, Kadence was going to be asked questions like these often. She had to be able to open up, or at least have a good story. Her reputation would be built by how she handled these situations, and Mallory really wanted to see her succeed. It was time for some professional advice. "This is good. I can see you're not comfortable talking about how you create your art. I can help you with that. You need to be able to share yourself with the world."

"I don't know about that. I mean, I'll share my work, isn't that enough?"

"It can be, but not if you want to have the kind of reception that results in sales. I mean, people are buying your experience as well as the physical art. Trust me. Those who share get a bigger piece of the revenue pie. People buy people, and the stories behind those people, as much as they buy the physical product."

She could see that concept made Kadence uncomfortable. That wasn't an uncommon reaction among some of the more humble artists she had signed. It was like they were viscerally connected to their work, like the thought of profiting from it made them somehow guilty of self-betrayal. The exceptions were there, of course. Artists like Sheva, who were already certain that what they created should be given its due. Mallory preferred working with the more grounded, authentic artists like Kadence.

"I know it feels weird, but the point of my bringing you to the gallery is to help you get noticed. To help you build a following we can both profit from. Frankly, you need to make money with your work so you can continue to create it. One goes hand in hand with the other. No sales, no following, and pretty soon no art. I don't want to see that happen to you."

Kadence was quiet. Mallory wondered if she'd said the wrong thing. She'd dealt with some fairly sensitive artists, but usually she could bring them around to her point of view.

The cab pulled up in front of the restaurant and they exited, Kadence as quiet as before. Once they were seated Mallory tried to bridge the silence.

"I hope I didn't upset you. I mean, I think the world of your work. It's amazing and you should be able to make a living from it. Don't you want that?"

"I'm sorry, I'm not upset. It's just that I never let myself believe I'd make it. I never gave in to the daydream of being a full-time artist. It was too scary. When you talk about profit and stuff, it makes it all so real. I'm just a little shocked."

"Well, you shouldn't be. You're going to be a sensation in some circles. You'll see."

"What do I need to tell people? I mean, can you help me figure that out?"

"Sure, that's easy. For now, just tell me about what inspires you. How does it feel when you're about to start a new canvas? Do you plan and sketch first, or just start painting?"

Their drinks arrived, followed soon by appetizers. She slipped a labne sphere into her mouth and let its sour rich deliciousness explode on her tongue. She sighed and smiled. This was a small sample of the wonderful adventure her palate had ahead.

Mallory loved exotic foods as much as she loved art. The creativity invested in food like this spoke to her soul. It was like the vibrant blending of paint on canvas, the emotions of the chef clear in the bite and tang of the labne. She was moved by the experience and she felt her face flush with pleasure. She watched Kadence take her own first taste. She wasn't sure how to interpret her reaction. She wanted Kadence to connect with the food as she did. She looked for that spark of understanding, that knowledge that she had just sampled something amazing.

"What do you think?"

Kadence furrowed her brow, and Mallory couldn't tell if she was happy or not.

"Um, it's different."

The shrug wasn't helpful. Mallory wanted to know if this exquisite little bite impacted Kadence the way it had her. "Different good or bad?"

"Good, I think."

"Tell me. Give me a taste of your passion, Kadence. Does it begin in subtle smooth flavors, or does it burst out of you like the taste of these little cheese balls, flooding the canvas with you?" Mallory knew she was being provocative, but she couldn't help herself. She was drawn to Kadence and wanted to ruffle her. The desire to see her react was so strong it shook her.

Kadence froze, her second labne ball halfway to her mouth. She let the hand drop back to her plate and stared at Mallory.

Mallory wanted to take back what she'd said, to undo her rush to connect. This was always her downfall. She felt the passion and emotion of creative energy in every cell of her body. Her nerve endings exploded when she found something that struck her like this. She wanted everyone to feel that power, that flash of energy that wrapped around her and made simple things like paint and canvas, like labne balls, into houses for souls. She'd been sure that Kadence would feel it, and in her hunger for connection, she'd set her off balance by pushing.

"I've made you uncomfortable. I'm sorry."

"What exactly is this all about? I mean, the dinner, the asking about my passions? What's going on?"

Mallory burned with embarrassment. She wasn't exactly flirting, but she was pushing. It wasn't fair or professional and she needed to stop.

"I'm sorry. Your work excites me, Kadence. You excite me, but that's no excuse. I had a rough afternoon, and I think my confidence is shaken. I really want to know your passion for your work, your process, so I can make that a part of introducing you to my world, but I don't mean to make you uncomfortable."

"Okay. So, can we set up some boundaries? Can we agree that discussions about my passion are only about my work? I'll tell you what motivates me, what grabs me by the soul and rips at my insides until I get it out of me and onto canvas, but you have to promise not to exploit that. You have to promise that the difference between sharing my process with you and anything else is clear."

"You've got my promise."

Kadence stared at her for a moment, as though trying to figure out if she was being genuine. She took a deep breath and started talking. "Okay. When I paint, I don't plan. I don't know ahead of time what I'm going to create. That's one reason I'm an abstractionist. I paint what I feel. Maybe I wake up in the morning and realize I can't make my rent, so I get swallowed up by fear and anxiety. What I do with that is pull it out and put it on canvas. Maybe I have a wonderful night with a beautiful woman. Maybe I see, in her, a reflection of self I'd forgotten or denied. I pull that out and put it on canvas. When I'm sad, angry, defeated, I make it into art. It's what I do, and when I do, I heal. I feel better about me, about them, about everything. It's all I am."

Mallory felt each word and knew it for truth. This was how Kadence managed to create such moving pieces with such muted edges. She painted her emotions. No wonder Mallory had felt so drawn to her work. She was putting all of herself into it.

"That's amazing. I feel all of that when I look at your pieces. When your show opens, that story is going to spark your sales. People these days shut themselves off from their emotions too often. Your work makes them feel. It's cathartic. Trust me, you're going to do well."

"I'll have to take your word for that. It feels really weird to think of my work opening other people's emotions. I guess I use my work to rip mine out, so I don't have to feel them anymore."

"Why don't you want to feel them?"

Kadence sighed and looked away from her. "They hurt. Not feeling is better than feeling. So, I take them out, put them on canvas, and I don't have to deal with them anymore."

Mallory didn't know how to respond, so she kept quiet. *How does that work? Denying your feelings?* Soon their entrees arrived, and Kadence asked her about running a gallery. She was glad to move into more comfortable territory, and opened up about her life a little. They chatted about different types of art, different openings, and various people Mallory had met throughout her time in the art world. When Kadence asked whether she was an artist herself, she smiled and shook her head.

"My mother was confounded that I had no talent. She tried everything she could think of to change that, but painting, sculpting, all of it, was beyond me. When I watched my mother paint, I felt connected to her, more than at any other time. The best times growing up were times I sat in her studio, watching her. I wanted that connection, and even though I'm a great disappointment to her, my mother's work and where it led are the single biggest influences on my life. I love what I do. I love art and the way it makes people see the world."

"I can see that. I'm lucky you discovered me."

Mallory lost herself momentarily in the depth of Kadence's eyes. *Like windows into her soul.* She felt her breath catch and coughed to hide it.

"Yeah, lucky for both of us. Let me get the bill and we can head out. I'll drop you back at your place."

"Thanks for this."

"Thank you. And thanks for not running for the door when I made you uncomfortable. I think we'll work really well together."

Mallory watched Kadence skip up the steps of her building as her cab pulled away. *She moves like a cat, sensuous and powerful, graceful.* Kadence Munroe was not only an incredible artist, she was sexy. Mallory smiled and hugged herself tight. *A sexy goddess who is only going to be your client, maybe your friend, but that's it.* It was a boundary she wouldn't be crossing again.

CHAPTER THREE

Kadence kicked the apartment door closed behind her as she pulled at the knot in her tie. What the fuck was going on? Why had Mallory really invited her to dinner and why did their conversation make her so uncomfortable? *Because she was getting too personal with you, and it made you uncomfortable, that's why.* She'd been careful with boundaries since Carlyle, and lately, with Mallory, she felt close to letting her guard down. Christ, she'd already told her about her mother and a little about her childhood. That was more than she told *anyone*, but she regretted it, and she wouldn't go there again for several reasons. She counted them off mentally, reminding herself. Number one, Mallory was kind of her boss, and that wouldn't work for her in any sense. Number two, she didn't do dating and such. Random encounters were much safer for her heart. Tonight felt way too close to a date. And number three, Mallory said she'd been stood up, so that meant she had someone to stand her up. *No can do.* It'd taken such a long time to get over Carlyle, and even longer to set aside her criticism of her work. Kadence wasn't ever going to let someone get close enough to rip her apart again. Her art and an occasional dalliance would be enough. It had to be.

She grabbed a beer off the counter and dropped into her chair. She'd set up her room so she could use most of it for working and storing her paintings, so it didn't accommodate much in the way of comfort furnishings. But she had her favorite overstuffed chair, crammed in against her bed. She toed off her dress shoes and sipped at the chocolate stout. She needed to figure out what to do with tonight. Should she just forget that it happened? Just erase the night from her memory? That'd be the best solution, probably. She could just go into the gallery on Wednesday and help with the setup of her show as she'd planned. She could force the respectful distance back into place between her and Mallory. But then she'd have to give up any sense of closeness she'd felt before things got uncomfortable Was it that big a deal? Could she just let it go and keep the friendship she'd felt with her? Maybe. Or maybe she was reading too much into it, and she was just out of her depth, as usual. Maybe this was how people in the big art world acted, and she simply needed to get used to it. It probably didn't mean anything, and she was making something out of nothing.

Her throat tightened and she knew there was no turning back now. She was in for the full emotional ride tonight.

She finished her drink then stripped out of her suit and hung it up. She pulled on her paint-stained jeans and ratty old CAA sweatshirt. She needed to paint, to get out the mix of anxiety and confusion flowing through her.

She chose a five-by-five canvas that had been prepped with a blue tinted gesso. She loaded her palette with the colors of her mood: deep blue, purple, and black, titanium white to mimic the unknown future. Heat rushed through her and she tightened her grip on her palette knife. She layered the paint thick in waves and ridges, sharp edges to match the wash of anxiety she felt. Her stomach churned and she clutched the knife harder as the memory of Carlyle and her words came back. She feathered the paint wildly, letting the pain direct her movements. She felt the sting of her mother's belt across her shoulders, heard her drunken railing at Kadence for things she didn't comprehend, much less cause. The deep cold blue of isolation that had saved her, that made it possible to survive those years. The stark white of the unknown when she broke away, when she secretly applied for a scholarship and won it, when she climbed on that bus and left Texas in the dust.

She felt the heat of her tears as they traced the contours of her face. They fell freely as she opened herself to her emotions. She scrubbed at them when they rolled over her chin and sped down her neck. Her throat felt like she'd drunk a cup of glass shards.

Finally, she couldn't take any more and she threw the knife onto the palette. She thrust her hands into the paint and tried to grab the past to capture it. All she succeeded in doing was covering her hands and arms in paint, but the effect on the canvas felt right. She slumped over the canvas and wept onto its surface until she had no more tears.

When she was able, she gathered the fractured bits and pieces of herself and pulled them together. She looked at the smeared, jagged peaks and waves of her painting and knew this was only the first stage of this piece. When she painted like this, the result was always too much, even for her. Tomorrow she would look at it again, and then she could build something that would last.

Her shoulders ached and her throat was drier than a salt flat, but the tension that gripped her gut was gone. Paint yourself happy, that's what her grandma had always said. It didn't make her happy anymore, but it was cathartic. *I can't control what happens. I can only guard my heart and keep living.*

She grabbed her paint-stained towel and cleaned her arms as best she could before going to the bathroom. She stripped off her clothes and slid into the shower. She leaned on the wall and let the warm water sluice over her. The blue tinted water swirled down the drain, and she tried to force the lingering web of emotion down with it. Her soul was like an empty husk, a shell, its edges lined in shards of hardened crystal. Allowing herself to feel put that shell at risk, and it was getting harder to tamp those emotions down. *If I can smile and function without feeling, I'll be okay. Just swallow it down and keep it locked in.*

Slowly, Kadence felt the emptiness fade and the mask she wore slip back into place over her heart. She wouldn't let anyone or anything in to hurt her. All she needed was to keep on relying on herself and moving through life. Her art was where she lived. That was where her feelings played and tore at each other. Here, in this empty place, she was free.

❖

Mallory was walking up the landing of her building when she heard Sheva's whistle. That had been cute, once, that wolf whistle she tossed out, but tonight it wasn't cute. It wasn't fun or sexy or any of the things Mallory had once felt when she heard it. She pretended she hadn't heard and pushed through the entrance without stopping.

"Hey, Mallory, wait up. I'm sorry, okay?"

Mallory kept walking. Sorry wasn't enough. She was going to have to do better than that. She hit the button for the elevator and hoped the building door would latch before Sheva could get in. No such luck.

"Mal? Are you mad at me?"

Count to ten before you say anything. The anger her dinner with Kadence had erased flared up, hotter than before. How could Sheva not expect her to be angry? Did she not get how rude she'd been?

"Look, I know I was an ass. That's part of my charm, right? I mean, I'm an artist, I can't help being a jerk sometimes. I feel like a total douche, if that helps. Can you forgive me?"

Mallory rushed into the elevator as soon as the door opened, Sheva right behind her. Sheva caught her by the arms and dropped to the floor on her knees.

"Please? I beg you, Mal. Forgive me?"

Sheva's eyes were red and Mallory could see she'd been crying. Maybe she was overreacting, the old tapes about her father making the circumstances bigger than they were, maybe she should cut Sheva some slack. She looked down into those dark pools of midnight, seeing her angry face reflected there. The fire went out of Mallory and her heart softened. Looking at Sheva like this made it hard to stay angry.

"Why did you do that to me?"

"I'm so sorry. I had a bad day in the studio. Nothing was going right. I haven't had a good casting since last April and I'm getting nervous. I need a new piece for my Geneva show. It was stupid of me to take that out on you. It's not your fault that I'm stuck. Please forgive me?"

That drained the last of Mallory's anger away. She knew how important it was for an artist to produce. Her mother had been unbearable when she'd hit lulls in her work. It was a part of the artist psyche.

"Okay, on one condition."

"Anything."

"That you never do that to me again. I know how hard it is, but you must keep your art and us separate. I can't let you treat me like that for any reason, okay?"

"Deal. Can I come up with you?"

Mallory thought about it. She should tell her no, for tonight, at least, but the thought of a night with Sheva was too tempting.

"Yeah, I'm good with that. But expect to be making it up to me all night."

Sheva gave her that rakish smile and she melted. Damn. Those black eyes and full lips could convince her of just about anything.

The trip from the elevator to the bedroom was a blur, so much heat coming off their bodies it mucked up her consciousness. When her back touched the cool sheets of her bed and Sheva slid on top of her, she knew she was home. Sheva's mouth was everywhere, kissing and sucking, driving Mallory insane with her teasing.

"God, take me!"

And Sheva did. She drove hard into her, fueled by their passion. Mallory cried out at the intensity. Sheva rocked her with deep powerful thrusts coupled with her unceasing kisses, and just when Mallory reached the peak of her climax, Sheva bit down on her nipple. The electric shock of pain rippled through her and entwined with the overwhelming pleasure of her orgasm. She screamed, her body arching off the mattress in response to the pain and pleasure combined. She was coming apart, flying out and away from the two of them, freeing her to feel the depth of the connection they had created.

When she came back to herself she looked at Sheva and really saw her. Her expression was one of power and control. There was no connection to the emotional roller coaster she had put Mallory on. Mallory could have been a slab of clay she was manipulating, a piece of art Sheva had created with her hands and mouth, but not her soul. The disconnect between them made Mallory apprehensive. She wanted to pull away, but Sheva held her fast.

"You're so perfect, Mallory. God, you're so perfect." She kissed her way down Mallory's body and slipped between her legs. Her mouth stroked the tender places she had so forcefully entered before.

Mallory tried to slip back into the moment, but she couldn't shake her trepidation.

"Stop. Sheva."

"Why stop?" She worked her tongue back and forth across Mallory's oversensitive clit.

"Just stop."

Sheva sat up, looking puzzled. "What's wrong? You haven't had enough already, have you?"

"Yes. I'm done." Mallory could hear the coldness in her voice. She knew that wouldn't go over well, but she couldn't help it. She felt manipulated, used.

"What the fuck? What's wrong? That was beautiful. Why are you upset?"

"I'm not upset. I'm just tired," Mallory lied.

"Tired? Yeah, right. Okay." Sheva stood and started pulling her jeans on.

"Why are you getting dressed? Lie back down with me."

"Nah, I need to go back to the studio. You've inspired me. I need to get the images in my head in clay. I'll see you at the gallery tomorrow."

"Don't go."

"I have to, baby. I need to create. Look, I'll see you soon, huh?"

Mallory didn't want her to go. She wanted to talk about what she'd felt during their lovemaking. Why had Sheva been so disconnected? Why the introduction of pain to their pleasure? If she didn't get answers, she knew she wouldn't sleep.

"Sheva, please stay. I need to talk to you."

"Talk to me in the morning. 'Night."

And then she was gone, the door closing softly behind her.

Mallory thought about what she'd seen in Sheva's eyes. She hadn't been in the moment with her, or at least not in the same way. Had it always been that way? She'd never bitten her before, but she was always intense in her lovemaking. Most of the time she liked to take Mallory forcefully, often instigating a passionate coupling in an unusual place. She liked tables, and counters. They always wound up in bed, so Mallory had written it off as intensity. Now she wasn't so sure. Did Sheva ever do gentle? Was she always disconnected? She thought about the first time they'd been together. It had been so hot, like something from a movie. Sheva had taken her against the door of her apartment after starting in the elevator. It had been exciting and different for Mallory, but would that ever turn to something more emotional? Was Sheva even interested in her emotionally? And the biting thing, that had hurt. Yes, it had exponentially changed her orgasm, but it wasn't something she wanted as a part of a loving relationship, or even as a regular part of sex. Pain definitely wasn't her thing. *Do we have a relationship or are we just fucking?*

She got up and went to the shower, feeling dirty. She made the water as hot as she could stand before slipping in. She soaped her body thoroughly, being careful of her tender nipple, then rinsed and soaped again. Why was she feeling like this? She hadn't done anything she didn't want to do, and Sheva had stopped when she asked her to. *It's because you feel used. She objectified you by staying separate from you emotionally. You were a thing to her, not a person.*

She flinched at the thoughts pounding through her head. The truth in them was harsh. That's exactly how she felt, like something used and tossed aside. *Has it always been this way, or is this new?* Sheva had really pissed her off about the dinner reservation, but she didn't think she had held on to that anger when they'd started making up.

She wrapped up in her robe, went to the living room, and poured herself a glass of wine. As she sipped, she went over every time she could remember, every moment she'd spent with Sheva.

She dug her nails into her palms, and her eyes burned as she thought about it. The anger from earlier came back, stronger than before. She finished the wine and poured a second glass as the memories replayed in her mind. Sheva, wild and passionate, kissing her and groping at her breasts in the elevator. Struggling to unlock the door as she felt Sheva's hands sliding her skirt up above her hips. Finally, in the apartment, closing the door as Sheva flipped her around, face to the wood and took her, with hot hands and whispered words in her ear. She'd come harder than ever before. And when she'd turned to embrace Sheva, seeking the contact of her body against her own, Sheva had dropped down and taken her in her mouth, making her bones turn to liquid as she came again and slid to the floor.

She'd scooped her up in those strong sculptor's arms and carried her to the bed, but had kissed her good night and left. In fact, Mallory realized now they'd never spent an entire night together. There was always work at the studio calling Sheva away from her bed. And the times they'd lain together after lovemaking had been spent in exhausted sleep. There had been no cuddling. No loving words exchanged over the pillows. It had been carnal and fierce, but not emotional.

I'm such an idiot. Sheva'd been clear about her needs from the beginning. Mallory understood then that she'd set this up herself. She'd put Sheva on that same freaking pedestal she'd put her parents on. No wonder it felt so wrong now. No wonder she felt used. She was trying to work through her daddy issues by letting Sheva walk all over her. Screw that. She might have made it happen, but she wouldn't let it continue. If there was one thing her mother had taught her, it was to be strong. That, she could do. Eventually, anyway. Right now, she just needed to be honest with herself about what she was feeling. Actions could wait.

The cold hands of shame wrapped around her legs and climbed her body, filling her with feelings of worthlessness. *I did that to myself. I gave her that power.* Her robe was no match for the chill that enveloped her. She pulled the throw from the back of the couch. *I let that happen.* She pulled her knees up and curled into a ball, wondering if she'd ever be warm again.

Sheva felt the energy of their coupling rocket through her body. She knew Mallory was upset, knew she wanted her to stay and talk things out, but that was the opposite of what Sheva needed. She had to get to her studio, to the clay, and re-create the image of Mallory arching off the bed. It was the perfect image for her next sculpture. Such a mix of passion and pain that it would blaze through in bronze when she had it finished. You wouldn't be able to look at the figure without feeling that perfect moment. She knew exactly how to re-create it for the bronze casting later. It was burned into her mind and would stay until she perfected it. The clay model was a necessary stage in casting. She had to have the full visual guide for her final cast.

She unlocked the padlock and slid the door of her studio open. The light flared as she hit the switch, illuminating her perfect world. This was the only place she kept clay maquettes of her sculptures, models that included all their features, on a small scale. When she cast them in bronze, though, they were always anonymous, those specific features captured in the maquettes missing from the final product. There was nothing recognizable beyond the torso and hands.

She ignored the call of the maquettes and went straight to her worktable. She pulled out the wire form she had created in the image of Mallory's body and manipulated it into the shape still dancing in her vision. She began to apply the clay in small spheres, then smooth them until the body became clear. With slip and time, she re-created the moment Mallory gave in to pleasure, the moment the pain hit her brain, the arch of her body. It was divine. Sheva was a god when she was at her craft. The power to capture these moments didn't feel like it came from within. It was like her hands were directed by something outside of her. It was ecstasy in its most exquisite form.

As she watched the moment come to life in her hands, she felt her excitement mount, and as she ran the slip up and down the doll-sized model of Mallory, she came, harder and more completely than she ever could when having sex in the flesh. She collapsed over the table, spent and exhausted. This was going to be her best work yet.

CHAPTER FOUR

Mallory woke cold and cramped. She was still in her robe and on the couch, the gray light of early morning filtered through the blinds. She stretched, working out the kinks in her muscles from sleeping on the couch. She'd tried to go back to bed the night before, but the smell of sex permeated the room. Her stomach tightened in anger at what she'd done with Sheva. She'd have to wash the sheets today.

It was Tuesday, which meant Tarin wouldn't be in until eleven. She needed to get moving. The robe pulled on her breast, reminding her of the night before.

She was dressed and out the door half an hour later and at the Gallery with five minutes to spare. She punched in the alarm code and moved through the space she loved, greeting the works that she had brought here. This was her place. She'd fought hard for her innovative ideas and her belief that new artists would bring new clients. The board had balked at the expense, but she'd won them over. There'd been lean times, when she'd forgone a paycheck so she could pay an artist, but her hard work and perseverance had won out in the end. She relished the success now.

She patted the smooth, white wall of the foyer, her good luck ritual. No matter what, she had the gallery.

The bronzes looked alive in the morning light, and she couldn't help but run a hand over their smooth surfaces. She looked at the six sculptures with a fresh perspective today. The torso being fondled from behind, the faceless head on the folded arms, all of them held a story. They were striking because of the emotions they captured. How could Sheva create such moving pieces and be so disconnected while making love? It struck her suddenly that she knew exactly how Sheva created her art. When she was making love, she was sketching out her next figure. That was why she was disconnected; she was studying, forming the beginning of her next sculpture. *Am I going to be her new piece? When her show moves to Geneva, will my image go too?* Anger flared again, her hands tightened into fists, and she wanted to hit something. *Damn her. I don't want to see myself in bronze. My body, my emotions, bared for the world? No frigging way.* She had to keep that from happening. She didn't want to be one of Sheva's bronze trophies.

Her mood didn't improve with her thoughts. She decided she would spend the morning on the second floor, planning the layout for Kadence's show. That was something she could pour herself into and not get angry. Kadence was genuine, and her show deserved Mallory's attention.

The loft space she'd chosen would be perfect for the minimalist paintings Kadence made. They were subtle but powerful. She needed to know exactly how many frames and what sizes Kadence would be displaying. It wouldn't work to plan the space without the specifics.

She called the number she had for Kadence, but the line rang without answer. Maybe she didn't have a voice mail. She was about to email her when her phone rang. It was Kadence.

"Hey, there. Good morning."

"Good morning. Did you just call me?"

"I did. I'm working on the display for your show, but I don't have the number and dimensions of your canvases. Could you help me with that?"

"Um, sure. Let me wake up a bit. Can I call you back?"

"Yes, no problem. Just call as soon as you can. Your pieces arrive tomorrow and I want to have the layout planned so we can arrange them as they come in."

"That makes sense. Can I come and help with the planning? I mean, I know what pieces will show best in different lighting and stuff."

"You'd be willing to do that?"

"Of course, why wouldn't I? Isn't that something everyone does?"

"Some do, but I've learned never to expect it. I'd love your input. What time do you think you can make it here?"

"Give me an hour."

"Okay, and, Kadence?" Mallory tensed, knowing what she wanted to say, but not sure how Kadence would interpret it. *Thank you for bringing your smile to me today?* That'd be cheesy and too personal. *Keep it simple.*

"Yeah?"

"Thanks."

"Sure."

Mallory smiled as she hung up. Kadence was just what she needed this morning. The feelings of shame and sadness that held her last night faded. She would be a breath of fresh air and help banish any lingering negativity. She pushed back from her desk and headed to the loft space. She wanted to showcase the larger paintings in the center of the space, moving outward to the walls with the subsequent smaller canvases. The natural light in the space would set the pieces nicely in the daylight hours, and she'd spent a fortune on a xenon lighting upgrade for the entire gallery. That would accent the paintings on cloudy days or at night.

She not only wanted the show to be a success, she needed it to be. Her first three shows at the gallery had been hits, but they'd all been recognized artists. Kadence would be her first discovery. If the show hit big, that would mean Mallory had proved her abilities and would guarantee her choice of placements should she ever leave the ARA. And her mother would hear. *There it is, the old desire to get Mom's attention.* She'd never managed to do that with her work.

Sanford Tucker never seemed to notice her successes. It wasn't original art, so she tended to be oblivious. *Is that because she's an egomaniac or is it just that wicked artist's psyche coming into play? Sheva is just like her.* At least her mother wasn't consciously being vindictive, she was just clueless. She had a good heart and loved Mallory. She wanted the bond Mallory craved; she just couldn't find a way to connect to her. Sanford was worth the awkward, painful moments, because she didn't know she caused them.

It would break her mother's heart to know how often she'd crushed Mallory's spirit. *And thank God she wasn't the kind of mother Kadence had.* The thought was sobering and made her cut her mom a little more slack.

It was the art, and only the art, that moved creative types. *Dammit, it moves me, too, but I share what I feel. I let people inside and invite them to find something more in the work than lines and movement. Why are they so cut off from the rest of us?*

It hurt, seeing the similarities between her mother and Sheva. Last night, more than ever, she'd wished she'd never met her. Her mother had made that feeling, like she was superfluous to the situation, the central theme of her life. Always outside the bubble and lacking the innate ability her mother and her artist friends were born with. *Why did it matter I wasn't good at it? I felt the work, I knew the stories they were trying to tell. Why couldn't I be inside?*

She sighed and took deep, steadying breaths. *Stop it. Get a grip. They live in their bubbles because they can't function outside of them. You can go in with them and draw them out. You've proven it to yourself, and Kadence's show will prove it to everyone.*

The bell signaled the arrival of a patron or an artist, so Mallory left the loft and headed to the main floor. She put on her best welcoming smile as she exited the stairwell, but she felt it fade when she saw Sheva walking among her bronzes.

"Hi."

"Oh, hey. How are you this morning?" Sheva said.

"I'm not sure."

Sheva raised an eyebrow. "You're not sure? What's that supposed to mean?"

"It means I'm not sure how I am with you, this morning."

"Huh? What are you trying to say?"

The bronze image of herself rose in Mallory's mind, and she forced herself to remain detached. "I think I'm saying I need some space. I'm saying I'm not sure I want to see you anymore."

"What the fuck? Where did that come from? Are you still pissed about that stupid dinner? Come on, Mallory, grow up." She caressed one of her sculptures like it was a lover. "You didn't seem angry when you were on your back."

Mallory watched her jaw clench and knew Sheva was stressed. "It's not about being angry, and it's not about the dinner. I don't like how being with you makes me feel."

Sheva gripped her chest like she'd been shot. "Ouch. That was a sucker punch. Look, fuck you, Mallory. I was getting tired of you anyway. I'm not even here to see you. I need some time with my girls. I need to listen to what they tell me so I can create their sister, get it? I'm an artist and this is me. You can't handle me, fine, fuck off. Now get the hell away from me and let me do what I need to do."

Mallory straightened and kept her arms at her sides, so she didn't look as defensive as she felt. She was not going to back down. "So that's it? You don't want to know *why* I feel this way."

"I don't give a fuck. Really. Just go on about your work."

Anger surged through Mallory. "I won't be dismissed like that, Sheva. You deserve to know why I felt like shit after last night, and I deserve the chance to tell you. I am a person, dammit. You don't get to set me aside like yesterday's leftovers."

"You're wrong. I don't owe you a thing. You got what you wanted from me, I got what I wanted from you. Now we're done. Simple as that, so yeah, I get to dismiss you like the bad memory you'll be in a few hours."

"God, you're such an ass. I can't even believe I slept with you. Get out of here. This is my gallery, just get out."

"Correction, Princess. This is the gallery you manage, and these?" She held her hands out to her bronzes. "These are my loves. I made them. I own them and I'll spend as much fucking time as I want with them. Good thing we've got that contract in place, huh?"

The dim awareness of the bell chiming hit Mallory as she stormed up the stairs to her office. *Good, maybe she's gone.* She tried to slam her door, but the gentle close didn't allow it. She wrenched it open again and tried to smash it with some force. She wanted some physical reaction to the anger that flooded her, but it was pointless. She ran to her desk and grabbed the crystal vase from its surface. She threw it with all she had to the floor and was tremendously satisfied by the tinkling crash as it exploded. She looked around for something else to throw.

The crystal plaque from the art guild would do. She yanked it from the shelf and wound up to crash it against her door when it opened. The door was as quickly closed as the plaque thunked against it and fell to the floor in one piece. *Not as satisfying as the vase.*

The door opened again and Kadence peeked around its edge.

"Is it safe or should I come back?"

"Argh!"

"Okay, not safe. I'll be out here when you're done."

Mallory fought to push the anger down, to let it go, but the fury shifted and she began crying instead. She dropped to her chair and let the tears come. She watched the door slowly open as Kadence came into the room.

"Hey, is there anything I can do?"

Mallory swiped at the tears and tried to pull it together. "Yeah, not be an asshole."

"Okay. Don't be an asshole. Check. Here, take this. Can I get you some water?"

Mallory saw she was holding out a faded cotton bandana, and for some reason it struck her as funny. She started laughing through her tears. "I'm not going to blow my nose in your do-rag."

Kadence looked at the bandana, then back at Mallory.

"Do I look like I'd wear a do-rag? It's a handkerchief. Take it and use it. You're grossing me out with all that drippy stuff."

Mallory laughed harder. "If you insist. Thanks." She took the bandana and wiped at her cheeks.

"No, really, blow your nose already."

She did and laughed again. "You chose the right time to walk through the door."

"You think? I was a bit worried you might take my head off, but I'm no chicken. What's going on? Why are you so upset?"

"Is she gone?"

"Who?"

"Sheva."

"Oh. I guess so. I didn't see anyone. What happened with the bronze greatness?"

She must have left right before Kadence came in. Maybe I got to her after all. The thought was vaguely satisfying. "Pft. Great asshole, you mean."

"Uh-huh? Do tell."

Mallory looked at the glass littering her office floor. *I might have overreacted.* "Never mind. Let's just say we had a little disagreement."

Kadence held her hands out in a gesture of submission. "Remind me not to disagree with you."

Mallory had to laugh. She looked so darn cute. Kadence's arrival was like walking into sunshine after a long, cold winter. "Deal. You want to go look at your space with me?"

"If you're okay. I mean, you don't have to stop your, um," she gestured to the shattered crystal, "whatever, just because I'm here. I'm a good listener, if you need someone to talk to. Just don't throw anything at me."

"I'm so embarrassed. I don't usually throw things, and dammit, I loved that vase." Mallory's shoulders slumped as she waved her hand at the fragments of crystal.

"Well, the award survived. You have a broom and dustpan around here?"

Mallory sighed. She wished she hadn't done that. "Yeah, I'll get it. You don't have to help me with this."

"I don't mind. I've had the same sort of thing happen with me and paint, so I get it."

Mallory went out into the hallway to a door marked private and pulled out a couple of hand brooms and dust pans. "Here, if you're sure you don't mind."

"I'm sure. What did Sheva do to piss you off so bad?"

"It's not so much what she did, it's who she is. We were, well, we were kind of seeing each other."

"Seeing as in dating?"

"Yes." Mallory caught the quick jerk as Kadence digested that. *Hm, that bugs her.* She wondered if she should have admitted to the relationship. Would Kadence think less of her professionalism?

"Is she the one who stood you up last night?"

"Yes. But that's not what this was about. Not really. It's just that you artist types live in your own world, so far above us peons that you forget we're human sometimes."

"Wait, hold on, not all artists are like that. I'm not like that. Definitely don't tar me with the same brush as Sheva."

"You're the exception, then." Mallory shook her head and dumped the crystal into the trash can by her desk. "I'm not being fair, I know. I've met some artists who are down-to-earth and relate in the real world. But right now, I'm not feeling love for you creative types."

Kadence dumped her dustpan and smiled tightly. "I get it. No worries. How about we go look at the space for my show and make some plans? When we're finished, how about I take you to my all-time favorite place in New York? I know you're busy, but I thought it'd be fun to spend some time together."

Mallory smiled. Kadence was obviously bothered by her revelation, but she was so sweet. If they'd been in the reverse situation, Mallory knew she'd never be so kind. "Give me a hint where that might be and I might take you up on that offer."

Kadence's smile was huge and so childlike, Mallory felt her own smile growing.

"You've probably been there, the Sunburst Cinema? I love that place. They're showing the new film by Alejandro. What do you say? You up for some popcorn and a good movie?"

The Sunburst? Sitting in a dark theater with Kadence might be just what she needed. "That sounds wonderful. I can't leave here until we close, though. Is that going to be too late?"

"Heck no, we can grab some food on the way and make a night of it."

"You're really a good person, Kadence." Mallory squeezed her arm, trying to convey how much her overture meant.

"Thanks, but it's really that I hate going to the movies by myself."

Mallory could tell she was downplaying the invitation and she appreciated the gesture. It made it easy to accept and not feel like things were going to go astray like the night before. They could do things together as friends.

"I'm buying the popcorn, though."

"I'll go for that. Show me what you're thinking for my display."

Mallory led the way to the loft space and told Kadence her plan for moving from large, more dynamic pieces to smaller pieces.

"The layout will draw the viewer into your work. What do you think?"

"Well, I like the idea, but my canvases don't vary that much in dimension. I do have some framed pieces that might work in the center area."

Mallory imagined the space filled with the essence of Kadence. She could feel the warmth the room would exude, so different from the main hall and the bronzes. This would be the heart of the gallery. "Hm, okay. I'll have Tarin help me set up the grid frames and we can build your show as it comes in. Do you have specific paintings you'd like to see in specific placements?" She watched the play of light on Kadence's face. Her serious brows drew together as she studied the space. Working with Kadence was like taking a walk on a warm beach. It was effortless.

"I have a series I'd like to highlight. It's titled *Colder than Blue*. The five individual pieces move through shades of ever darkening blue. The first is barely tinted except one dark circle of pthalo. The final piece is almost completely dark with only the echo of light on the edges. I'm not sure how to set them up here. The room is a nice size, but there are only four walls."

"That sounds intriguing. I can't wait to see your collection unloaded. Here, look at this. This is called flex grid. It's a malleable grid structure that allows us to redesign the space on a whim." Mallory held out her tablet. There were images of previous show layouts on the screen. "This is the arrangement I was thinking for you, but since you have a series," she flipped through the images to one where the grid frame was molded into a spiral, with framed pieces leading into the center, "this might work for you."

"Oh, I like that. I think that will be perfect for the *Colder* series. We can use the other paintings on the square walls. This is going to be amazing."

"Good, I'm glad you're excited. When Tarin gets in we can start the setup." She clicked off the tablet and smiled at Kadence. She loved the way her eyes sparkled and her body radiated enthusiasm. She took her arm and led her back to the office.

"Can I stay and help with that? I'd really like to be involved in the whole process, if that's okay."

"You can supervise, but I can't let you do the build out. Our insurance won't cover you if something happens."

Kadence looked disappointed, but Mallory knew she had to stick with company policy. If Kadence was injured it would be bad news for the gallery.

"You can be as involved as possible, short of moving the grid frames, okay?"

That brought the smile back to her eyes. "Yes! Thanks, Mallory. I'm a hands-on kind of person, so it matters to me."

"I get that. As long as you keep the hands off the big stuff, you can stay. When your pieces arrive, you can help hang them, since that falls under artist contribution." She'd have to warn Tarin. It would be a challenge for Kadence not to jump in. She loved her enthusiasm, but needed to follow the gallery guidelines.

"Awesome. Thanks."

"Sure. Look I've got to get some work done before Tarin gets in. Do you want to hang out here, or come back?" Mallory wished she could shelve her work for the day and spend time with Kadence, but knew she couldn't. She liked watching her and seeing her excitement about the show build.

"Is it okay if I stay in the gallery space?"

She looked so hopeful, like a kid asking for a puppy. Mallory's heart flipped and she had to push down the impulse to hug her, just because. "Of course it is." She handed over the tablet again. "Here. You can flip through the other images and see if the spiral is what best suits you. There's also a directory in there that will guide you through the other shows currently in house. Have fun. I'll be in my office if you need anything."

"Okay, thanks."

The desire to snuggle up against her and look through the grid guide, experiencing every option with her, was overwhelming. She pivoted and walked deliberately to her office. She had to focus. Kadence would be here when her work was done. She might just have to sneak in that closeness later, at the movie.

CHAPTER FIVE

Kadence walked through the loft space, imagining her paintings set up for the world to see. The shows she'd been in before had been exciting, but she'd only had one or two pieces featured. This was going to be all about her. *Colder than Blue* would be her signature series. Would it touch people the way she imagined? Would they feel the emotions she felt when she painted them?

She had painted the first, *Cold Blue Emptiness*, in the month after she and Carlyle broke up. She'd been lost and used the canvas to find a way back to herself. It had been therapeutic to ply the work with paint and let the emotions wash away into the painting. The off-center circle of white was the only bright spot on its surface. Each subsequent painting had been a tool in healing that pain. Would the critical words Carlyle had thrown at her ever be excised from her memory? No, but the worst of the pain was gone. If only she could talk to her one more time and close the book on their relationship once and for all, she would be able to move on.

She hadn't had a real relationship since then. She'd been happy to socialize and hang out, but not willing to give any part of her heart to anyone. She'd had brief physical encounters with women who, like her, had no interest in anything beyond immediate gratification. *Is a relationship what I want?* It was hard for her to determine. She knew she was missing something, that her life was out of balance, but she wasn't sure if risking her heart would help. Maybe she was meant to be alone? Some people were. She could have a full life without having another person to quantify it.

Kadence looked at the tablet, dark in her hands, and brought it to life with a quick slide of her finger. The images were of several loft space shows and the grid framework that held their pieces. She glanced at each, looking for something that connected to what she envisioned for her work. There was a serpentine layout that wove through the space, artwork on both sides. She liked that, but it wouldn't capitalize on her chronological sequence with *Colder*. There was a maze-like framework that was fun and funky, but not quite right. She closed the tablet and wandered down to the first level of the gallery.

The rooms on either side of the main display held two completely different styles of art. The right was all textile work, with a cool scene of felted, rainbow-hued full-size forms at a table with crocheted coffee mugs in front of them. There was a similar scene, smaller scale, of a felted person sleeping, bundled under a blanket of riotous colors with a felted pooch at its feet.

Kadence smiled at the simplicity and joy of the pieces. *This room makes my heart happy.* She sat against a bare space on the wall and let herself be engulfed by the positive power of these sculptures. They held her, cradled her in their expression of happiness and joy. She hugged herself, feeling as if she could slip into these scenes so easily, vanish into imagined serenity.

She sat there taking it all in for a good fifteen minutes before levering herself up and walking to the left wing of the gallery. This room was given over to conceptual reality pieces by various artists. It wasn't as warm as the textile room, but Kadence enjoyed the clever way the artists had used everyday things to create new and different works. The overall feel of the room was steampunk. Gears and pulleys used for building figures and machines. A futuristic cityscape made from trash got her attention.

She spent less time with these works than the happy room. Finally, she steeled herself and walked into the main display area. Sheva's area. She couldn't deny that the bronzes moved her. They sparked with life and movement. The light glinting off the perfect forms warmed them and through that warmth, struck her soul. She made a point of ignoring the bronze torso being groped from behind. That one stirred such a chaos of emotion in her that she knew if she gave in to its call, she'd be a wreck. Something about it, more than the others, unnerved her. She ran her fingers lightly down the arms of the figure emerging from the waves. It was so lifelike she expected it to jerk back from her touch.

Pushing down her reaction, she increased the pressure of her touch, hoping to find it more mundane in its reality. The longer she held the arm, the more overpowering the sense of living form became. It was almost creepy in its intensity. She pulled her hand back and walked to the far wall. She sat against it and opened the tablet again. What was the story Sheva built around these pieces?

It took her a moment to find the gallery guide Mallory had spoken of. Once there, she pulled up the section of the bronzes. The show was titled *Human Ecstasy: Moved and Unmoving*. The six sculptures had been produced over the past two years, the earliest being *Torrid Heat*, the torso she was avoiding. She read about Sheva's lost wax and bronzing process and the amount of time each piece took from conception to final product. *Torrid Heat* had been completed six months after conception, the first of Sheva's non-abstract sculptures. She finished it as her residency at CAA was ending. She had dedicated it to the students of CAA, and so in a way, to Kadence. Maybe that was what drew her to the piece? It was probably modeled by one of her classmates.

Kadence jumped up from the floor and hurried to the piece in question. *Do I know you?* She looked again at the form, the lay of the hands, the shape of the breasts and the navel. She could see that the skin showed goose flesh, a striking detail she had missed earlier. If only the face had been there. She felt like she knew this form, but she couldn't be sure. *Carlyle?*

She reached out and ran her hand down its side, but the contact did nothing to stir up a memory. It probably was one of her classmates; wanting it to be Carlyle and it actually being her were two separate things. She moved back to the wall and used the Internet browser to search Sheva. She didn't know what she was looking for but felt compelled to know more.

As the links populated the screen she heard the chiming of the gallery door. A slim, neatly dressed man walked into the gallery and headed for the stairs. She rose and he jumped, startled by the movement.

He jumped back and clutched his chest. "Oh! You scared me."

"I'm sorry. Hi, I don't think we met the other day. I'm Kadence Munroe." She smiled and held out her hand.

He shook it and immediately relaxed. "Ah, the abstractionist. Wonderful, I'm Tarin. Glad to meet you. What are you doing in the corner?"

"I was just enjoying the bronzes. They're phenomenal." She meant it. Whatever else Sheva was, she made fantastic art.

He looked at the sculptures, breathing in their presence. "They are, indeed. Is Mallory upstairs?"

"Yes. She's doing paperwork, I think." Kadence turned toward the stairs, wondering if she should ask him about the grid for her show.

"And you're here to help plan your layout, right?" He smiled knowingly.

Kadence felt herself warm to this man. He radiated kindness. "That's right."

"Good. Shall we go discuss it with Mallory? I can get the grid framing started as soon as I know the plan." He waved her up the stairs, and then followed.

"Great. She and I talked about it a bit. I want to be as involved as possible without getting in the way."

He paused, mid-step and gazed up at her, his expression curious. "You did? Okay. Well, we like an artist to be involved. Come on."

Despite the weirdness with Sheva's sculptures, Kadence's tension had mostly dissipated. She liked Tarin's calm energy, and the gallery itself felt like a perfect home for her work. Mallory looked up as she entered and waved her to a chair. Tarin closed the door and sat in the chair beside her, waiting patiently while she finished what she was working on.

"Good, you're here. Has Kadence filled you in on the layout details?"

"Not yet"

"I didn't know the procedure, so I left that to you," Kadence said.

"Okay, here's what we worked out." She swung her display around and showed him a three-dimensional image of the spiral they'd talked about.

Kadence gasped. It was perfect. She could picture her works laid on the framework. This was exactly right for her. "Oh my God, I love it! How did you do that?"

"It's part of my job. So you think this layout will work?"

"Perfectly." Kadence could hardly contain her excitement. This was really happening. Her show was beginning to come together, and Mallory's ideas were going to make it soar.

"Can you print that out for me so I can get started?" Tarin said.

"It's on the printer. I had a feeling it would work. Kadence has volunteered to help with spacing and detail. Make sure she doesn't touch any of the build." She gave Kadence a firm look, to let her know she was serious, but there was a gentle smile in there too.

"Got it, boss." He nodded to Kadence. "Come on."

They spent the next two hours moving and arranging the framework. Even though she wasn't allowed to touch it, Kadence was fascinated by the durable, lightweight structure that conformed so easily to the direction Tarin gave it. It was strong enough to support her paintings, but light enough to be malleable.

"That stuff is amazing. I've never seen anything like it." She was mesmerized by the flowing, almost liquid way the walls undulated.

"It's pretty cool, huh? Mallory is always on top of new innovations when it comes to the gallery. I think that's part of her charm and why she's perfect as director. She's not afraid to take a chance on something. She found this stuff through one of her mother's friends. I'm not sure about the exact details, but I know it's cutting edge and no other gallery has it. It's refreshing to have someone in control who's focused on presenting the art in the best way. Our last director was only interested in making connections to move up to a bigger and better posting."

"I think she's great. I don't know why she picked me to feature, but I couldn't be happier."

"If she chose you, then there's a reason. It's in your work. All you have to do is let her show it. She's amazing."

Warmth rushed through her as Kadence realized, again, how lucky she was.

When Tarin was satisfied with the placement of the framework, he asked her what colors were predominant in her pieces. She rattled off the blues and purples she used most heavily. She described the smaller pieces that would adorn the outer walls of the space. He nodded, plugged something into a floor outlet, and the framework flashed with color.

"Watch and tell me when we get to a color group that's close to what you've got in your series."

The colors flashed and scattered across the framework. Pinks, reds, oranges, yellows, greens, and finally, blues. She watched as they shifted and moved. "Stop!"

He looked up as the darker hued blues flashed on the screen. He nodded and entered something on his key pad. The framework seemed to shimmer, then lit in a wave of contrasting color. Kadence was dumbfounded. The shades were the exact complement to the blue hues still frozen in the upper corner of the right wall.

"That's unbelievable. How?"

"Don't ask me. I just type in what Mallory told me to type in and the magic happens. Your walls are officially 'light goldenrod' as per the color matcher. Wait."

He entered a few more commands and the entire wall was washed with the subtle golden light.

"Do you like it?"

Kadence was blown away by how perfect the buttery yellow would be. Chills chased up her arms. "I love it."

"Good. Let's do the exterior walls."

"Seriously? The walls are on that system, too?"

"You bet. But only here in the loft. The lower gallery is due to be upgraded to the light-wall fabric next year. What works best here? You said teal and turquoise, yellow, red and orange, right?"

"Yes. I don't know what would work best with all of those." Her stomach twisted, and she wished she had contained her color scheme a little. Those colors were so varied, it wouldn't be easy to find a hue that would work for all of them.

"That's what the program figures out. Here, come and watch."

He held the pad to the side and made room for her to squeeze in close. Kadence watched as he entered each of the colors and hit a series of commands. The screen mimicked the walls and flipped through a series of colors, settling on a wash of color that started as pale orange and darkened in the center, then lightened to a deep turquoise.

"So. The paintings with more teal and turquoise go on the orange and the orange and reds go on the turquoise?"

"Exactly. Once we have the actual pieces on the wall, we can tweak the colors to make the best fit."

"I'm blown away by all of this. It's going to be surreal seeing my work here." She felt a surge of panic at the thought of her work, her deepest emotions on display. How would that feel, having strangers walk through her emotional life? Would they understand her point of view or would they see only empty rectangles? She was unnerved by fear and had a sudden desire to run. *What am I doing here? This may be the biggest mistake of my life. I'm not good enough for all of this.*

Tarin seemed to read her mind. He stopped fiddling with the tablet and looked at her sharply. "You're here because you belong here. Your show is going to be a hit, just wait and see."

Kadence wanted to believe him, but fear was powerful. Somewhere, somehow, Mallory had seen her work, and in that viewing, had found something that gave her belief in Kadence's talent. That was a huge responsibility, and also a huge source of anxiety. *I hope I can prove her right.*

"Hey, nerves are natural. Don't be too hard on yourself. Let's finish up, huh?"

"Guess you've seen it before, huh? The agony of the self-defeating artist?" She tried to make it sound like a joke but knew she'd failed when he looked at her sympathetically.

"Absolutely. But I promise, you have no reason to worry."

Kadence nodded, grateful for his unsolicited comfort. They continued to work on the spacing for each painting and decided to hang the exterior wall paintings at oblique angles to heighten interest in each one. When they finished, Kadence looked at the space and imagined her work, the lighting, the gallery patrons moving through the space.

Tomorrow the paintings would be moved and the reality of her show would be undeniable. Anxiety and pride warred inside her, but she forced the anxiety down. *If they didn't think I was good enough, I wouldn't be here.* She thanked Tarin for letting her help and left him to his other responsibilities. There were several people in the gallery, and he needed to be available to them.

She returned to the bronzes and watched the afternoon light play on them. A feeling of sadness nearly overwhelmed her. What was it about these figures that drew her? Why did they have such a hold on her? She walked through the space, pausing in front of each one. The melancholy increased exponentially as she drew near *Torrid Heat*. She knew she shouldn't, but she ran her hands down either side and pressed herself to the torso. *Why are you so familiar?* She touched a small imperfection on the hip of the sculpture, a small round bump, the size of a peppercorn. She leaned down to look, but voices from the textile room made her step back.

It wouldn't do to be caught molesting the sculptures. She moved past *Torrid Heat* and on to *Broken Wave*, then out the door and onto the street. She'd go grab a bite to eat and come back closer to closing time so they could go to the theater.

Why can't I keep my hands off those sculptures?

Sheva had unbalanced Mallory, just as she'd planned. She would be completely in her hands soon. Confusion was key to her success. It had worked in the past and it would work this time as well.

She had new rubber molds ready for waxing. This one would be called *Pride*. The model had been a dancer she had dallied with in Atlantic City, someone who appreciated her skill both in the bedroom and in the studio. Her perfect moment was when she realized Sheva was going to capture her soul in bronze. She'd considered leaving her face intact because her expression had been so perfect, but it wouldn't fit with the others, so she settled for leaving her face below the nose. The impact of her partial expression was going to be transcendental.

The difficult process of creating the rubber molds behind her, she brought in assistants to help with the wax figure production. She had the three prepare the microcrystalline wax, melting and carefully pouring it into the mother molds. They helped her move the molds around to fill the entire inner surface of the rubber molds with wax. They repeated the process until the wax was a quarter-inch thick.

She sent them home afterward, knowing the cooling process took time. Tomorrow they would return to help unmold the wax castings. This one was going to be beautiful. She would spend the rest of her evening cleaning her kiln. It needed to be pristine for the firing since it wouldn't do for them to see what she had to remove. Some things you had to do yourself.

CHAPTER SIX

Mallory hit send on the initial order for catering the opening of Kadence's show. She needed to double-check the numbers from the invitation returns. There had been good response so far, but it never hurt to follow up with those less likely to RSVP. *I should invite my mother. She'd really enjoy Kadence's work, but would I enjoy having her here? Would her presence detract from Kadence's big moment? Maybe if I could trust her not to upstage Kadence, but that would be like asking a tiger to change its stripes.* She struggled with the idea. Her mother had come to Sheva's opening, but Sheva was a recognized name already. Besides, even Sanford Tucker would find it hard to upstage Sheva. She dominated a room.

Why are there such disparities in artists' personalities? Kadence had shown none of the overreaching ego her mother and Sheva shared. The same was true for about half of the artists she'd shown. She'd always suspected it had to do with self-confidence and recognition, but that hadn't always held true. Her childhood on Monhegan proved that to her. Her "uncle" Jamie and his wife had been so real, so connected to life and had given her a sense of self-worth her parents hadn't. Her father, consciously, her mother, obliviously. So why? *Is there something fundamental missing in some of them that makes it impossible for some of them to relate to and treasure other people?*

A hollow feeling swallowed her. It was the same feeling she had when she thought of her relationship with her father. He would have dismissed her career as a hobby. No matter what she achieved professionally, it would be diminished by the lack of appreciation from her mother. *That's why I'm torn about inviting her. Do I want her here for Kadence or for my own selfish reasons?* Did it matter? If she came, it would guarantee press coverage for the show, and that could only help Kadence. It was the smart thing to do. If she built in false hopes of receiving her mother's praise, that was her problem to deal with. Her job was to show artists and create a buzz about their works. That was where she needed to focus. Having Sanford Tucker at Kadence Munroe's opening would be a good thing.

Resolved, she sent the email invitation to her mother. She knew it would be a while before she heard back from her, but she'd opened the door. Now all she had to do was armor herself against the personal disappointment she knew she'd invited.

The door chimed, and she knew the gallery had several patrons currently in house. She got up to help Tarin. He was engaged with a young couple in the textile room so she met the new arrivals at the foyer and led them to the bronzes they'd come to see.

The clients were regulars at the gallery, and Mallory was glad to see them. They'd been in several times to see the bronzes, and she was sure she'd close the sale on one with them soon. The question was only which piece they would select.

"My favorite is *Torrid Heat*," the older woman, Christina, said.

"I don't know. I'm torn between that and this one," the younger woman, Chas, said.

"*Love's Birth*." Mallory supplied the name of the sculpture. It was an outstanding piece. A nude woman emerging from rock, visible from mid-thigh through the torso, and ending in abstract flames just above the chin. "It's my personal favorite. How can I help you ladies come to a decision? This show ends in five days so the remaining sculptures will move on to the artist's next show."

"Five days? That's so little time to decide." Christina looked worried. She put an arm around Chas's shoulder and gave a squeeze.

"I know, but they've been with us since July." Mallory didn't want to pressure the women. They were good, dependable clients, and she wanted it to stay that way.

"Do you know where the show will move?" asked Chas.

"I believe the shipping orders are Geneva, so my guess would be the Baffler or Salutations. I can ask Sheva, if you like."

"Yes, please. We definitely want one now, but we may have to have both."

"Well, you certainly have the room for them." Mallory knew the women had an expansive estate in Greenwich. She'd already helped them acquire several pieces for their collection. "I do hope you'll come to our opening Saturday. I have a hunch Kadence Munroe is going to be the next big thing in the art world."

"Do tell? Are you going to give us a sneak peek?" Christina said.

"You know I'm not able to do that. I'll be sure and mark the paintings I think best suited to your collection in your guide."

"You're so good to us, Mallory. Will your mother be here?" Christina looked at her hopefully.

"I've invited her. I'm not sure of her schedule, but if possible, I know she'll make an appearance."

"Good, we don't see enough of Sanford. So, shall we take *Torrid Heat* or *Love's Birth*?"

"*Torrid Heat*. It must be *Torrid Heat*," Chas said.

Christina looked at Chas fondly. "All right. Mallory, will you draw up the paperwork and send it to me?"

"I will. Of course, I need to clear the sale with Sheva, but I'm sure there will be no complications. I can have it delivered following the close of the show."

"Perfect. We're off now, ta."

"Ta, ladies. Do come on Saturday."

"Indeed, we're looking forward to it."

Mallory felt a pang of envy, watching them walk out. *Will I ever have someone look at me like that?* She sighed, then wanted to high-five someone. She'd just sold two of the bronzes. A nice day's work, provided Sheva didn't play any games. Mallory loved knowing the bronze would go to a place it would be appreciated. She hoped Sheva would be cooperative. She wasn't sure how Sheva would react to anything. Her connection to her sculptures was intense. They'd had to scuttle a sale on *Broken Wave* because Sheva didn't feel like the buyer appreciated the sculpture. She'd challenged their contract and won with the board of directors. This one shouldn't be a problem. These ladies worshipped their art, and it would lead to future sales for Sheva. Surely, she couldn't make waves about this sale. *I hope.*

She went to the office and wrote Sheva an email detailing the sale and the patrons. Her stomach churned as she hit send. She wished she'd never gotten involved with her. It had brought her nothing but pain, and now, it weakened her position as gallery director to artist. The acid in her stomach was wreaking havoc, so she looked through her purse for an antacid. She'd just popped a tablet into her mouth when her phone rang.

She tensed, willing the conversation to go smoothly. "Hello?"

"Mallory."

Cold, but not openly hostile, this might go okay. "Sheva. Did you get my email?"

"Yes. You have a buyer for *Torrid Heat*?"

Sheva's voice had risen, showing she was upset. Mallory used her own tone to try to calm her. "Yes."

"And what do we know about these buyers? I don't let my work go to just anyone."

Stay calm. Don't react. "I'm aware. These patrons are regular buyers at ARA. They come to almost every opening, and I'm sure you've met them. Christina Lorde and Chas Drummer? Here, let me send you their profile." She opened the gallery page on her browser and signed in. When she found the file she emailed it to Sheva. There was silence on the line while she presumably read.

"Greenwich? That's kind of out of the way for one of my pieces."

Peeved, Mallory shot off an answer, then wished she could take it back. "These ladies host parties regularly with the art set. You'll get lots of buzz from this sale. They're also very interested in *Love's Birth* and may end up wanting to purchase that as well."

"Two? No one should have two of my pieces. They each deserve their own domain. I don't think I can sign on to this sale."

She ground her teeth in frustration. *Not again.* "Seriously? Why are we showing your work if not to sell it?"

Sheva sighed as though put out. "You know I have influence with your board."

"Correction, you *had* influence, but allowing the cancellation of the sale of *Breaking Wave* cost the gallery a pretty penny. If you think the board doesn't have the bottom line in mind, you're kidding yourself. There is no reasonable cause to cancel this sale. If you insist on bringing it up to the board, understand, I'll fight you on it."

"Oh! I'm so scared. Not. Ask the ladies to come by and I'll interview them to see if they're a match for my beautiful girl."

"I won't do that. I've submitted the paperwork for the sale. The contract is binding and I'll deliver the sculpture at the show's end. If you want to challenge the sale, you'll have to go to the board on your own. I've got to go." She hung up before Sheva could engage her in an argument. This was getting ridiculous. How could she function at this level if she wasn't willing to sell her pieces?

She wanted to punch somebody, her every muscle taut with annoyance. *Damn her and her ego.* She shoved away from her desk and thought about her earlier reaction to Sheva's asinine behavior. *Don't throw anything. Just let it go. The board can deal with this.* If they let her crash the sale again, they would only have themselves to blame. She walked down to the main floor just as Kadence was coming in the door. *Thank goodness, she'll help me get over this.* "Hey there."

Kadence smiled up at her and she felt a flutter in her chest. That smile was powerful, and Mallory liked being its recipient.

"Hi. It's almost closing time, right?"

"Yes. I'm looking forward to getting out of here, too. Are we still set for the show?" She waved, signaling Kadence to come upstairs.

"We are." Kadence took the stairs two at a time and was beside her in a heartbeat. She smelled so damn good, Mallory was tempted to pull her down and nuzzle her neck.

"Good. Let me see if Tarin can handle closing with the staff and we can head out."

"That sounds good to me."

Tarin was happy to close, so they were out on the street moments later. They walked to the train station. Kadence was easy to be with. Mallory knew the tension from her conversation with Sheva was still radiating from her, and it was nice not to be asked about it before she processed it. As they settled into their seats, she finally relaxed and felt human again.

"I'm sorry I'm such poor company."

"On the contrary, you're real. You're feeling something and I'm giving you space. That's what friends do, right?"

The smile that accompanied her easy words warmed Mallory's heart. She smiled back. "Yeah, that's what friends do. What did you do with your day?"

"Oh, I had a great day. I helped plan the framework for my show. Man, those panels are amazing. I've never heard of anything like them. Where did you find them?"

"I can't give away all my secrets. They're awesome, huh?"

"Yeah, they are. Then I spent some time with the other works in the gallery. I hate to admit it, but I can't get Sheva's sculptures out of my head. They're so powerful."

Kadence's face flushed as she spoke, but Mallory couldn't tell if it was embarrassment or something else that caused it.

"I know what you mean. They really are something. It's too bad she doesn't want to sell them."

"What? That makes a gallery show kind of pointless, doesn't it?"

"I think so, but I'm only the director. The board members don't always agree with me." She was getting hot again, and that wasn't fair to Kadence. She tried to shut off her emotions.

Kadence touched her arm. "Don't do that. Don't feel like you have to stifle your emotions around me. It's okay to be mad. I'd be mad, too. I mean, you make us sign a contract with the idea of selling our work. It would piss me off if my job was being undermined."

"Exactly! I can't believe they sided with her on the last sale she torpedoed. Now, two of my best clients want to purchase and she's balking again. The fact that they let her get away with it once is going to make it that much harder to secure the sale now." Mallory tightened her hands into fists in front of her. Sheva was a problem, there was no other way to say it. She needed to solve the problem or she'd be the one covered in crap. Her instinct was to call the board right now, to do something to keep the sale. When she saw Kadence's worried expression, it made her pause. "I'm sorry. You don't need this dumped on you."

"No, you're right, that sucks. Why won't she sell? It makes no sense."

Mallory appreciated Kadence even more. She needed to talk about this, and Kadence was willing to listen. "Ugh. She must be sure her 'girls' are going to the right homes. She wants to interview my clients! I can't allow that."

"What are you going to do?"

"What can I do? If they approve her scuttling the sale, I'll have to break it to my clients. I hope that doesn't happen, but it might." She dreaded the thought that she might be put in that position again.

"That's harsh. I hope you don't have to do that."

The real concern in Kadence's eyes warmed her heart. She was so glad they'd gotten so close these past couple of weeks. "Thanks. At least you're my next big thing. You won't be giving me these kind of headaches, will you?" Mallory looked at her with a raised eyebrow.

"Not a chance. If someone wants to buy my work, I'll be honored. You'll have no problems with me."

"If? Believe me, people will buy your artwork. It has its own power."

"If you say so."

She knew so. Kadence underestimated the elemental force of her work. The way it drew you right in and twisted your heart. That would make people buy, she had no doubt. She leaned into Kadence, letting the anxiety and anger waft away with the passing tunnel walls. She needed to let it go and enjoy this time, enjoy Kadence. She wouldn't give Sheva the power to get between them.

Kadence reacted by sliding her arm around Mallory's shoulders in a gesture of comfort and friendship.

Their station came up and they left the train. They walked the short distance to the theater. When they got into the lobby, Kadence rushed to the concessions stand like a child. Mallory laughed as she put both hands on the glass and pressed her face against it.

"Cut it out, silly. Don't you know these poor attendants have to clean that glass? You're such a kid." It made her feel like a kid again herself, being with Kadence. The light way she looked at life, her easygoing spirit. Mallory needed this. It was the perfect antidote to Sheva.

"But picking the candy's the best part. Come on, get down here with me. What'll it be? Mike and Ike? Dots? What's your favorite?"

Mallory squatted down beside her and looked at the colorful candy packages under the bright counter lights. *I haven't bought candy at the movies in a decade.*

"I know what I'm getting. Raisinets. They're healthy." Mallory pointed to the yellow and red box on the top shelf.

"Ha! You're funny. If those are healthy, so are Sno-Caps." Kadence nodded at the neighboring box.

"Raisins are healthy."

"Um, so is dark chocolate. Can we get that fruit and nut chocolate bar? That has fruit and protein, very healthy." The sad eyes Kadence gave her were too much. *Who could resist that face?*

"Oh yum! I didn't see that. Okay. That and some popcorn."

"Sounds good."

They took their spoils and found the theater. Mallory was carrying the popcorn and her drink. As she walked into the darkened theater, she walked straight into Kadence, who'd stopped in the middle of the aisle.

"Why are you not walking forward?"

"Well, because."

"Because why?"

"Because I don't know where you like to sit. I mean, are you a front row person, a back of the house person, or a mid-level person?"

"I'm an about to spill the popcorn person. I can sit anywhere, so you choose."

Kadence clearly agonized over where to sit, but finally settled into a seat near the middle of the theater. Mallory handed down the bucket of popcorn and sat down beside her. Kadence was too sweet. *Worried about where I like to sit? Who does that?* All the tangled, poisonous vines of her relationship with Sheva fell to dust when she was with Kadence. She mattered every moment with her, and she knew it. This thing about not going further than friends was starting to chafe. If she let this opportunity go without boldly saying what she wanted, she'd always regret it. *But what if it goes to hell? Haven't I learned my lesson about dating my artists?* She looked over at Kadence, the light from the screen reflecting on her rapt face. *I want you.* But she waited. What she wanted wasn't always good for her, as Sheva had proven. She needed to stay professional.

"I'm so jazzed to see this film. Do you like Alejandro's work?"

"I love it. Thanks again for the invitation. You turned this day around for me."

Kadence smiled. "My pleasure. Oh, cool, here come the previews."

Mallory felt better than she had in ages. She felt like she could sit beside Kadence all day. As the film began she found the story drawing her in, pulling her attention away from her immediate problems.

The movie was excellent, exciting and funny at the same time. Kadence had this habit of grabbing her arm when the tension ratcheted up. It made her all fuzzy inside when she did that. *Don't make anything of it. She's just enjoying the movie, and she doesn't even know she's doing it.*

The movie ended and Mallory waited to see if Kadence would jump up to leave. She hated being in the crush of the crowd exiting a theater. She liked to wait for the end credits to finish. She steeled herself to push through with the herd, but Kadence sat patiently, watching the screen.

Her body relaxed, and comfort, like an old friend, washed through her. She slid her hand over Kadence's arm, and smiled when she folded it in her own. When they stood to leave, Kadence tightened her grip on Mallory's hand and smiled. A sense of rightness came over her. Her hand belonged in Kadence's. There was none of that awkward, sweaty palm stuff that she detested, just smooth, warm togetherness. She willed herself not to make a big deal of it. *We're just friends.* Being attracted to Kadence didn't mean she had to act. The thing with Sheva had been a mistake she didn't want to repeat. *Just chill. Be the professional you are.*

"That was fun. Do you want to get some coffee?" Kadence said.

"I'd like that. You're so easy to be with. Thanks for helping me get over this day."

"Aw, it was nothing. You'd do the same for me, right?"

"Sure I would. Do you know of a coffee shop nearby? Or we could go to the deli." Mallory really didn't want their time to be over yet.

"Let's walk to Ink. They have great coffee. It's only a few blocks."

"That sounds good to me."

They walked hand in hand the four blocks to the shop. Mallory kept expecting Kadence to realize they were still holding hands and shake hers free, but it didn't happen. Her whole spirit lightened as they walked along. *This thing that shouldn't happen is happening. Now what? I should pull away.* She didn't.

Ink was a coffee shop/tattoo parlor. The rustic charm appealed to Mallory, and it was clear Kadence was something of a regular. They greeted her by name and asked if she'd come for liquid or needle.

"Liquid today, but I need to get back here soon for ink."

"Yeah, you do. That dragon isn't complete and I'd hate for you to show it off unfinished," called a bleached blond from the studio area.

"I know, Jake. I promise, I'll be in next week."

Kadence led Mallory to a small scarred table near the window. "You save our table, I'll grab the coffee. How do you take it?"

"Strong with a splash of chocolate milk and cinnamon."

"Nice. Okay, I'll be right back."

Mallory watched her walk to the serving counter. She had an undefined grace in the way she moved, like a tiger, unhurried but deliberate. Her pulse sped up as she watched the play of Kadence's long muscles in her tight jeans. Catching herself ogling, she looked around the room for a distraction. She found one in the riotous colors on the arms of a man sitting a few tables away. He had intricate designs tattooed into sleeves on both left and right. She studied them, finding a mermaid and a dragon entwined around his elbow. What did the guy mean, her dragon? Kadence obviously had a tattoo, but where? Would she be okay with Mallory asking about it, or was it too personal? Was her dragon like the one on that man's arm? She looked closer, noting the detail in the artwork.

"What're you looking at?" Kadence said as she slipped into her chair.

"Those tattoos. How long do you think that took to complete?"

"That? Wow, could be anywhere from seven months to more than a year. It depends on how long he could sit for sessions and how quickly he healed in between."

"Healed?" Mallory didn't realize there was healing involved.

"Um, yeah. You don't have any tattoos, do you?"

"No, but I've thought about getting one." *But not if it hurts.*

"Each time you get one you're basically dealing with an open wound. You have to let that heal before you can add more around it." Kadence ran a hand over her left shoulder, tapping the area lightly.

"Wow, I had no idea."

"Most people don't. Until you have a tattoo, you don't think about it."

"So, you have tattoos, right?"

Kadence grinned and chuckled. "Yeah, I have a few. The biggest one is on my back and around to my upper chest. It's a rainbow dragon."

Mallory suddenly wanted nothing more than to see that dragon. She looked at the collar of Kadence's shirt, hoping for a peek.

"Nope. You can't see it unless I have my shirt off. Everything but the neck and head is on my back. Right now it's only a third of the way colored."

"Would you show me?" The thought of her shirt off made Mallory's stomach flip.

"Uh, maybe. If it gets hot enough in the gallery to wear a tank."

"You mean you won't just take off your shirt for me?" Mallory batted her eyes in an imitation of a junior high kid flirting for the first time.

Kadence blushed the shade of a radish. "No. I mean, you're kind of my boss right now. That wouldn't be appropriate."

Mallory enjoyed her reaction. It felt like the teasing of the week before, but without the overtones. More of a friendly teasing. "Why not?"

"Mallory. You know why not. When my show ends, if you haven't seen it, ask me again. For now, that's off the table." Her smile was gentle, taking some of the bite out of her words, but it was obvious she meant it.

Mallory shrugged off the refusal, but she couldn't help the sting of disappointment that it brought. *I'd really like to see that dragon. Maybe I'll turn the heater on at the gallery tomorrow.*

CHAPTER SEVEN

The movie had been better than Kadence had hoped. And being with Mallory had been great. She was fun and easy to be with, not to mention gorgeous. She'd opened up a little, but nothing serious, and built their friendship. It felt good. The only moment that threatened to push beyond them, Kadence had turned aside pretty easily.

It was a shame she couldn't have shown Mallory her dragon, but that would have gone beyond her comfort level. She was proud of her ink. The best thing about it was that Jake was trading her art for art, so her bank account wasn't taking a hit. It was only costing her two walls of murals. *One day I'll show her, when there isn't that weirdness of being in her debt.*

They'd taken the train back to Mallory's apartment and walked her to her door, then, after the briefest kiss on the cheek, she'd said good night and headed home. It was still early, and the streets around Mallory's place were full of people looking for fun. If she wanted, she could go back to Ink and get some work done. She considered it, not feeling like being in her apartment, but it might not be a good idea having a raw tattoo on a day she had to haul her paintings. Blood seeping through a bandage under her shirt would probably put people off. Not exactly the impression she wanted to make.

Tomorrow she'd help with the realization of her show. *My show. How awesome is that?* She had to pinch herself every time she thought about it. It was happening. After Saturday, she'd either be a flash in the pan, or an up-and-coming artist. Which one would it be? She felt the jitterbugs bopping in her gut, warning her that this line of thinking wasn't going to help her sleep tonight.

She shut it down and crossed to the train station. It would take her forty minutes to get back to Bushwick, and she needed to find something to settle her mind. A sleepless night would make a painful morning. She slid into a seat and put her earbuds in, pulled up the book she'd been listening to, and let the narrator's voice carry her away.

By the time they reached her stop, she was lost in a world of dragons and evil men, her earlier anxiety gone. She put away her stuff and headed up to the street. It was quieter here, but the foot traffic had increased since she'd moved in, with more restaurants keeping later hours.

The scent of fresh basil filled the air as she walked past Berta's. They always had a line at that place, but Kadence rarely stopped to eat there, since she was pretty careful with money. She wanted the term "starving artist" to stay a concept rather than a reality. It smelled divine and briefly made Kadence reconsider. *Maybe after the show, if I've managed to sell anything.* She turned onto her block and skipped up her stairs to her apartment. The roomies must be out, as no light shown in the place. She made her way through the shared hallway and unlocked her room. Just as she'd left it, the blue-black painting watched her from the far corner. Maybe she could add to that tonight? She wasn't feeling it, though. When she painted, she wasn't in control; it was in the hands of her emotions and they directed when, and what, she would create. Tonight, she was lackadaisical. She had a full stomach, a happy heart, and no worries. In her world, that added up to no creative drive. Better to shower and try to get some sleep than to try to paint. It never worked to push her muse.

The water felt good on her charged skin, hot and hard, the way she liked it. She ran her fingers through her hair, working at the tangles as the conditioner softened them. As the water washed down her body she looked at her arms and legs, remembering how thin they were when she was younger. They were still thin, but at least she didn't look like she was a day away from starving anymore. She traced the crisscross scars on her thigh, feeling the sting of the switch her mom had used. She'd made her go out and pick one off the shrub in the yard. That had been almost worse than the stinging blows, having to pull and tug at the thin branch, knowing its purpose. Her mother had taken every sour thing in her life out on Kadence. If she hadn't gotten the scholarship that took her to California, she had no idea where she'd be now.

She shook off the unpleasant memories and grabbed the small blue vial from the rack. Lavender essential oil poured into the stream of hot water gave her a therapeutic end to her nightly ritual. Standing with her back against the ceramic tiles, breathing it in, she imagined Mallory standing there with her. Her nipples tightened and she shuddered as the vision washed over her. Mallory naked, her hair damp against her face, her body compact but strong. Her breasts would be fuller than Kadence's with smaller nipples. The thatch of hair at the top of her thighs, thick and golden brown. Her lips, so often canted to the side in humor, would be full and moist, waiting for her kiss. Kadence slipped into the fantasy, wanting it to be a reality, but knew she couldn't let it happen. She slid her hand between her legs and gave in to the only release she would take from this relationship. When she finished, she slumped forward, allowing the water to pummel her head and dash the thoughts away. She climbed from the shower and wrapped up in her Egyptian cotton oversized bath towel. It was her one indulgence, a towel that was more of a blanket.

When she was dry and in her comfy T-shirt and cotton pajama pants, she plopped down in her chair. Why was it Mallory had filled her mind? Why couldn't she keep the wall she constructed around herself intact? It was so much better not to have connections like the one she was building with Mallory. So much safer and less painful. Her thoughts went back to Carlyle and the emptiness that experience brought her.

I need to get some resolution with her. I need to call her, find her, and say the things I should have said back then. If I don't, I might never be able to let anyone in.

She walked to the closet and pulled out her messenger bag. One more time, she dumped it out, found the notebook, and stared at it. She made herself look for the number. *Don't stop this time. Don't. You need to do this.*

She entered the number into her phone and hit call. She tightened her grip on the phone as the other end rang and rang. *What if it's not her parents' number anymore?* She was about to cancel the call when there was a voice in her ear.

"Hello?"

"Um, hi. I don't know if you remember me. My name is Kadence Munroe. I'm trying to find Carlyle Goodwin."

There was silence on the other end, broken only by the sound of the other person's breathing. If Kadence had wanted to cancel the call before, now she wanted to more than ever.

"I went to school with her, a few years ago. Is she there? Or do you know where I might find her?"

Finally, Kadence heard something, a sound like muffled crying. *What the heck?*

"I'm sorry, I must have the wrong number." She started to pull the phone away from her ear, but the voice on the other end stopped her.

"Wait! Please, don't hang up. It's just that you shocked me. Please."

"I'm still here."

"Oh, thank God. It's just that, well, no one has called about Carlyle in more than a year. It took me by surprise to hear her name."

"Has something happened to her? I mean, she left school midterm. We'd all assumed she went home."

"No, she never came home. We haven't heard from her since Thanksgiving two years ago. She was so excited about her life back then. She called to let us know she wasn't coming home for Christmas. Told us not to worry, that she was going to New York with an artist friend. That was the last we heard from her."

"Really? Wow, I promise you, everyone at school thought she was going home. And then, when she didn't come back, well, we thought it was because of the breakup." Her stomach tightened. Carlyle hadn't gone home? Hadn't been heard from since that Thanksgiving? How was it possible that she didn't know that?

"Breakup? What breakup?"

"The breakup with the sculptor who was the visiting artist that year."

"This is the first I've heard of it. She said her friend was taking her to see the galleries in New York. They were going to spend the holidays there."

"Did she mention the friend's name? I knew most of the same people." It had to be Sheva. Who else? What had happened? Cool sweat covered her as she realized her anger and disappointment with Carlyle back then might have kept her from knowing Carlyle was in trouble.

"Not that I can recall. Her father and I assumed everything was fine when she didn't call to let us know how her holiday had been. When she didn't call on my birthday at the end of January, I was heartbroken. We tried not to worry. She was twenty-two and able to take care of herself. We thought she wanted space, freedom, you know what I mean? Then spring break and still, no word. We couldn't believe she wouldn't want us at her graduation. Her phone number was disconnected, and we were at a loss. We loaded up the car and drove to California. When we got to the campus, no one had seen her since before Christmas. It was devastating. We didn't know what to do. It had been five months. The police were helpful, but they really had no leads to follow. We hired a private investigator to search for her there and one in New York, but we've had no luck."

"But no one told me. I mean, we were very close. Someone should have asked me something." Guilt poured through her, making it hard to think. If they'd asked her, what could she have said? Carlyle had refused her calls and changed her number a few weeks after they broke up. As close-knit as the campus was, she'd not seen Carlyle again. Carlyle had been the social one, making tons of friends. Kadence only had one real friend from school, her roommate, Tara. Tara was so pissed at the way Carlyle treated Kadence that she'd written her off. "I'm so sorry. I wanted to talk to Carlyle about something that happened that last year. I hope I didn't cause you too much pain by calling."

"Oh, no, that's okay. The pain is a part of every breath I take. I'll never stop looking for her."

"I'm sure you won't. If I ever hear anything, I'll contact you."

"What was your name again? And how did you know Carlyle?"

Kadence swallowed the bile rising in her throat. "Well, we dated. We were together for a year and a half." She waited to see how that would settle. She knew Carlyle had been in the closet at home. She'd hardly ever gone to visit, and Kadence had seen her ignore calls from her parents. But if Carlyle had gone missing, it wasn't the time to worry about outing her.

There was a sharp intake of breath on the other end of the phone. "What? Excuse me, what did you say?"

"I was Carlyle's girlfriend, junior year and for the first part of senior year."

"You were her…I'm sorry, I'm having a hard time processing this. Are you saying my daughter was in a same-sex relationship with you?"

"Yes, ma'am." Kadence felt like she'd been punched. Why were some people so blind to their own children?

"Oh dear. Oh. Tell me your name again." She could hear the shock in the woman's tone, but she didn't seem angry, just confused.

"It's Kadence Munroe."

"Could you give me your phone number? I need to sit down, but I'd like to talk with you later."

"Of course." Kadence gave her the number and hung up. She felt the tension in her shoulders and neck and figured it would probably be there for a while.

How could this have happened? Why wouldn't the police, or at the least the private investigator, have contacted her? Carlyle's friends knew about them, didn't they? They had to. The first nine months they were together they were never apart. Except for classes. And well, Carlyle had her design labs on some weekends. But they'd never hidden the fact that they were together. At least, Kadence hadn't. But what about Carlyle?

She thought back to that time and how busy they were, how excited about school and friends. Everyone kind of hung out in a group most of the time, and Carlyle hadn't been a fan of public affection, so they hadn't even held hands. But Kadence respected her wishes on that, knowing full well how important boundaries were. When they'd been alone, it had always been after being with the group. They'd always gone to Kadence's room, Carlyle's roomies being more in number and less likely to give them privacy. Maybe she'd never been open at all.

The realization rocked her to her core. *Did Carlyle really never tell anyone about us? Is that why no one ever contacted me?* She felt the old scars from the betrayal two years ago rip open and fresh red pain well out. It was like she'd been eviscerated. She'd never been anything real to Carlyle. She wanted to vomit.

The shock of finding out Carlyle hadn't been safe in Nebraska all this time wiped her out. Every muscle in her body felt like jelly. If she'd had to get up, she didn't think she'd be able to. What happened to Carlyle? What did Sheva know? Had anyone asked her, or was their relationship a secret, like hers and Carlyle's?

Kadence had to do something. It wasn't right that she'd just disappeared. She sent emails to a couple of Carlyle's friends from that time, asking what they knew. She hoped some would answer. She hadn't kept up with anyone from school. She knew what she needed to do was confront Sheva. She had to know something. It was clear she was the friend who was supposed to take her to New York.

Anxiety ballooned in her gut, destroying the good feeling she'd had before. She wasn't good at confrontation. Her only model growing up had been her mother. She would never give in to violence like her, so what did she have left? She avoided conflict like the plague, but she couldn't this time. She had to find out what Sheva knew.

The first email response came in, and Kadence hurried to open it. It was from Tara. She had nothing new to share, and was as surprised by the news as Kadence had been. She said she'd ask the friends she had that knew Carlyle. Like Kadence, she'd simply assumed Carlyle had gone home and cut ties with her schoolmates.

Helpless and wired, Kadence sought release in her painting. Now she had something to put into it. The canvas was rippled with waves from her physical dive into the wet paint. There were peaks of color that spoke to her of fear. *Now I can elaborate on that fear.* She squeezed some Winsor deep yellow onto the palette and, using a fan brush, washed the ridge tips with streaks of yellow. She pulled it down, making the ridges appear as if they were weeping yellow tears. Gathering the different trails, she drew them into an odd shaped mass, like a pool of despair. While this was still wet, she took her palette knife and cut jagged lines through it. She'd fill these with red and orange later. The whole piece was a frenetic mess, and it captured exactly what she was feeling. Jagged, broken, cast into a world of uncertainty by the knowledge that her chance at closure was possibly gone forever, and that something terrible might have happened to Carlyle.

She took the titanium white and loaded her knife with it. She stood back from the canvas and flung the paint, hitting the ridges with elongated circles of white. She watched as some of the larger blobs of paint rolled sluggishly down the uneven surface.

It was so satisfying to see her representation of uncertainty flow into the pool she'd created. It made sense. Something had to make sense. Before she could do anything to change the work, she grabbed her palette and tools and took them to her sink. *Wash it away. Wash the uncertainty away. Don't look at the painting, just wash this down the drain.*

She carefully rinsed the brushes, feathering the tips a bit under the water. The palette washed clean in a few seconds. She kept the painting to her back, knowing looking at it might make her want to jump back into it. She needed to give these new movements time to dry. Give herself time and distance from these emotions. When all was clean, she stacked the palette and stood the brushes in a cup. She dropped onto her bed and flicked the light off.

She needed to sleep, but it wouldn't come. She had to get Carlyle out of her head, not to mention the possibility of confronting Sheva. She'd never sleep if she couldn't push those thoughts aside. She rattled through song after song in her head, but finally gave up and turned on her audio book. When it claimed her, sleep came on dragon back, with a fierce warrior queen astride it.

CHAPTER EIGHT

Mallory couldn't get Kadence off her mind. It had been a nice evening with her after the shitty way Sheva had made her feel. And Kadence didn't ask about that. *She let me decide what I was comfortable talking about. She was present but not controlling. Nice.* She knew Kadence had strict rules about their relationship, and she'd agreed, but cracks were starting to appear in that "be professional" argument. Her desire to be more to Kadence than a friend was growing stronger every time they were together. She felt like she was going to explode with it. Would it be so bad? Sheva popped into her mind and she knew it could be.

But Kadence and Sheva were complete opposites. She'd never felt such a strong emotional pull with Sheva. It had been all about excitement and control. Her feelings for Kadence came from a much deeper place, a place she kept firmly locked down in every other relationship. Kadence drew out that part of her effortlessly. But she knew she couldn't give in to her desires; the stakes were too high. She'd worked so hard to become a gallery manager, and she couldn't put that at risk, no matter how badly she wanted to.

Why couldn't Kadence have come along before she ever signed Sheva? Things would've been so much easier. This hesitation to push for more than friendship wouldn't exist. *Dammit, that's not me. When I want something, I go after it. Shit.* She couldn't though. That would be a mistake. Kadence had been clear about where she stood, and pushing would only damage what they had, and possibly ruin her career. Her best bet would be to nurture their friendship. Once

Kadence's show closed, she'd be completely free to explore her feelings.

She dropped her bag on the couch and started to unbutton her blouse as she walked to her bedroom. A thump on the other side of the door made her freeze. *What the hell?* She took off her shoe, holding it like a weapon, the stiletto heel a wicked point. If somebody had broken in they were going to be sorry. She edged closer to the door and pressed an ear to it. Another thunk, as something heavy hit the floor. She stood with her hand poised over the doorknob, afraid to go forward, and afraid not to.

"Mallory? Is that you?"

What the hell? Sheva? She shoved the door open, making it crash into the far wall.

"What are you doing here? Get out!"

"Chill, I know you're pissed, but—"

"Fuck what you know. Get your damn boots and get the hell out of my apartment. How'd you get in here anyway?"

"Oh, well, you told me where the extra key was, so I let myself in."

"Fine. Give me the key." Her hand shook with suppressed anger as she held it out.

Sheva slid to the dresser and scooped the key up.

"This key?"

"You know perfectly well which key. Give it to me." Her hands balled into fists. If she didn't leave right now, Mallory wouldn't be responsible for her actions.

"As I see it, this key is a negotiation tool. I have it, you want it. So, it's a point of power. Let's sit down and talk about why you're so angry."

"I am done talking. You have thirty seconds to put that key in my hand or I call nine one one."

"Seriously? Come on, you're going to call the cops over a key?"

Sheva looked perfectly relaxed, her arms crossed nonchalantly in front of her. She had that stupid half smile on her face.

"I'm going to call them because you broke into my apartment."

"Technically, no. But look, I can take a hint. You don't want to talk to me and make nice. Fine. I'll go."

She grabbed her boots and tried to rush past, but Mallory stuck out her foot and tripped her. Sheva fell hard and landed with her metal tipped boots under her. Air whooshed out of her and she grabbed her midsection.

"The key. In my hand, now."

Sheva dropped the key into Mallory's upturned palm.

"Geez, you're such a bitch." Sheva was still holding her stomach as she rose.

"Now get out."

When Sheva had stumbled out the door, Mallory locked it behind her, throwing the deadbolt closed. What the hell had that been about? How could she show up after all the ugliness between them? No sane person would expect a warm welcome after that. She couldn't possibly be so self-centered that she was blind to such simple societal norms. *What's wrong with her?*

Her good mood completely blown, Mallory tried to shake off the anger. It wouldn't help the situation, so why waste the energy? She needed to do something with this. If it were earlier, she'd have gone out for a run, but not at this hour. Maybe she could run the stairs? She did that sometimes, when she couldn't sleep. Her building had a back fire safe stair, so when you were in it, the sound was muffled. Her neighbors would only be disturbed if they happened to be using the back stairs rather than the front.

She stripped out of her work clothes and pulled on some leggings and a T-shirt. Finding her athletic shoes was a bit of a chore, since she hadn't used them in two months. She found them under a stack of towels in the closet. When she had them on, she slipped her key onto her shoelace, double knotted it, and headed to the stairs. She ran down to the first floor before starting her count. She started up at an easy pace, one floor, two floors, all the way to the eighth floor, then back to the bottom. Over and over until sweat trickled, then ran down her back, soaking her shirt and the top of her leggings. Still she went, pounding against the cement, feeling each riser like a hard slab of rock sending shockwaves through her body.

When fatigue began throwing off her depth perception, and she could no longer be sure of her footing, she sat on the fifth-floor landing. Breath rattling in and out, fast, then slower, sweat beginning to chill, she stood and went through her cool down stretches. The deep sensation of heat running through her calves and thighs was satisfying. She undid her shoelace and pulled her key free. She slipped into the hallway and walked to her door. Her mind was pleasantly free of thought, beyond water and a shower.

She kept only the sense of satisfaction in her head as she drank, then cleaned up. Comfortable emptiness surrounded her, and she welcomed it. She wanted no more drama, no more tension, and emptiness was the perfect antidote for the day. Curled into her pillow, the night's sounds a chorus to lull her, she felt the gentle hands of sleep reaching out to claim her. She went without struggle, easily.

The hands grabbing her leg brought her out of sleep with a start. *Sheva, back again? How?* She felt her pulling at her, trying to drag her from the bed. She tried to scream, but her words bounced around inside her head without finding an exit. She kicked at her, trying to break her hold, but her hands were like steel and Mallory felt her body beginning to slide toward the foot of the bed. The hands now gripped her waist and she came face-to-face with Sheva.

Her eyes were wild, dilated. Her grin, phantasmagoric. *She's a monster. She's going to kill me.* Mallory drew her knees up, levered Sheva away from her, and broke free. She scrambled to the floor and ran out of her apartment. Now she could hear her screams, piercing the heavy night air. Why weren't her neighbors flinging open their doors? She ran down the hallway to the landing and flew down the stairs. She could hear Sheva behind her, almost feel her breath on her neck. She grabbed the balustrade and pivoted down the next flight of stairs, satisfied to hear Sheva sliding in overcorrection. *Fourth floor, keep moving, don't stop.* She pivoted again onto the third-floor landing and on down. Sheva pounded along behind her, sometimes closing in, sometimes missing her timing and falling behind. *First floor…wait? Where is the door?* More stairs leading down. Did she miscount?

She picked up her pace, knowing she'd wasted time she didn't have in her confusion. One more flight, but no, here too, more stairs leading down. *Keep moving.* This had to be the last flight of stairs. She ran as fast as she dared, but felt Sheva gaining on her. As she reached the landing, knowing this had to be the first floor, she pivoted toward where the door should be. Nothing but more stairs.

She was a ball of electric fear, and tension and panic tasted like copper on her tongue. She was poised on the top of another stairwell, one foot about to step forward when she heard the scream, like a circular saw cutting through wood. It ripped at her sanity and the hands hit her, full force in the middle of her back. Then she was flying, falling, watching the steps below her blur. Flipping, she could see where her body would hit and break.

There was no time to do anything but surrender to the motion. She hit with a jarring impact. Her body became a solid flare of pain. She screamed, but her mouth filled with liquid. She couldn't move, couldn't breathe. She could only watch as Sheva slowly descended the stairs, light glinting off a knife in her hand. *Die.* She needed to die before Sheva reached her. She prayed to be released, but still she came. When she stood above her, Mallory could see the knife was actually a chisel, honed razor sharp. Sheva's other hand held a hammer, red with gore. She placed the chisel over Mallory's heart, laughing. The other hand raised up, above her head and then—

Mallory sat up in bed, her heart racing, the sheets wet with perspiration. *What the hell?* She hadn't had a nightmare since she was six years old. *Why now?*

Obviously, the tension with Sheva was weighing on her subconscious. Such a vivid, horrible nightmare. Why would she dream something like that? Her hands were shaking and she still had the taste of copper in her mouth. She got up and stripped the bed, putting fresh sheets on. It was four in the morning and she wondered if she should even bother trying to get back to sleep. Maybe some coffee and browsing the Internet would help her nerves settle.

After an hour of cat videos and two cups of dark roast, she was ready to face the day. Her morning would be full, so no reason not to start early. She took a car to the gallery because she didn't like taking the train before it was full daylight. Walking into the space she loved usually inspired her, but today, the sight of the bronzes made her go cold. She needed to call a locksmith and change her locks. She didn't really think Sheva would do her any harm, but her uninvited entrance and the dream made Mallory uneasy. The woman was unbalanced, at the very least, and Mallory didn't need that in her life. Another reason not to mix the personal with the professional.

She arranged to have her super meet the locksmith at nine. He would hold her new keys in his office. She might be able to run over and get them after Kadence's work arrived. If not, she could send Tarin for them. She'd have to find a new place for her extra key. *Maybe just leave one here at the gallery.* She couldn't shake the feeling that something was wrong, and she wasn't going to take any chances.

She plowed through some paperwork, trying to get caught up before the movers arrived. She was deep in thought when Tarin walked in, making her jump.

"Hey, what's up with you?"

"Nothing." Mallory sucked in her lips, not wanting to talk about why she was jumpy. *It was just a dream.*

"Yeah? Why'd you nearly jump out of your skin when I came in?" Tarin raised an eyebrow.

"I didn't hear the door chime. I guess I was engrossed in this report. You scared me." She indicated the papers in front of her.

"Huh. I didn't think you scared so easily." He slid into the chair in front of her.

"Normally, no. I'm nervous today." She curled into herself, gripping her sides, as if for protection.

"Really? Why?"

"Oh, I don't know, maybe because someone broke into my apartment last night." Mallory heard the waver in her voice and knew she was close to losing it.

"What? Are you okay?" Tarin reached out to her.

She put her hands in his and felt relief wash through her. Tarin always knew how to make her feel safe. She took a deep breath, letting his presence calm her. When she spoke again her voice had steadied. "Yes, it was only Sheva, but shit. That wasn't okay."

"No, it wasn't. What can I do?"

Not knowing how to answer, Mallory went for humor. *What can anyone do?* "Just make noise when you come in the room."

He smiled, and she saw the tension in his face relax. "I can do that. Now, do you want to come down and meet the movers with me?"

"Oh! I lost track of time. Yes, let's go. I can't wait to see these pieces."

They went down to the loading dock and met the movers. Kadence was there, too, looking tired. *I wonder if she had nightmares too?*

The process of unloading was slow by nature, every care taken to insure no damage came to the paintings. Each painting was double wrapped in brown paper, bubble wrap, and hard foam corners. They were cradled in specially designed moving trays to keep them from bumping each other during the drive over. As each was unloaded, Kadence and Mallory inspected the packaging for damage, then tediously unwrapped them.

"Oh my gosh, these are so amazing. You've outdone yourself, Kadence. I can feel how this series moves from such a dark, painful beginning to a more hopeful, healing place. Outstanding. I hope someone buys the lot. It would detract from their power to separate them."

"Ah, that's okay. They served their purpose for me, I can let them go. They helped me through a rough time, but now, I'm better and they can stand alone."

Mallory caught the slight tensing of her lips. She might be okay with selling her paintings, but she was worried about something. "Still, I'm going to package them as a group. I'll bet I can find the perfect buyer for them."

"Suit yourself. You're the one who knows this side of the business."

Kadence's eyebrows were drawn together. She was an open book, and Mallory wanted to reach out and smooth the tension away. She studied her face, and each line of worry struck at her heart. A bright speck on her chin caught Mallory's attention. "What's that?"

"What?"

"That, on your chin. Looks like orange paint?"

Kadence rubbed at her chin, her fingers finding the spot of dried paint. The movement was so childlike that Mallory was overwhelmed with the desire to embrace her, hold her, and wipe the worries away.

"Oh, that. I was painting late into the night. Guess I missed a spot in the shower."

Mallory reached out and cleaned the spot of paint off. Her body thrummed with attraction, and she had to force herself not to slide into

Kadence's body space and snuggle against her chest. "Hm. I'd like to see your new work, too."

Kadence must have picked up on the undercurrent. She straightened and moved away. She cleared her throat. "Sure. You can have a look once it's finished."

Mallory and Kadence helped Tarin and the crew to position and hang the canvases. Mallory was even more pleased than she expected with the beauty of the exhibit. This was the beauty of Kadence, the core of her. It was powerful to realize how much of herself Kadence had laid bare in these paintings. This show was going to be a knockout. And it wouldn't have happened if she hadn't been willing to look in unusual places for emerging artists. Kadence deserved this show, and the world deserved her gift. She was gratified to see the show come together. This would be her defining moment as a director. Her gift for seeing what an artist was trying to express would be on display as well. This would be her success as much as Kadence's.

The final touch was the lighting of the framework, and it was perfect. Mallory watched Kadence's face as the lights came up above and behind her paintings. Her eyes sparkled and the smile on her face was pure happiness. It was like the light filled Kadence, too. Mallory felt her own smile grow to match Kadence's. She leaned toward her and slipped her hand into Kadence's. The warm squeeze she received in return warmed her.

"Thank you," Kadence said.

"Thank you. This is all you."

"No, it's not. I mean, it's my work, but you've taken it and made it something more. It's like my paintings are ideas and you've woven them into a story. It's beautiful."

Mallory was taken aback. No one had ever given her that much credit in setting up a show, and certainly never one of the artists. She didn't know how to respond, so she just gave Kadence's hand another squeeze.

"It is something, isn't it?"

"Yeah, it is."

The crew bundled out the packing materials, and Tarin went off to sign their receipt. Mallory and Kadence were alone in the loft, surrounded by the evidence of Kadence's soul. Mallory felt small in the space, superfluous. She anchored herself in the hand still holding hers, and cemented that by slipping closer and leaning against Kadence.

Kadence turned toward her and drew her against her.

"This is so beautiful. Just like you." She moved her head until her breath was hot on Mallory's cheek. "Just like you."

She leaned in the final inch and they were kissing. The warm softness of Kadence's lips captured hers and held them briefly. Mallory raised her hands to hold her there, to keep her from pulling back from the moment. She deepened the kiss, wanting the contact. She could feel Kadence beginning to move away.

"Don't. Please don't stop."

"Mallory, we can't." Kadence breathed against her lips. "I'm sorry. I shouldn't have done that."

"I know, but—"

"No, we can't. Not now." She broke the contact, leaving Mallory aching for more.

Mallory knew she was right, this wasn't the right time, but the power of their kiss blinded her to reason. "Why not? We both want it. Why can't we?"

"I told you, you're my boss. It feels wrong. I mean, it feels wonderful, but not right. I can't get involved with you. Not that way. We're friends, right? Can't we stay there for now?"

Mallory didn't want to stay in the friend zone. She wanted more, but she knew she had to agree. It had to stay this way, for now. Her career and Kadence's integrity required it. She pulled her shoulders back and took a deep breath. "Yeah, of course we can. How about we go get some lunch?"

Kadence's body straightened and she looked relieved. "That sounds good."

"Okay, let me get my bag. I have to stop by my building and get keys from the super. I hope you don't mind the detour."

The tension gone, Kadence's familiar comfortable nature asserted itself. She visibly relaxed and her smile returned. "Not a bit, but what happened to your keys?"

Mallory felt the anxiety from the morning well up. "It's a long story. Let me tell you while we eat."

"Okay."

They went to a small sandwich shop around the block from the gallery. It was a beautiful, sunny day, so they took their food to a nearby park and sat on a bench, side by side. Mallory watched Kadence as she ate. She seemed perfectly at ease in this setting. Sheva would be crawling up the wall sitting out here in the open. She couldn't stand being "on display" as she called it. *As though people don't have better things to do than watch her.* Mallory had missed casual lunches like this.

"Look at that guy." Kadence pointed to a squirrel. He was inching closer and closer to them, moving sideways. He had his eyes on the half sandwich Kadence had set beside her on her bag.

"He looks dangerous. Maybe you'd better pick up your sandwich."

"Nah, I want to see what he does." She moved the bag forward, egging him on.

"Don't do that. He's going to steal your lunch."

"I don't mind sharing. Here, watch this." She pulled a corner of the sandwich off and tossed it closer to the squirrel. He froze, looking at her, then in a rush of movement, grabbed the corner and was gone. As she laughed with Kadence, happiness washed over Mallory, a sense of joy that she wasn't familiar with. *This is how life is supposed to feel.* She wanted to grab Kadence and dance with her, spin in a circle until they were so dizzy they couldn't stand. Laugh until her stomach hurt and then do it all over again. *What would she do if I tried that? Would she humor me or shut me down?*

She had to do it. She stood up and pulled Kadence to her feet, still laughing, then held her hands and began to spin. Kadence looked surprised, but not upset, and she went along with it. Mallory laughed as she watched the blur of the park zoom past, then finally, she stopped and fell back on the grass. The trees above wavered and blurred until they settled into their natural shapes. Her sides sore from laughter, she turned and saw Kadence looking back at her, laughing. She sat up and pulled Kadence to a sitting position.

"Well, that was fun. Kinda weird, but fun," she said.

Mallory wrapped her arms around her middle and hugged herself. She looked at Kadence, wishing it was her she was holding.

"Wow, I haven't had so much fun in years. I knew you'd be willing to be crazy with me."

Kadence looked surprised. "You did?"

"Well, I hoped, and you didn't disappoint me." She grinned at Kadence and ran her hands through the sun warmed grass. If she could, she'd run her hands across Kadence's abdomen, slide over into her lap, and kiss her.

"I'm glad. I haven't been this dizzy since I was four."

"Me neither. Thanks."

"For what?"

"For being real." Mallory looked down, wanting her to feel how much that meant to her. She slid her hand over and squeezed Kadence's.

"Are you going to tell me about your keys?"

"Not now, this is too perfect. Let's go get the new set and go back to your exhibit." She wanted to stay in this moment, sun shining, Kadence beside her, but their idyll had to end.

Kadence pushed off the ground and stood, then leaned down and pulled Mallory up. "Okay."

It was so nice that was all it took. She asked not to revisit her night and Kadence just agreed. No argument, no feeling of consternation, just peaceful companionship. She slid her arm around Kadence's waist as they walked to the train station. Maybe Kadence was right. Maybe friendship was a better option. Relationships could end and people would go their separate ways. She didn't want to lose this easy connection with Kadence, and if that meant staying just friends, perhaps that was good enough.

CHAPTER NINE

Kadence was getting nervous about the show. Everything looked amazing. It was surreal to see her paintings in the loft space. Mallory and the crew did an unreal job of highlighting her work.

"You're so good at this. You make my work so much more than it is."

"No, we just give it the appropriate setting. Your work stands alone. If we hung these paintings on dull white walls, they'd still be as powerful as they are now. The tricks I use just bring their power out. You're the one who made them what they are." Mallory smiled, looking at one of the paintings that really popped against the colored wall.

"Well, I'm blown away. I hope I can live up to this show." She tugged at her suddenly too tight collar. She couldn't shake the fear that something would go wrong, or that people would read the wrong things into her paintings. *Are they really just paintings of rectangles?*

"Of course, you can. You're just as amazing as they are. Remember, I'll be here the whole night. If you get anxious, all you have to do is look for me or Tarin and we'll boost you right back up."

"Thank God." She wondered if following Mallory around all evening would be acceptable. Somehow, she didn't think so. When she was with Mallory, she believed in her work, but on her own, she wasn't sure how she'd be. The ball of anxiety in her had grown to encompass every part of her. *How can I possibly come off as professional and secure?*

"I think this is as ready as it's going to get before tomorrow night. What are you going to do with your evening?"

"Ugh, probably go home and throw up a few times." She knew she was making a fool of herself, but she couldn't help it. She didn't want to be the center of attention. That wasn't her. She just wanted to paint. If she could only have Mallory beside her, that wave of confidence she gave would make it okay. But how could she ask that? Mallory was the gallery director. She'd be so busy tomorrow Kadence would be lucky to see her at all. Nausea rose again, and she really might need to go home and be sick.

Mallory laughed and squeezed her arm. "No, don't do that. You deserve this show, and it's going to be fabulous. You need to take your mind completely off tomorrow night. Do something to distract yourself."

"Like what?" Kadence looked at her hopefully. Maybe they could do something together?

"I don't know, go see a movie, go to a club, listen to music, read? Whatever you think will do the trick."

She tried to hide her disappointment. She was hoping they could do something together. She had to be okay with entertaining herself. "I'll try. What are you up to tonight?"

"I'm here late, working on the final details, then I'll head home for a good night's sleep."

"So, I can't talk you into a movie?" She had to try.

"Not tonight, but any other night I'd jump at the chance. I have to get things completed. Listen, I'll make you a deal."

"Okay." Kadence waited, holding her breath. *What kind of deal?*

"Tomorrow night, after your opening, I'll take you out to celebrate."

She let her shoulders slump, knowing she'd be on her own tonight. "That sounds good, but it doesn't help me now."

"True. You're on your own tonight."

Kadence sighed. She'd wanted to spend more time with Mallory. Being with her made everything stop. She didn't think about her inadequacies when they were together. It was so different from what she'd expected. Any other time she got close to a woman, she'd lock up, be a jerk, and ruin things. Ever since Carlyle, she hadn't been able to trust her instincts. She torpedoed anything promising. Mallory was different. She made it okay to be herself. It was comfortable, even when things went a little beyond her boundaries.

"Okay, I'll see you tomorrow." To her own ears she sounded like a dejected two-year-old. *Yeah, I'm sure that will impress her.*

"Sounds good. Try to get some sleep. I'll send a car for you at five. I don't want you getting smudged on the subway."

She could only mumble, "Okay."

Mallory surprised her by wrapping her in a hug and kissing her cheek.

"You're going to be a hit. This will be smooth as silk. Go relax."

Kadence hugged her back, her whole body alive at the feel of Mallory in her arms. The scent of Mallory's perfume, like jasmine on a sea of orange blossoms, surrounded her. It was intoxicating and she felt her body reacting. Her skin ached to be against hers, her lips, on Mallory's. As good as it felt, it scared her. Was she setting herself up for more hurt by letting herself care, just a little? Was even thinking about Mallory in those terms healthy? She'd had that thing with Sheva. *Maybe she does this with all her artists?* If she did give in, could she finally grow past the pain of the breakup with Carlyle? *What happened to Carlyle?*

She broke the embrace, but gently, and smiled. "I'll see you tomorrow."

"Yes, sleep well."

As she walked past the bronzes, heading for the exit, a sour taste rose in her mouth. Carlyle's face flashed in her mind. *Not until after my show, please?* She pushed down the anxious feeling and focused on Mallory. She left the gallery and headed to the train, wanting nothing more than to relive the feeling of Mallory in her arms. She caught the subtle scent of her perfume wafting up from her jacket. She breathed deeply, wanting to hold the lingering memory of her. Her body was overly hot, pheromones charging and discharging, heating her. It had been more than two years since she'd let anyone affect her this way. She knew she should shut it down, deny what her body craved, but she wanted to relish it tonight. She'd reinforce those walls tomorrow, before her opening. Tonight, the idea of Mallory, the scent of her, would be a comfort.

She indulged herself in the fantasy of Mallory during the ride home. How it would feel to have her in her arms for more than a moment. What it would be like to dive into the warmth of her, the soul of her. She could feel how perfectly they would fit, like they'd been made for each other. She closed her eyes and imagined each touch, every caress they would share. By the time they reached her stop, she was completely involved in the fantasy.

The jerk of the train stopping was a rude awakening. She trundled out of the station and walked the few blocks to her place, aware that she was still half gone. If she'd been confronted at this point, she'd probably be an easy mark, but she made it home, unaccosted.

When she opened her door, the reality of what she'd been doing struck her. Fantasizing about someone who should remain untouchable. That was dangerous. Mallory was in control of her show, in control of her, basically. She lived through her painting, and if this show became a negative experience, it would wreak havoc with her self-esteem. She couldn't afford that, not even the fantasy of that. *Mallory is your friend, period. Don't sabotage yourself.*

She checked her emails, partly looking for distraction, partly to remind herself of how easily she'd let Carlyle destroy her self-confidence. Carlyle had disappeared, but not before shredding her self-image. *Don't forget how many times you had to tell yourself you were more than a painter of rectangles. Hold on to that truth. Letting people in opens you up to pain you can't afford.*

There were a couple of responses, but nothing new. No one had heard from Carlyle since that Christmas. The last person she knew who'd seen her was the last person Kadence wanted to ask. Sheva might know something, but could she bring herself to ask her? The anger she felt for the sculptor was still as hot as it had been two years ago. But was that fair? Did Sheva even know that Carlyle had been her girlfriend? Kadence doubted it. Carlyle seemed to have kept their relationship hidden. She wouldn't have wanted to risk mentioning her to Sheva, so maybe asking about her could be no big deal. Maybe letting go of the anger would be a good thing.

But how to approach her? She didn't really know Sheva other than as a sculptor. When she was the visiting artist at school, Kadence hadn't had any personal contact with her. *Maybe through Mallory?* That might work. It would be an awkward conversation, though. How did you ask someone about a person they dated two years ago? She'd have to figure that out. If she didn't do it, she'd never feel like she'd done all she could to gain the closure she needed. And she wanted to be sure Carlyle was okay, that she'd found someone new and run off with them. Something like that. She had to know something bad hadn't happened. Not knowing would leave so many things unresolved. She needed closure now more than ever. She wanted to be open to something with Mallory, unhampered by the past. She'd ask Mallory for an introduction at the show tomorrow, if Sheva made an appearance.

Right now, she needed to try to get some sleep. It was going to be a big day and rest was imperative. She showered and slipped into her bed, and turned on her audiobook to help ease her way into sleep. Her dreams were troubled. Images of Carlyle, her face a mask of fear, and then Mallory, being chased by something, filled her night.

Kadence woke the next morning, nervous but excited about the show. Her strange dreams quickly dissipated under the excitement of the day to come. She spent the morning alternating between forcing herself to relax and panicking. Opening her artwork to the eyes of the world was like giving away a piece of her heart. It would hurt if it wasn't received as well as she hoped. The anxiety about meeting Sheva was there, too, but she couldn't focus on that. In an hour, she would be out there and whatever happened would happen. She wished the knots in her stomach would unwind, but knew that wasn't likely. Her hands were damp with perspiration, but luckily, only her hands. Her suit looked good. *I can do this.* If only her grandma could be here to see this. To know how her paint box had ended up here. Kadence swallowed the lump in her throat. Her grandma would be proud, and she'd want Kadence to look her best, so no tears.

She'd never been so anxious. When the call came that the car had arrived, she took a deep breath and locked the apartment. The black town car was waiting at the curb. She slid inside and tried to calm down. She closed her eyes and listened to the pounding of her heart, willing it to slow down. *Breathe.*

The gallery was all lit up for the opening, with one of her paintings on a poster announcing the show on a marquee out front. She thanked the driver and went in. Her heart stopped and her sweaty palms became sweaty everything when she saw Mallory. She was gorgeous, dressed in a shimmering gold evening gown that hit mid-calf. Her hair had been pulled into a chignon and a rhinestone comb held it in place. Her pulse quickened and everything tensed as Mallory began to walk toward her. Kadence fought down the urge to sweep her into her arms. Instead she was frozen in place by the power of Mallory's beauty.

She met Kadence near the door and hugged her, giving her a kiss on the cheek. "You look marvelous. That suit is perfect."

"It's the only one I have, sorry."

"Seriously, it looks divine on you. Come on, let me show you the layout."

She took Kadence by the hand and led her through the sculpture room. There was a bar set up and the bartenders wore white jackets and black pants. The stairwell was lined with candles, creating a warm ambience as you went up to the loft. And then, they were among her paintings. They were amazing in this setting. Three service people stood by the far wall, waiting for them. Mallory introduced Kadence to them, so they would know to look to her during serving. The hors d'oeuvres and canapés were plated and ready to go.

"God, I'm so nervous," Kadence said. She rubbed at her hands, trying to dry them before anyone arrived.

"That's only natural. You'll be fine, wait and see."

"I wish I had your confidence in me. I'm so going to make a fool of myself."

"Why would you think that? You're poised, you know your work, you'll make a great impression. I'm positive."

Kadence tried to choke down her nerves. It wasn't working. "Ugh."

"Come with me." Mallory led her into the office. "Now, sit."

Kadence sat and tried to relax.

"Okay, I want you to imagine the worst possible thing that could happen. Visualize it, think of how you'd react."

The worst thing she could think of was getting sick in the middle of the show, maybe on someone. That would be horrible.

"Now. Think about what you'd do in that worst-case scenario."

If she felt sick, she'd excuse herself and go to the restroom. No big deal. She could breathe again. She opened her eyes and smiled at Mallory. "Got it."

"The thing about nerves is they always happen and they're rarely justified. Try to remember, you're not in this alone. I'm here. Tarin is here. You'll be okay, and if not, you make an appearance and step out. That's okay. I'd prefer you to be here the entire night, but if you can't, it's okay."

That was a relief. Knowing she could make a break for it helped immeasurably. "I'll be okay. I promise."

"Good, I'm glad to hear that. Now, I have to go down and greet the guests. You can stay here if you like. I'll send Tarin for you when it's time to introduce you."

"Okay. Thanks, Mallory." Relief washed over Kadence and she could breathe again. She could do this. She felt the anxiety wane, but sadness filled its place. She had no one to share this night. Jake and his wife were going to come, but they were casual friends, not family. She'd been on her own a long time, but this was the first time not having a family mattered. Why now? Was it because of her growing friendship with Mallory? The news about Carlyle and hearing how her mother ached for her return? Why did it matter now?

She should be happy tonight, over the moon because she had made it, not wallowing in self-pity because she didn't have a family. What did this mean?

She didn't hear the door, but she felt Mallory's hands come around her shoulders from behind. Her breath was in Kadence's ear, then she kissed her cheek and whispered, "You're going to be okay."

And just like that, the sadness melted away. Kadence wished they could stay in that moment. The feel of Mallory's hands lingered on her skin and warmed her to her core. The scent of her perfume was a natural mood stabilizer, and she breathed it in, holding on to it. She heard the click of the latch as the door closed and knew she was alone again, but the peace that had come with Mallory remained.

She had no idea how long she drifted in the calm, but when Tarin knocked and called her, she was ready. She walked out, confident and strong to meet her possible patrons. The first person she met was Sanford Tucker. Her anxiety flooded back in like a tsunami. She took Sanford's hand in her sweaty one and said hello.

"Ms. Munroe, so nice to meet you. Come, walk with me. Show me your work."

Kadence swallowed hard and led her to the spiral. "This series is called *Colder than Blue*. It represents two years of my work."

"Hm. I see. So, what inspired this series? What drove you to fill your work with so much melancholy?"

Kadence was taken aback. She'd never thought of the work as melancholic, but Sanford was right. The whole emotional life she'd lived since that October was in this series. It *was* sad.

"Well, I guess—"

"Come, come, no need to guess. You should know what inspired you. Your vision should flow in your paintings, but also out of your mouth. Tell me what makes you, you?"

Kadence responded automatically, trying not to self-censor. "My life has been shaped by sadness, and melancholy molded me. It's no wonder that it's the first thing you note. But look deeper, don't stay on the surface. That would be the easy way. Look beyond the sadness and tell me what you see."

Sanford stopped to study one of the blues. "I see, you're right. There's so much more. There's hope, there, in the yellows, and passion in the deep purples. Yes, I see it. Good, now, what else?"

Kadence moved her to the center of the spiral. Here the blue was shoved to the extreme edges on the canvas, the center completely occupied by the play of titanium white and lavender. Cross-hatchings of cobalt and black scored the peace of the inner circle.

"What does this say to you?" She watched Sanford's face as she took in the painting. She was getting it, Kadence could tell. She winced at the blue and black lines, smiled at the white and lavender. *She understands*.

"You've had some struggles, yes? But you came through them, and you're kind of…what? Drifting now? Am I seeing this correctly?"

"Yes, that's it. The pain, the scars, they're a part of who I am, but they don't define me. I won't let them. But yeah, I suppose I'm also not entirely sure who I want to be yet."

Sanford turned and grasped both of Kadence's forearms. She leaned into her and spoke quietly. "You're an amazing woman, Ms. Munroe. Your work is moving and deep. I want you to come visit me on Monhegan. I'll set aside a room for you. Come anytime. Now, show me your happier work."

Kadence felt a ripple of shock at the invitation. To work on Monhegan would be unreal. She was blown away by the offer. She led Sanford to the side walls, where her paintings became brighter. These were the paintings that reflected her childhood before her father left. When she was light and carefree. It showed in color and schema. Sanford waved her off to visit with other guests, lingering in the happy works.

Kadence felt like she needed to retreat after that. Sanford was the picture of elegance, and so kind, but her spirit took so much energy. Kadence felt like her soul had been excised, examined, and returned. Somehow the fit wasn't quite the same as it had been before. No wonder Mallory was such a strong woman. How would it feel to be consumed like that as a child? It had to have been disconcerting. Kadence shook off the strange feeling and took a breath. It might have been uncomfortable, but it was so worth it. To be invited to Monhegan was an amazing gift. She'd dreamed of visiting the island since she'd heard of it. If nothing more came from this experience, this would still be the highlight of her career.

Mallory approached her then, to introduce her to Christina Lorde and Chas Drummer. They were interested in *Colder than Blue* and wanted her to talk to them about the series. Mallory left her with them in front of the paintings. Talking about the paintings came easier than Kadence expected. She talked about every emotion she felt when she painted them, and why she created a series as opposed to one piece. It was a great experience, to share this with these women. Their appreciation was obvious, and they not only thanked her profusely, they hugged her as well. That was a surprise and she handled it with grace, but hoped it wasn't typical of the patrons.

The evening went on, with many more introductions and lots of talking about her work. The few times panic reared its head, she looked for Mallory, and seeing her, she felt the peace from before. When she looked for her, Mallory often seemed to know, and would catch her eye and smile reassuringly. Kadence liked this invisible connection.

When Kadence had a free moment, she snagged a bottle of water from one of the servers and watched the crowd absorbing her work. She saw Mallory and her mother, heads together, bodies leaning in.

They were like a single unit. Mallory talked like her mom was a problem, but the love they shared radiated from them, warming the space. Sanford was an imposing spirit, but so, too, was Mallory. They probably didn't see their similarities, only their differences. Kadence watched until Mallory felt her gaze and turned her way. She smiled then and nodded, then walked to some patrons to talk about her work.

By the time the night ended, Kadence was exhausted. Mallory looked equally spent, and Tarin was dozing in a chair in the office. The caterers had cleaned as the evening waned, so they were out the door shortly after the guests, and it was just the three of them.

As she dropped into the chair next to Tarin, Kadence realized that Sheva hadn't shown up. The other artists had been there and she'd met them, but not Sheva. A wave of guilt washed over her; was it bad to feel relieved? If she'd met Sheva, she'd have felt compelled to bring up Carlyle, and this wasn't the time or place. She shook her shoulders and stretched. It had been a great evening, but she was beat. Tarin looked as tired as she felt, but Mallory looked as gorgeous as she did the moment Kadence walked in.

Mallory slid into her desk chair and sighed. "That was a great show, Kadence. You're going to sell out."

Kadence sat up straight, the words like a jolt of electricity hitting her system. "What? No way. I mean, maybe a piece or two, but not a sellout."

Mallory had a funny little smile on her face, almost smug. "I wouldn't be surprised. You've sold close to half already."

Kadence felt hollow. It was like her whole middle fell out, just dropped right onto the floor. "What? How could that be?"

Now Mallory's smile widened and her eyes sparkled. "Well, you charmed the pants off Madams Lorde and Drummer. They bought the *Colder than Blue* series right after you spoke with them. That was five pieces. Two others were sold outright, and three are under consideration. You're a hit."

Kadence couldn't believe it. It was too much to hope for. *They liked my work.* "Unbelievable. I'm floored. I really didn't expect this."

"But it's good, right?"

"Of course it's good. It's amazing."

Mallory's voice took on a teasing lilt. "What are you going to do now that you're famous?"

Kadence laughed and blushed. "Not famous, just full of myself."

Mallory leaned toward Kadence. "For now. But mark my words, this is going to change everything for you. Is there anything you'd wished for tonight that didn't happen?"

Anything she'd hoped for? Did wishing for her grandma count? There was no one who could give her that, and Mallory had made everything else a dream come true. "Well, let's see, I got to meet your mom, got invited to Monhegan, sold a lot of paintings, it was pretty perfect…"

"But?"

"But I was hoping to meet Sheva. I thought she might be here." She wasn't being completely honest, since *not* seeing her had been a relief.

Mallory frowned.

Kadence noticed the subtle tightening of her muscles and the way she went from relaxed to ramrod straight in her chair. Something about Sheva was still bugging her.

"Oh, well, she has her priorities. She'll be here tomorrow to discuss the sale of two of her bronzes. She's meeting with me and the chairman of the board at nine. If you'd like, you can come around at, say, eleven, and I'll introduce you," Mallory said.

"I'd like that. We have a mutual friend I'd like to talk to her about."

"Great. I'll see to it. Now, are you ready to go home?"

The tightness didn't go away. Obviously, Mallory didn't like thinking about Sheva and Kadence together. *Does it bug her that I want to meet Sheva? Is she worried we might hit it off, or does she still have feelings for her?* That stung, and the image of Mallory with Sheva made her blood boil. She sighed, feeling a little bit of their connection fade away. "Yeah, I'm beat."

"Good, we can share a car if you like. Tarin, honey, wake up."

Tarin sat up, rubbing his eyes.

"Shall we go? The car can take all of us."

Kadence was happy to see the tension fade. She didn't want anything between the two of them. She helped Tarin up from the chair and they walked down the stairs.

They locked up the gallery and slid into the comfort of the town car. Tarin sat on one side with Mallory in the middle. Kadence couldn't hide her reaction to having Mallory against her. Her skin prickled with electric pulses and her nipples tightened. She was thankful she had her jacket on. When Mallory leaned her head onto her shoulder, it was natural for Kadence to put her arm around her. Mallory's easy breathing against her throat charged Kadence even more, making her wish it were just the two of them in the car.

By the time they reached her apartment, Mallory was snuggled so deeply into her, that Kadence hated to move.

"Mallory, hey, wake up." She shook her gently.

Mallory sat up, startled. Her face was flushed with sleep, and the imprint of Kadence's jacket was on her cheek. Kadence's heart melted at the sweet, sleepy look on Mallory's face. It made her feel tender and mushy inside. "This is me, so I better go."

"Mm, okay. I'll see you tomorrow?"

Kadence gently moved Mallory's arm and leaned in to kiss her cheek. She smelled so good, it was all Kadence could do to move away from her. "Yes, at eleven."

"'Kay. Tarin? You still with me?"

Tarin yawned and nodded. "Yes, boss. I'll make sure you get in your apartment then have the driver take me home."

"Okay. Good night, superstar."

"Good night," Kadence said, stepping away from the car and closing the door. She watched the taillights until they made the corner, then hurried up to her place.

Snuggled into her bed later, she let the memory of Mallory in her arms surround her. The weight of her head on her shoulder, that glorious jasmine-citrus perfume, the silky touch of the hair that slipped from her chignon, it all added up to the best part of her night. Yes, she'd been a hit, she'd sold paintings, but her night was special because of Mallory's place in it. The way she looked at her. How their eyes would meet across the room in silent communication, the gracefully beautiful way she moved across the room. Her smile, her perfume, the dress, everything…Mallory made the night for her. She let herself enjoy the feeling of contentment that being with Mallory gave her. Tomorrow she could think about why she shouldn't act on those feelings.

Chapter Ten

Mallory felt a little guilty about her pretend nap on Kadence's shoulder last night. It was so nice to be held by her, feel her reacting to their closeness, she couldn't help herself. When she was with Kadence she felt free, whole and herself. She didn't have to adapt to Kadence's preconceived ideas of who she should be, because Kadence was real. She had expectations, boundaries, but not judgments.

Watching her tonight was mesmerizing. She moved through the crowd, drawing everyone's gaze in her close-fitting suit. Her smile was quick but genuine as she spoke to prospective buyers. As nervous as she'd been before the opening, Mallory had worried for her, but she'd been amazing. And the way she was with her mother, that was surprising. It took a spine of steel to endure a Sanford Tucker grilling, and Kadence had handled it with panache. Mallory had been struck by the contrast of self-conscious Kadence as opposed to Kadence on display. It aroused her, watching Kadence work the crowd. And those times she felt Kadence watching her she'd blushed, hoping her desire wasn't obvious.

She thought about the what-ifs while she showered and got ready for the day. What if she could convince Kadence to give them a try? What if she could have that comfortable connection with her and take it somewhere further? What if Kadence still refused her advances? That made her stop. Why did that have to come to mind? It hurt to think it. Her stomach tied itself in knots. It was silly to even think about it anyway. She'd made a big mistake getting involved with

Sheva, and Kadence was right. They needed to wait. As long as she was showing in the gallery, Mallory had to resist Kadence. It didn't matter what she felt, she had to keep her promise. Friends, for now, would have to be enough. Accepting that, especially after last night, was hard. Her chest tightened and she knew tears were coming soon. Why did she have to complicate things by starting up with Sheva? Now she had to spend her morning dealing with her. At least she had Kadence's visit to look forward to.

She stood under the showerhead and let the water mix with her tears and wash them away. She had to pull it together. The day wouldn't wait for her, and dealing with Sheva was going to require her full attention. She pushed down the emotions that she'd released and made herself get through her routine and off to the gallery.

Millie Fletcher, the chairman of the board, was waiting at the gallery door when she arrived. She nodded a greeting and opened the door. Millie was in good spirits, having attended the opening the night before and seen the positive reception Kadence had received.

"Oh, Mallory, what a great event last night. So many people for an unknown artist. I think she did quite well, don't you?"

Mallory smiled, happy with the show's success. "Yes, she was quite a hit. We've sold about half her pieces already. I think she's going to sell out."

Millie almost jumped with enthusiasm. "That's fantastic. So, tell me what's going on with Sheva? Is there a problem with the sale you've made?"

Mallory felt her stomach sour. Sheva was going to be trouble, she knew it. "Oh, well, I don't think so, but she has other ideas. She wants to interview the buyers, make sure they are *worthy* of her work."

"You're not serious." The shock on Millie's face was clear. This wasn't how things were done in the New York art scene. Artists were happy to make sales, and both the galleries and the artists benefitted from it.

"Completely. That's what she told me on the phone the other day when I told her about the sale. And that's why I asked for you to come today. I know she was able to convince the board not to go through with the sale to Sims and Martel, but this is different. This isn't a corporate group. These individuals truly value the art and will protect and promote it. There's no reason for her to object." Mallory straightened her back and crossed her arms in front of her. She wasn't going to give this sale up without a fight.

"Who are the buyers?"

"Lorde and Drummer." She knew that would get Millie's attention. The couple were their biggest patrons. The board wouldn't want to be part of anything that made them uncomfortable.

"Oh, of course. True patrons. She should be thankful for their interest."

"I agree. Now we have to convince her. Although, to be honest, it irks me we have to. What's the point of showing her work if she won't sell it?" Her frustration with the way the board handled the corporate sale made her a little snarky.

They retired to the office and Mallory brought up Sheva's gallery contract. There were agreed upon prices for every piece in her show. She'd signed the contract, making the gallery her agent in sales. The gallery would split the price fifty-fifty with Sheva. Nowhere in the contract did it make stipulations about who could or could not purchase, or require artist's approval of sale. So Sheva had no grounds to object.

Mallory pointed out the pertinent clauses to Millie. They had to stand firm on this. If Sheva balked, she would be in violation of the contract and the gallery would litigate to recoup lost sales.

"This isn't going to be a fun meeting. I should have had the attorneys present." Mallory felt queasy thinking about the confrontation they were likely to have.

"Maybe it won't come to that. Let's see how it goes. The legal team is available should this not go our way." Millie appeared confident.

Mallory hoped she was right. "Okay. I'm glad you're here."

"Yes, well, let's hope for an easy resolution."

Mallory rose and walked toward the door. "I agree. Would you like some coffee? I was going to get a cup."

"That would be nice."

"I'll be right back." Mallory filled two mugs with coffee and was on her way back to the office when the door chimed, announcing

Sheva's arrival. She should wait on the landing for her, but she didn't want to be alone with her, so she hurried back into the office.

Mallory held out a mug, her heart racing. "She's here. Shall we go greet her?"

"Yes, of course." Millie rose, taking the mug and placing it on the desk.

Sheva was down with the bronzes. They joined her, but waited until she turned toward them to greet her.

It irritated Mallory that Sheva hadn't turned right away. *She's already being difficult.* "Sheva, good morning. You remember Millie Fletcher, right?"

Sheva gave a big smile and held a hand out to Millie. "Yes, hello, Ms. Fletcher. There was no reason for you to be bothered today. I'm sure Mallory and I could work this out."

"Well, I felt a board member should be present if there were a dispute," Mallory said.

"Ah, well, there's no dispute. I have no problem moving forward with the sale to Ms. Lorde and Ms. Drummer."

Shock like a brick wall slammed Mallory. *What? Did I just hear that?* No problem? What was her game?

"Mallory? I thought you said there was going to be a problem," Millie said.

"My mistake, I apologize. I understood you were hesitant about selling. I believe you said you wanted to interview the buyers?" Mallory raised an eyebrow at Sheva, daring her to contradict her.

Sheva shrugged. "Just an artist's volatile temperament, nothing more."

Mallory tried not to let her irritation show. "Then let's sign the paperwork, shall we?"

They followed her up to the office, Mallory fighting to hide her anger at Sheva's shifty behavior. Why had she done this? She wouldn't relax until Sheva had signed the bill of sale and the deal was complete. This was going to take the shine off her star for the opening last night.

The meeting took only a few minutes, they reached an agreement on price, and Millie said her good-byes. The small changes meant

Mallory would have to rewrite the sales contract. That meant she'd still need to get Sheva's signature. This wasn't over yet.

"What is your game?" Mallory said as they made their way back to the bronze room.

"What do you mean?"

Mallory's voice rose as her anger forced its way through her careful façade. "What do I mean? You had a complete fit when I told you the ladies wanted to buy your sculptures. You were adamant that you wouldn't sell."

"Well, I changed my mind. No big deal. I decided I had what I needed from *Torrid Heat* and *Love's Birth*. I'm ready to let them go. I have a new project in mind. The perfect figure to complete this series."

Sheva looked like she'd never made waves about the sale. Mallory was filled with trepidation. "Really? Well, good. Chas and Christina will be very happy."

"I couldn't care less. I do need something from you, though."

Mallory physically took a step back. There was nothing she would give Sheva, not again. "From me?"

"Yes. You're my inspiration for my next piece."

Mallory was repulsed. After the last time they'd been together, she wanted nothing to do with Sheva. *How can she possibly think I'd model for her?*

The door chimed, keeping her from saying what she was thinking.

"Excuse me." She went to the foyer and was happy to see Kadence. Looking at her face made much of the tension and anger dissipate. "Good morning. I'm glad you're here."

Kadence gave her a warm smile. "Thanks, and good morning to you. Am I too early?"

"No, you're right on time. Follow me." She took her hand and led Kadence to the bronze room and Sheva. Mallory gripped Kadence's hand tightly. She was worried about this introduction. Sheva could be so nasty, and Kadence was so open. She felt protective of Kadence, didn't want Sheva to hurt her in any way.

Pulling Kadence forward, Mallory introduced them. "Sheva, this is Kadence Munroe, our new abstractionist."

"Nice to meet you," Sheva said, holding out a hand.

Kadence shook her hand. "Same."

Mallory noticed the change in Kadence's body. She was suddenly tense, almost wooden. *What's up with that?* "Kadence asked to meet you."

Sheva looked surprised. "Oh?"

"Yes, I know this is going to sound crazy, but we have someone in common."

Mallory was confused until she remembered that Kadence had mentioned this the other day. She hadn't thought to pursue the question at the time. But why was Kadence's voice so hollow?

"We do?" Sheva said.

"Yes. Carlyle Goodwin." She spit the words out in a clipped tone.

Mallory was shocked. She took in Kadence's posture, trying to find her footing in the suddenly shaky environment. Kadence stood with her legs braced apart and her chin thrust out, like a kid on the playground starting a fight. Mallory could see the cords of muscle standing out in her tense forearms. Who was this Carlyle? Why hadn't Kadence told her about this? Mallory twitched with discomfort. Kadence was angry, confrontational. *Why is she acting this way?* She didn't like being in the dark, and this might as well be a black hole.

"Hmm. Doesn't ring a bell."

Kadence's already stiff body became so rigid Mallory was afraid of what might happen next. She was practically vibrating with anger. *What the fuck is going on?*

"From CAA? Two years ago? She modeled for you, you dated her?"

Mallory felt things slipping out of her control. This wasn't okay. It was too confrontational. She needed to stop this before it escalated. She could cut the tension in the room with a butter knife. Kadence looked like she was barely keeping herself in check, and Sheva had a surly expression, completely confrontational.

"What? No, I don't remember."

"You remember her. She's right here in this room with us."

Kadence's voice was as cold as ice. Mallory had never seen this side of her. "Hey, let's take a step back from this, okay?" She grabbed at Kadence's arm, but she shook her off.

"What?" Sheva said.

"This, *Torrid Heat*, this is her. Exactly. Her body. Her breasts, her navel, *her*. Down to the mole on her right hip. It's a perfect model of her body."

Sheva held up her hands and stepped away from Kadence. "I don't know what you're talking about. That was modeled after a woman I knew in San Tropez."

Kadence took a step forward, menacing Sheva. "No, it wasn't. This is Carlyle. I know it's her. But what I don't know is what happened to her after you were finished with her. No one has seen her since she was supposed to go away with you for Christmas. So where is she?"

"Stop this, Kadence. You're scaring me." Mallory tried to get between them, to make Kadence look at her.

Sheva moved farther back. "You're crazy. That isn't this woman you're talking about. I don't know anything about her."

"You do. She was your model."

"Mallory? Could you get her away from me? Please?"

"Kadence, come on." Mallory grabbed her arm and tried to move her away from Sheva, but she shook her off again.

"No. I'm not leaving without an answer. What happened to Carlyle?"

"I don't know any Carlyle. I never have."

"Liar. Why are you lying? You dated her, for Christ's sake. You were the visiting artist at CAA and you dated her. She modeled for you when you started your figure series, and then she disappeared. You dedicated this sculpture to the students at CAA. It's obvious you're lying, but why? What happened to her?"

"Kadence, stop this. You're not being rational. You have to stop." Their voices had risen, and Mallory had to think of the other patrons in the gallery. Where was Tarin? She needed to get Kadence away from Sheva, right now.

"She did something to her, don't you see? Why else would she lie?" Looking desperate, she pointed at Sheva. "You were the last person she talked about. She said she was going somewhere with you, and none of us ever saw her again. What are you hiding?"

This was unreal, she needed to reach Kadence, make her stop. "You're jumping to conclusions. You need to cool off and think this through. Stop attacking Sheva and calm down."

Kadence looked at her with so much anger, Mallory felt her stomach drop. Adrenaline pumped through her, and every nerve was on end.

"I will not calm down! I want to know what happened. Her parents want to know. Have they got any idea that you've got her body here, in bronze? Have they been told that their lost daughter is here?"

Mallory felt her own anger rising. "Stop it. You're acting crazy. You have to stop."

"You have to tell me. You have to."

Sheva backed up against the bronze, holding her arms protectively in front of her. Kadence advanced on her, and Mallory jumped between them. What the hell was wrong with her?

"Kadence, stop." She put her arms out to block her approach. "You need to back off. Just go. Go home and cool off."

Kadence didn't seem to hear her, just pushed forward until Mallory had to grab her arms and hold her back. Sheva was squatting down under the torso of her statue, her arms wrapped around her. But her eyes were a different story. They were as hard as agates, and although her body language said victim, her expression said something else entirely. This thing was going to explode if she couldn't stop it.

Mallory didn't know what was worse, seeing Sheva like that, or Kadence losing her mind. This was way too much. She struggled to keep hold of Kadence, but she was losing. What would happen if she got loose? Would she physically attack Sheva? The adrenaline from this craziness was helping, but she couldn't hold her much longer.

Suddenly, Tarin was there, helping her pull Kadence back. They got her into the textile room and pushed her inside.

"What in the world?" Tarin said. He held Kadence by the arms, his body pushed against her to keep her from leaving the room.

"I'm not sure myself. Just don't let her go." Tremors started in Mallory's legs and quickly moved upward. She needed to sit down before she fell down, but she had to make sure this thing was really over. They heard the chime of the door, and Mallory wondered what next, but no one appeared.

Kadence seemed to be calming a bit, fighting less to get away. She was rocking side to side, hugging herself.

Mallory was torn. She wanted to go to Kadence and comfort her, but it was her job to make sure things like this didn't happen. *Shit.* "Can you manage her? I'm going to check on Sheva."

"Yes, I've got her."

Mallory went back to the bronze room, but it was empty. *That must have been Sheva leaving.* At least now she could relax a little. She returned to Tarin and Kadence, worn to the bone with this bizarre behavior, and worried about what caused it.

Kadence had slid to the floor and was continuing to rock. Mallory got down on her knees and put her hands on her shoulders. "Kadence? Can you hear me?"

She nodded but didn't speak. Her rocking was subsiding.

"What the hell was that all about? Do I need to call nine one one? Is she off some medication or something?" Tarin said.

"No. Don't call, I'm okay." Her voice was weak, subdued.

Mallory's heart ached for her. Why had this happened? "Can you explain to me why you just attacked Sheva? Help me understand. We're worried about you."

"I lost it. I'm sorry. I didn't mean to attack her. I just wanted to ask her some questions. But when she denied knowing Carlyle, I lost my mind. I just wanted to hurt her. How could she do that? Just deny her existence like that? She can't be allowed to do it." Tears streaked Kadence's face and she scrubbed at them with the back of her hand.

"And there's the problem. You can't go around attacking people, no matter what they say. It's illegal. They call it assault. I could press charges against you on behalf of the gallery. You need to help me understand why you did that."

Kadence nodded again, tears streaming down her face. Mallory was upset and angry, but she knew Sheva could push all the right buttons as well. She wanted to hear Kadence's side of things, but only once she'd calmed down. "Okay, here's what you're going to do. You're going to go with Tarin. He'll take you home. You get yourself together, take a pill, or whatever, then come back here at five. You and I are going to sit down in my office and calmly talk about this, okay?"

She nodded. Tarin gently led her to the door.

"Tarin, stay with her until you're sure she's going to be okay."

"Yes, boss. How'll I know when that is?"

"Use your judgment. I'll be here, holding things down."

Mallory watched as Tarin half supported, half led Kadence out the front door. She was suddenly weak and needed to sit down, every nerve frazzled. Why had Kadence done that? Her hands shook as she sat at the desk to drink her coffee. *Get a grip*. But she couldn't, the whole thing was so upsetting. Now that it was over, her nerves let loose and she felt like jelly. How was she going to function like this? She needed something to brace herself, so she went to her cabinet and pulled out the bottle of Chivas Tarin had given her on her birthday. She poured a finger into a glass and tossed it back. The burning sensation gave her boneless body something to focus on and she felt her nerves begin to settle.

A trip to the powder room repaired her makeup and made it possible to go on with her day. She needed to call about the sale of the bronzes, but she wasn't sure she could hold it together. She'd call tomorrow.

She catalogued the sold pieces from last night's show, marking each description card with a small blue dot. Only seven pieces were left in Kadence's show. Of course, they'd keep the work together for the three-month duration of the show, that was standard. They made exceptions occasionally, but for the most part, they kept the work as a unit until the shows closed.

She went down to the bronzes and did the same for the two she'd sold this morning. They were amazing sculptures, well worth the asking price. As she placed the sticker on *Torrid Heat's* description card, her breath caught in her throat. It was as Kadence had said. This sculpture was completed at CAA and dedicated to its student body. Why would Sheva lie about that? Had she forgotten? Not likely. There was something more to this whole situation. Still, it didn't justify the attack on Sheva. She thought about Sheva's behavior, breaking into her apartment, expecting to pick things right up after treating her like shit. She was definitely an ass, but did she have anything to do with the girl Kadence was yelling about? And if so, why did Sheva lie? She thought about the hard expression on Sheva's face when she was cowering, and it sent a chill through her.

The emotions from earlier welled up. What am I going to say to Kadence? How could they move forward, professionally, much less personally after this? Was Kadence unstable? Did she want to continue any relationship under these circumstances? Maybe she needed to find herself a nice dentist to date or something. Artists were all crazy.

She had to hear what Kadence had to say, then she could decide about the future. *Shit. Why?* She was such a good person, so calm and down-to-earth until today. She fumbled through the rest of her morning, dreading the meeting ahead.

CHAPTER ELEVEN

Kadence was a wreck, but she managed to convince Tarin she'd be fine and would see him later. He patted her shoulder awkwardly, but looked sympathetic as he turned to leave. Waves of guilt buffeted her as she climbed the stairs to her apartment, like solid walls of brick, plowing into her. *What were you thinking? Idiot.* The idea was to ask Sheva what she remembered about Carlyle, not to attack her. *Now everyone thinks you're crazy. Hell, you were crazy. What were you going to do if you got away from Mallory? Punch her? Geez, Munroe, you've fucked things up but good.* She'd never forget the look on Mallory's face, the shock and fear. *You did that. She'll never let you back in to her life now.*

What had made her lose it? The realization that the bronze was Carlyle? She knew Carlyle had modeled for Sheva. Sheva's denial? Hell, maybe she just didn't remember her. It was two years ago and Sheva probably slept with a ton of people. Now she'd never get a chance to try asking again, not after the way she'd yelled at her. And she had her own show to worry about. Did her irrational behavior cost her the show? God, she hoped not. She couldn't blame Mallory if she terminated her contract. She wouldn't fight it, if that's what happened. She'd been so stupid.

She been just like her mother. That had always been her worst fear, and when it happened, she'd had no control. Why had she felt so enraged? Was it repressed jealousy because Sheva wooed Carlyle away from her? Was it something as foolish as that? She didn't think so, but she had no rational explanation for her outburst. *What am I going to say to Mallory?* Losing her was going to hurt. As much as she'd tried to keep things on the friend level, she hadn't succeeded in guarding her heart. It hurt to lose friends, too. She was going to have to face whatever was ahead. She'd created the mess, so the consequences were hers. It had taken so little to push her over the edge. To make her into the one thing she'd promised herself she'd never be, her mother.

Her stomach soured and she felt like throwing up when she thought about it. She'd been exactly like her, loud, overbearing, and threatening. At least she'd managed not to physically injure Sheva or Mallory. She hated that the ghost of her mother lived inside her. It was like she'd spent her life vowing not to let that happen, and the first time she was confronted, all her guards and defenses crumbled.

When Sheva had denied knowing Carlyle, it infuriated her and she lost it. So, how was she going to keep that from happening again? She needed to get some help, see a doctor and find out what to do. She didn't have insurance, so she looked up free clinics and found one nearby that offered therapeutic counseling on a sliding scale. She spoke to the receptionist and made an appointment for two that afternoon.

It felt like her head was full of mud. Sludgy and slow, unclear. She made herself eat something, then walked the mile and a half to the clinic. It was a squat building with construction netting covering the façade. She found the office without much trouble and signed in. They had her pay the minimum before ushering her into the back. The moldy smell of the reception area was replaced by the light scent of jasmine. The room she was placed in was pale blue with a couch, an office chair, and a coffee table with fresh flowers in a vase in the center. She chose the couch, thinking that the doctor would prefer the chair.

When the door opened, a young Asian woman walked in. She didn't look much older than Kadence, but as soon as she started talking, Kadence could tell she really knew psychology, and she was very reassuring. They talked for an hour, and the doctor helped her decide that the behavior she'd exhibited wasn't in character with her personality. It was repressed anger and talking to Sheva had triggered it. She gave her some exercises for anger management and advised her to return the following week to discuss her strategies. It felt good to talk to someone about Carlyle, to expose those buried feelings.

The weight of guilt was lifted by the time she left the clinic. She had just enough time to get to the gallery for her meeting. She could handle that now. She had a grip on what caused her outburst. It might still cost her the show, probably would cost her Mallory. This was so much like what happened with Carlyle, but this time it was on her. She'd been the one to blow it all up. Anger rose up inside. She'd lost control and thrown it all away.

The train was half empty on the ride there, so she used the quiet time to consider what questions Mallory might have, and how she'd respond. Mallory was walking someone through the exhibits when she arrived, so she waited in the bronze room. The statue that had shielded Sheva drew her. She walked boldly to it this time, ran both hands down its sides, feeling every inch of Carlyle in its hard, cold surface. This was her, no doubt. It was almost too perfect a casting. Why add the small imperfections of skin? Why the ridge that mimicked the scar she'd gotten falling from a fence? Would Kadence have included such minute details if she'd done portraiture?

She didn't think so. Carlyle had hated that scar, the mole on her hip. She wanted to get them removed. How had Sheva convinced her to leave them? *Maybe that's part of the reason they broke up.*

She moved to the other figures, examining them with the same care. They all had little things that marred them. Small details that most probably wouldn't notice, but they stood out to Kadence. This one had a broken fingernail. That one had a vaccination scar. Why wouldn't she smooth those out? Was she that much of a purist? Who were these other girls? Sheva had begun this series at CAA, maybe one or more of these were also classmates of hers.

"What are you doing?" Mallory said.

She snatched her hand back like a guilty child. How could she make this less painful? Her shoulders fell and the effort to make her mouth form words was huge. It was like her lips weighed a million pounds. Besides, there wasn't anything she could say to fix this, not really. She simply had to accept the consequences. "Oh, sorry. I was waiting for you to finish."

"What were you doing with the sculptures?"

Kadence felt that like a punch. Did Mallory think she'd damage the artwork? Probably. "I was just looking at them. I knew this girl. Maybe some of the others, too."

"That isn't a girl. It's a statue. Let's go to the office." The tension Mallory carried washed over Kadence, but she pushed it back. *There's nothing I can do but accept the consequences.* She followed her up the stairs.

When she sat opposite Mallory, she saw her contract on the desk. So, this was it. She would lose her and lose the show. Harsh, but understandable.

"We need to talk about the incident this morning."

Mallory spoke gently, making Kadence feel even more guilty. *This is all on me. She's trying to make it easy.*

"Um, I apologize. I don't know what I was thinking. I guess I wasn't. I kind of lost my mind." She hung her head, her body numb.

"You think? That was completely unacceptable and unwarranted. You attacked a fellow artist with no provocation."

She deserved whatever Mallory did. There was nothing she could say to change that. "Yes, I did."

"I'd like to understand why that happened. I can't excuse your behavior, but I'd like to know why."

She should tell her everything, but it would just make her sound even crazier. She needed to calm down and be in a better state of mind before she told Mallory about Carlyle. She was too raw right now. "I lost my mind. I can't really tell you any more than that." Mallory looked at her for a long moment. Kadence knew her answers were disappointing her.

"Okay, well, we have to figure out how to keep that from happening again. I know you artists can be a little temperamental, but that was extreme, don't you think?"

Kadence could see what she was doing. She wanted to give her an out, but Kadence didn't want an out. She'd become her mother and wanted the consequences. She hung her head and waited without saying anything.

Mallory continued to watch her, her irritation showing in the fast tapping of her foot. "Look, I want to work with you, but you're not making this easy."

"Don't make it easy. I don't deserve that. When do you want me to pick up my work?"

Mallory's foot stopped tapping. "What?"

Kadence looked up. *Is she going to make me say it?* "My pieces, I'm sure you want to cancel my show."

"Oh, no. That's not my plan. I still see the value in your art and want to promote it. However, we have to amend your contract."

Kadence felt something shift inside. Her heart stuttered as she realized she wasn't going to lose the show. "Okay, how?"

"Here." She pushed the paper across to Kadence.

There was a new paragraph attached to the end, a kind of restraining order. Kadence's show would run the entire three-month period, but Kadence would be banned from the gallery until further notice. The restriction would end at Mallory's discretion.

"Here's the deal. Either sign this, or we return all work and sue you for breach of contract to recoup possible sales."

Kadence felt the floor slip away, like she was falling, nothing but air between her and the ground. She was relieved she wouldn't lose the show, but not seeing Mallory would be hard. Her face burned with shame. She'd brought this on herself. It was fair.

"I'm sorry," she whispered as she signed the document and pushed it back across the table.

Mallory sighed. She took the paper and slid her hand over Kadence's. "I'd like to know you're going to be okay. I wish you'd tell me everything, so I could really understand. But if you're not going to, then I've got no choice. I've got to protect the gallery and the other artists, no matter how much I like you. I'm sorry." She looked so disappointed, so sad. "You'll keep in touch, right?"

Kadence nodded and rose to leave. Her heart was breaking at the finality of the good-bye. It hurt like hell. She loved spending time with Mallory, but now that was gone. Well, she always had her painting. Paint yourself happy, she thought, but somehow, she didn't think it would work this time.

Back at her apartment, she tried to channel the emotions into a painting, but it wasn't going to happen. It was too real, too big to transfer to canvas. She'd let Mallory in and now she had to feel the pain of her loss for real. *I knew better. Letting people in only causes pain.* She collapsed on the bed and rolled into a fetal position, her knees drawn up to her chest. Grief cascaded through her, making her stomach sour and her muscles lock. *I've destroyed any chance of anything with Mallory. Stupid. And all over a girl who tossed me aside for the glitter and flash of Sheva.*

Sheva. Why had she denied knowing Carlyle? What was she hiding? Who were the models for the other statues? She was going to have some time on her hands now that she was banished from the gallery. She could touch base with one of the sculpture professors at CAA and see if they knew anything about the other figures in the series. If Sheva had done something to Carlyle, maybe she'd done something to the other models as well.

She unwound herself from the bed and grabbed her laptop. She pulled up the website for the school and looked at the sculpture faculty. There had been some changes, but the two professors she'd known were still on staff. She sent them both an email asking how they were doing and if things were still the same on campus. If she got a reply, she'd ask if they remembered Sheva's time as visiting artist.

The reply from Frances Barton was quick and friendly.

Hey there, stranger! How are you doing in the big wide world? Campus life is just as exciting as it was when you were here. We've been dedicating a lot of time to found object sculptures. You'd love it. When are you coming back to visit?

—FB

Kadence smiled. Barton knew her so well. She'd love to be on campus creating art out of junk. Hearing from her made the day feel less depressing. She sent back her question about Sheva and waited, hoping Barton remembered her. This time the reply was longer in coming. Kadence had time to get some water and put on her cuddly sweats.

Yes, I remember Sheva Diva. She was a piece of work, but really gifted as an artist. Why do you ask?

She gave Barton her whole story, except for the breakdown. She asked if she remembered any of the other students who modeled for Sheva.

How great that you've got a solo show at ARA! I'm so proud of you. Hooks is going to be off the chain. Why no invites for your

people? We'd have flown out for you, you know. Right? Models for
Sheva. Well, she had a type she liked. Those were her first figures,
remember? She liked blondes, busty, medium build. There was
Carlyle Goodwin, and I think, Jackie Bondi? Carlyle was the first, in
the fall semester, then Jackie in the spring. She was here all summer,
so maybe one other. I'll ask around.
—FB

Kadence remembered Jackie. She was two years behind her, so she should be finishing her degree this year. Maybe Barton could give her Jackie's email. She wanted to talk to her about the modeling process. She asked Frances for contact details.

I can't help you there, pal. Jackie left school after that spring
break. She never even came back to get her projects. I haven't heard
from her since. Check with dean of students. They may have a contact
number for her.
—FB

Jackie left school after spring break the same year that Carlyle disappeared? And they both modeled for Sheva. All the hairs on the back of her neck raised and her skin prickled. She had to know if there were any other women who vanished after modeling for Sheva. What if they disappeared *because* they'd modeled for her? What if she had done something to make them disappear?

Stop it. You're going off the deep end. Jumping to conclusions
because of a coincidence is stupid and crazy. Don't be crazy. She didn't know anything about Jackie Bondi. It could be that she just dropped out like so many underclassmen did. She was probably back home, content with her life. It was ridiculous to assume she was missing like Carlyle. But she could try to find out more. She emailed the dean of students to see if she could get contact information for Jackie.

She hadn't known much about her. Nothing beyond her name, really. So she ran a search to see if it brought anything up. There were the typical sites claiming to have found Jackie Bondi near her and such, but nothing of substance. She added California to the search line and waited. The same sites came up first, but as she scrolled down, she found something more real. Something that scared her.

Jacqueline Bondi Missing, Chico CA

She hit the link and read the article.

Jacqueline Bondi was last seen leaving her home in Chico, California, at 9 a.m. on March 12. Friends said Bondi was despondent over a failed relationship and feared she might harm herself. Parents, Mike and Liz Bondi, reported that Jackie had left the house to spend some time with friends and do some shopping but never made it home. Her car, a black Mazda 6, was found in the parking lot of the Chico Mall on the morning of the 15th. No sign of Jackie or her handbag was found. Police are asking anyone with information to call the Chico police department.

It was dated March of two years ago.

Kadence's scalp prickled and all the hair on her arms stood up. *She disappeared.* She clicked on other links with later dates, hoping Jackie had been found, but there wasn't any resolution. She was still missing, like Carlyle.

Her email pinged and she opened the response from the dean's office. It was brief, saying only that they had no forwarding address for Jackie Bondi. Jackie's car had been found in Chico. That was more than five hours from Oakland. It was probably a weird coincidence and nothing more, but she couldn't shake the feeling that the two were connected. Both women had modeled for Sheva and disappeared. Carlyle had dated Sheva and they'd had a loud breakup. She had no idea if Jackie was even a lesbian, much less if she'd dated Sheva.

She needed to stop thinking about this. It was crazy to be obsessed with Sheva and create this whole drama around her models and disappearances. Was she going insane? She needed to calm down and be rational. *Don't blow this all out of proportion. You don't like Sheva, so you're finding reasons for what you did to her. Cut it out.*

She closed her laptop and got up. She needed to do something else. Stalking Sheva online wasn't going to help her with staying sane. Determined to stop dwelling on Sheva, she changed into jeans and a hoodie and headed to Ink. A good meal and spending time with Jake would be a welcome distraction.

The coffee parlor was in full swing when she arrived. Tables were crowded with hipsters and artsy types in their habitat. She fit. Jake was working on a shoulder tat for a young guy, but looked up when she called his name. He gave her a sign, indicating an hour before she could expect him to have room for her. She found a seat at the bar and ordered a Rueben and a coffee-infused beer.

Before long, the girls next to her were chatting her up, asking if she was there for the coffee or the ink. She indulged them and talked about her dragon tattoo. They were considering getting their first tattoos.

"Jake is the best there is. His work is amazing. If you decide to go for it, you won't be disappointed."

"But what should we get? I mean, I was thinking I wanted a gecko. Would that be weird?"

"Nothing you want is weird. Just get something you know you'll love forever. Something that really means something to you."

"Thanks."

They moved off to look at the tattoo books in the back area. Kadence finished her sandwich and drink, watching the clock for her turn with Jake. She ran her hand over the Malin tattoo on her wrist, its meaning particularly strong today. *I must face setbacks to move forward.* She traced the arrow from the fletching to the down loop, then crossed over and traced the up loop to the arrowhead. This was a setback, a replay of a past detour. If she made different choices this time, she'd move forward stronger and better than before.

The dragon perched on her shoulder reminded her of what she'd overcome. It was a symbol of creation and destruction. It was strength and wisdom. She'd survived the destruction of her childhood, the loss of her father, her grandmother, the abuse and anger of her mother. She'd come through it because of her creativity, her art. That's why she needed her dragon.

He finally called her over. She slipped in the back room and took off her shirt. They were doing the green, and she was jazzed to see how it would look when finished. Her ribbed undershirt followed, and she sat backward on the chair, her chest against the back pad.

The door swung open and Jake entered.

"You ready for some fun?"

"Bring it on," Kadence said, but her voice didn't have its usual playfulness.

"What's up? You sound a little down."

She didn't want to talk about her day, but Jake was a friend and talking might help. "Just screwed up my life, that's all."

"How so? You were all smiles last night. That was some big deal, your show. Thanks for including me."

Kadence winced. Was it only last night? The feeling of euphoria that had filled her last night was gone, dashed to bits by her outburst. "I fucked it all up. Destroyed it."

He looked puzzled. "What? How?"

The feelings from this morning came back. She felt numb and hollow. "I lost my mind. Totally and completely lost it. I attacked one of the other artists showing at the gallery."

His eyes widened and his mouth opened in a silent o. She'd shocked him, and that wasn't easy to do. "Holy crap. Seriously? Did they cancel your show?"

The guilt weighed on her, pressing on her shoulders and making them slump against the chair pad. "No, but I'm personally banned."

"Geez. Not good. I'm sorry, man. What made you do that? You're a level-headed person, I'd never figure you for something like that."

"I don't understand it myself. Something snapped and I went off on her. We have a common past, and old stuff came up." *Ghost of my mother.*

"Ah, an ex?"

"Kind of, I guess. She's a one-time rival. It's hard to explain. We have this girl in our past, my first love. She dumped me to get with this sculptor, so yeah."

"Hm. Not good. What are you going to do about it?"

"What can I do? I'm shut out."

"You can try. There has to be something you can do." He put a comforting hand on her back.

"I don't think so."

"Did you explain why you went off? I mean, it's not like this is typical of you."

Kadence wanted to tell Mallory her story. Maybe not now, but after a few days. Disquiet filled her. Maybe being banned was the best thing. If she stayed away from the gallery, she'd be away from Mallory. Being with her threatened the walls Kadence had built around her heart. She'd let her in, a little, and had been stung. Maybe staying away was a good idea. For some reason, the thought depressed her. It was like a wave of sadness hit her square in the middle of her heart.

Jake finished up the work he could, then put a waterproof bandage on her back and shoulder. The sting and burn of the new color was enough to take her mind off Mallory and what might have been.

"Okay, we just have the blue left. Give it two weeks to heal and then come back and see me. Well, come back before then, but don't expect work."

"Yeah, I know the drill. Thanks, Jake."

"Thank you. The murals look awesome in the baby's room, so this is a fair trade."

Kadence had painted scenes from *The Runaway Bunny* on the walls of Jake's apartment. His wife worked in finance and traveled a great deal. Jake's gift to her, after learning the sex of their baby, had been the nursery.

"Did Brenna like it?"

"She loves it. That was her favorite book, growing up. It's perfect."

"Well, I just hope the baby agrees."

"Tough luck if she doesn't. I better go. I've got clients waiting." He tapped her on the shoulder to get her attention properly. "Look, I don't know what happened, but I feel like I know you. And when you're making dreams come true, you have to keep chasing them, you know? Don't give up." He grinned. "My two cents."

"Yeah, I hear you. Thanks again."

Jake hugged her, making some of the black cloud around her recede. She had her friends, she had her art, why did she need anything else? She tried to believe it, but the heaviness didn't shift. The longer she tried to fool herself, the worse this was going to get. She cared about Mallory and losing her hurt. It was worth it to try to explain. To make some effort to mend the breach. But how?

CHAPTER TWELVE

Sheva arrived at the foundry early. She wanted everything to go smoothly with chasing the new wax. Her assistants arrived, and the careful process of unmolding the models began. The wax was checked for imperfections, soldering irons and small tools were used to remove any flaws. They added the sprues, gates, and vents with sticky wax and heat to prepare for the bronzing.

Sheva finished the slurry, and with great care, the four of them dipped the wax models carefully into the liquid ceramic. After sufficient draining, they applied the fine silica sand "stucco" that would capture the details. This step required several hours of drying time, so she dismissed the assistants until five that evening.

Now that she was alone with her newest girl, she could appreciate the beauty she was creating. *I'm a God. I, alone, can create this perfect form, this symmetry of life and death. Pride* was going to be breathtaking. Her erect figure, poised to reach a hand to the observer, with flames lapping at her lower extremities, her face a mask of absolute dread. *This one will be a statement piece. It will shock people, make them question themselves and each other.* She could almost feel the praise that would be showered on her at its unveiling. And with *Malice*, the name she'd chosen for Mallory's bronze, soon to follow, she'd have the public flocking to her shows.

No more selling her work off to complete strangers. After these two, museums would be lining up to purchase her work directly. She'd be done with the simpering and fawning personalities of gallery managers. She'd have the acclaim she'd worked hard to earn.

Need flooded her. She had to have someone right now, to give the excess of power the moment held a physical outlet. Mallory was out of the question. That would undo her careful preparations. She had to find a willing body on short notice, so she used her Pure app. In minutes, she had six potential sex partners willing to meet her in her zip code. She chose the one least like her models and set a meeting place. She'd have her gratification and not risk wanting to capture her partner in bronze. She shut down the foundry and locked it up before heading to her rendezvous.

Mallory stayed busy, trying to avoid confronting her feelings about Kadence, but it was no use. Any time she had a down moment, her mind went right to the attack and the conflicting images she had of her. Kadence had been so considerate and undemanding in every interaction they'd had before the blowup with Sheva. It was strikingly out of character for her to react that way. Confusion and turmoil ran through her. *How could I be so wrong about her? Was I? What happened to make her go off like that? Am I being fair to her, to myself, by not trying harder to get her to talk to me? Is this some by-product behavior from her childhood?* She shoved a paper from her desk. *What do I do?*

When she'd met with Kadence after the incident she'd tried to get her to open up, but Kadence had been so shutdown. She'd had to restrain her from entering the gallery, that was necessary, in her role as manager. But what about her role as friend? When Kadence had walked in on her throwing crystal around her office, she hadn't jumped to unfair conclusions. She'd been calm and understanding. She'd helped clean up and distracted Mallory from her troubles. That was what friends did.

She needed to reach out to her on those terms. Separate from the gallery and policies, she needed to offer support to Kadence. If she didn't she'd risk losing her friendship, and that mattered to her. She wanted her connection to Kadence. She needed to listen objectively and speak reflexively. Be there for Kadence the way she'd been there for her.

As soon as the gallery closed for the day, she called Kadence. There was no answer, so she left a voice mail.

"Hey, I'm feeling pretty bad about the way we left things yesterday. I'd like to get together and talk about what happened, but not at the gallery. Call me."

She hoped Kadence would call. If she didn't, it would hurt, but she wouldn't be able to blame her. She'd had to lay down the terms with her yesterday, and if that meant she'd lost Kadence on a personal level, it was her own fault. This was the price of mixing business and pleasure. *When will I learn?*

She was walking to the station when her cell buzzed. She grabbed it out of her pocket, hoping, but it was Tarin. He asked her if she was up for some company. He was solo tonight because his partner was on a business trip. She texted back that she'd love some company. The distraction would be welcome.

She got home and changed into jeans and a linen pullover. When her bell sounded, she buzzed Tarin in. He brought pizza and, knowing her taste, a bunch of old Hitchcock films on Blu-ray.

"This is great, Tarin. Do you know how badly I needed this?"

"Well, I figured after yesterday you could use some time away from reality. What'll it be? *Rear Window*, *North by Northwest*, or *Spellbound*?"

"Oh, *Rear Window*. You know it's my favorite."

"I know, but I was hoping to broaden your horizons. You'd love *Spellbound*."

"Okay, I'll give it a try. I don't usually like his earlier films."

"This one is different. You wait and see."

They munched on pizza while they watched Ingrid Bergman and Gregory Peck in the psycho-thriller. Tarin was right, the movie was fantastic. Mallory was on the edge of her chair, her stomach in knots by the final scene. Right as Bergman was walking away from the killer who held her at gunpoint, her phone rang, making her jump. Tarin hit the pause and she took her phone to her room to answer.

"Hello?"

"Hi."

Mallory felt her whole body relax as she recognized Kadence's voice. She'd been worried since she hadn't heard from her. "Kadence? I didn't recognize the number."

"Yeah, I'm calling from Ink. I guess it's a little late for coffee, huh?"

Mallory wanted to say no, but Tarin was in the next room, and he'd been great tonight. It wouldn't be fair to bail on him.

"Maybe, but there's tomorrow." She hoped Kadence would agree. She needed to hear her, to do something to make sure she wouldn't lose her because of what happened.

"Yeah, tomorrow sounds good. Do you want to meet early or after work?"

She sounded so down. It hurt to hear that sadness in her voice.

"Let's meet after work. At Ink?" Mallory tried to be peppy, to bring Kadence up a bit. She didn't like the dull pitch in her voice.

"Sure. Let's say, seven?"

"I'll be there."

"Great. Thanks, Mallory."

"I'm glad you called back. I've missed you. See you tomorrow."

Mallory hung up. She felt somehow dejected; even though she knew she could hash things out with Kadence, the idea of waiting until tomorrow was depressing. She wanted resolution. She wanted to reconnect with Kadence, and she really had missed spending time with her. But after the attack, and how shut down Kadence had been, she'd keep things on a professional level. No more crazy artists in her personal life. Tonight, she owed Tarin her time and attention.

She walked back to the other room and slid back onto the couch.

"Everything okay?"

"Yeah, or it will be." *I hope.*

"Okay, let's finish this show." He started the movie, Bergman walking away from the evil doctor, then rescuing Gregory Peck and finding their forever, together.

"That was a great movie. I wish real life could be like that sometimes." She liked the idea of happily ever after. Why shouldn't things work out in the end? It was easy to give up when things got hard. *Don't give up on Kadence.*

"Huh? Crazy doctors shooting other doctors and letting amnesia patients foot the blame?"

"No, silly, happy endings."

"Oh, yeah. They have been known to happen, you know."

"For you, maybe. Not for me."

"Come on, Debbie Downer, don't give up on happily ever after. You just haven't found your Princess Charming, yet."

She laughed. Sometimes Tarin was just what she needed. They started *Rear Window*, but both fell asleep before the best scenes. When Mallory woke, the film was rolling credits and Tarin was snoring beside her.

"Time to go, sleepyhead." She shook him gently.

After he left, she went to bed, hoping to pick up where she left off on the couch, but tossed and turned all night. She kept running scenarios in her head. Meeting Kadence, things going well, things not going well, things blowing up in a public place. She finally gave up and took a sleep aid. Tomorrow was soon enough to worry about things she couldn't control.

❖

Sheva and her assistants had applied the coarser stucco in three processes separated by two hours each. She now had the shell molds and they could be fired to melt the wax casting inside. They wheeled the molds to the kiln and loaded them, upside down, into the large boxy oven. She quickly brought the temperature up to thirteen hundred degrees, which melted the wax out and vitrified the ceramic particles in the slurry enough so they fused together. Tomorrow morning, she would inspect the molds for cracks that might have formed during the burnout process. If none were found, they could do the metal casting. For now, they were done.

Sheva left the foundry, exhausted. It had been a long day. Her afternoon adventure had proved pleasurable, and she could barely move. She would sleep the sleep of the dead tonight, satisfied completely. She made her way across the deserted metal scrapyard to her studio and let herself in. Her room was here, where she kept her maquettes, souvenirs of all her girls. She walked to the table and looked at each one. *Torrid Heat*, Carlyle Goodwin. She remembered her well, not that the painter needed to know. Carlyle had been her first, her gateway to the acclaim she was about to receive. How could she forget her? Never. Then there was *Love's Birth*, Jackie Bondi, beautiful and innocent Jackie. Trini Nguyen, *Broken Wave*, her third and almost final statue in the series. She'd loved Trini, just a little, and that had made the completion of the statue a challenge. *Sunburst*, Nicole Flemming. Ah, Nicole. *Sea Dancer*, Alyssa Shern, her mermaid. Those were all in the gallery, together as they should be. *Fragmented Humanity*, Elia Montoya, was her latest piece and the first to reflect the darker side of Sheva. She loved them all as statues, as maquettes. Each was a testament to her genius, and she would never forget any of them.

Carlyle had been the design student with an attitude. She'd been the whole reason Sheva had started down the path that led her here. She'd been a firecracker of a girl, exploding in every aspect of her life. Her design ideas were unconventional, her skills in the bedroom, phenomenal, and her anger at Sheva, acerbic. If things hadn't gone off track with her, maybe Sheva's work would have never taken the path it had. She was the key to creating Sheva's unique process. *I owe her everything. Funny, the painter knew her. Strange for her to lash out at me because of that. Was it because I denied knowing the girl? Whatever, she's a flash in the pan abstractionist. I am a god.*

It was evident in everything she did. The way women threw themselves at her. How easy it had been to collect each soul for her work. No one but a god could do all she'd done so easily. Look at what happened with the abstractionist. She'd played right into her hands when she started being aggressive. Sheva knew all about aggression. You have to be certain of triumph before you show your cards. She knew if she played the victim and let the painter rage at her, Mallory would come to her rescue. It worked like a charm. Now, she had the painter out of the way, and Mallory would be inclined to cooperate with her plans for a new statue.

Still, she knew Carlyle Goodwin had gone missing, and that made Sheva nervous. She needed to silence the painter for good. She had to guard her secrets, after all. A little more winding up, and that abstractionist would blow. She could collect the pieces and move on. She only had three and a half weeks until she left for France, and then Geneva. Time was ticking for Mallory, and she'd have her, as long as she could keep the painter from ruining everything.

Tomorrow they would do the metal casting and *Pride* would be born. Once she finished the removal of the mold, the welding, and finishing, she would add the patina and it would be ready for display. It would be the first new piece for the Geneva show. The gallery there was paying all shipping costs. *Malice* would be the second piece, and then she would move to Europe to create two or three additional pieces. She had a studio and foundry leased in Paris beginning next month.

A few days from now, she needed to be ready to start on *Malice*. Mallory would be perfect by then, angry, confused, maybe despairing. Her expression would live forever in the maquette Sheva would create.

She said good night to her girls and climbed into her bed, ready to face tomorrow.

CHAPTER THIRTEEN

K adence sat on her couch staring at the computer screen. She hadn't been able to verify the name of the last girl from CAA to model for Sheva, but she had found something equally chilling. Another young student in her first year at school had disappeared during that summer. She hadn't attended CAA but UC Berkeley. She had been a scholarship student from Boston, and her disappearance was the only one of the three that made national news. Trini Nguyen, eighteen, had been reported missing by her roommate in early July. She'd been expected back that evening after working her shift at a local coffee shop. Trini was a focused student who never missed a class and always showed up where she was supposed to. Her roommate became alarmed after she was two hours late and called the shop. Trini had never shown up for work that day. The police suspected foul play and had instituted a search immediately. They'd never found any sign of her.

Kadence hit the link to the national story. It gave a more detailed description of the investigation into the disappearance. Carlyle's and Jackie's names came up in the article, and speculation was made about possible connections. In later links, the police had halted that talk by pointing out that Jackie had disappeared from her home, five hours north, and that Carlyle was suspected of having disappeared while vacationing out of state. They were confident the disappearances were coincidental and unconnected.

What chilled Kadence was the photo included in the article. It was a picture of a petite Asian woman in short-shorts and a tank top. Her delicate bone structure was striking, and it rang a bell. This woman was the model for the sculpture of the woman coming out of the wave. She couldn't remember the name of the work, but it was her, she'd swear to it. If Trini hadn't been a model, how was it that her body was an exact match for that sculpture? She disappeared, like Jackie, like Carlyle. The police had brushed off any connection because they didn't have bodies, nor did they have leads.

They didn't know about the connection to Sheva, and Trini wasn't one of her official models. She wondered where Sheva had found the girl, if not through a university. *The police would see it if they saw the sculptures. I see it. I know they're connected. They're all at the gallery, together.* Three women who disappeared.

Am I going crazy again? Making something out of nothing? Why am I so certain Sheva has something to do with their disappearances? And what can I do to prove it? Nothing. That's what she could do. She had no proof, only her gut instinct. Bringing this to the attention of the police here wouldn't work. These things had happened in California, and they'd just write her off as a loony. What about the other three statues in the show? Who were those women? She'd be willing to bet they'd disappeared as well.

She closed the laptop with a snap. She needed to get photos of those sculptures and send them to the police who investigated the disappearances, along with a description of their connections to Sheva. That was the only way she could do something about what Sheva might have done. The families of those women deserved it. She deserved it. Kadence might be the only person close enough to this to make the connection, and it was her responsibility to do something. But she was banned from the gallery. How could she get the pictures? Mallory was giving her a chance, opening herself up to Kadence's explanation and maybe to their friendship. If she could explain everything to her, make her see, maybe they could stop Sheva together.

She shoved off the bed and jumped in the shower, trying to forget what she'd read. *There's nothing you can do about it right now. Push it away until you can do something about it.* She tried, she really did, but she couldn't help wondering if Sheva was making new sculptures here in New York. The thought was enough to push her over the emotional edge. She doubled over and retched, thinking more women would disappear into that psycho's world of bronze.

She washed herself off and cleaned up the shower, then dressed and headed out to Ink. She wanted to get there before Mallory, to have her coffee with cinnamon and chocolate milk waiting on their table. She had so much more reason to convince Mallory she was worth the risk. Focus on the positive, she told herself, make your way forward.

She carried their cups to the table and sipped at hers while she waited. She was nervous and her hands were shaking. She needed to calm down. Mallory needed to see that she could hold it together. *What if she doesn't believe me?* Her stomach cramped and her mouth was suddenly bone dry. *She has to believe me.* By the time Mallory came in about five minutes later, she was calm.

"Hey, over here," she called.

Mallory turned and smiled, then joined her. She seemed like the old Mallory, and it made Kadence stronger to think she had a chance. She nudged the cinnamon coffee toward her.

"You remembered. Thanks for the coffee."

"My pleasure. Thanks for calling me, meeting me. I appreciate it." Kadence was happy her voice didn't betray her nervousness.

"It's good to see you."

"You too." Everything was too stiff, too formal. She needed to do something to break this tension, but what? "So, anything exciting happen at the gallery today?"

Mallory's eyebrows shot upward. "Nothing like the other day." She laughed.

Kadence felt the shift and laughed with her.

"No? Dang, I was hoping someone outdid me."

"I don't see that happening. You kind of have the gold star for shocking moments. I think your record is safe."

"Ouch. Okay, I deserve that. I lost my mind, literally and figuratively. I'm ashamed to say that, but it's true."

"What I don't understand, and I want to, is why? What made you attack Sheva like that? I know she can be a world class ass, but I had just introduced you two."

"I can explain, but the explanation might not sound rational. Remember, I plead insanity." Kadence held her hands out, palms up, asking for understanding.

"I'm here to listen."

"Okay, well, it all goes back to art school. Sheva was the visiting artist my last year at CAA."

Mallory nodded. "That was the year she started doing figures."

"Right. I had a girlfriend back then, and we'd been together for nearly two years. You know, first love and all that."

"Uh-huh, go on."

"She volunteered to be a model for Sheva, then she dumped me and started dating her." Kadence rolled her shoulders. Saying it out loud brought back the pain from that day.

"So that huge reaction was about a breakup?" Mallory looked incredulous.

"No, let me finish. This all happened in the fall of our final year. Carlyle was a design student. She had an internship set up with a top fashion house in New York. She was good, really good, and very ambitious. She had a plan and was so excited about her future, then she met Sheva."

Mallory interrupted her. "So, Sheva broke her heart? Is that it?"

"You're not very good at letting people tell stories, are you? I don't know that part. She left for Christmas break, but never returned to school. I found out a couple of days ago that she never made it home. She's been missing since that December." Kadence heard the quaver in her voice as she said it.

"Wait, I'm confused. She left school for the holidays and disappeared, okay, but what does that have to do with Sheva?"

"I…well…I don't know for sure, but I suspect Sheva knows something about her disappearance. Carlyle called her parents and said she was going to New York with an artist friend, and then she disappeared. It doesn't seem like a huge stretch to assume it was the woman she was dating. I want to know what Sheva knows."

"And you thought you'd beat it out of her?"

"No, nothing like that. It was her denying she ever knew her that made me lose it. I know Carlyle's body. She was the first girl I ever slept with. I know every inch of her. That sculpture is her. How could she deny knowing her? It was like she didn't even matter." The anger from yesterday beat against her ribcage, trying to break free. Kadence reined in her emotions. She couldn't lose it, not again.

"Oh, Kadence, people forget these things. She's probably met and had so many women that one model, a few years ago, might not have made a lasting impression on her. I don't mean to diminish your memory of Carlyle, but the impact she had on you might be very different from the one she had on Sheva."

She was dismissing it. *How can she?* She had to make Mallory see the connections. "I don't think an artist forgets the person that inspired a piece, I really don't. But it's more than that."

"More how?"

Kadence hesitated, unsure she could trust Mallory to believe her. "Well, there are others. Women who modeled for her who dropped off the face of the earth after. They're all in your gallery."

"Come on, you can't mean that."

"I do mean it. I'm not accusing her of anything, but it's weird that they all modeled for her and then disappeared, and all within the same time period."

"Okay, I'll buy that it's strange, but there could be any number of explanations."

"I know, it's just a feeling I have about her. And they're all connected to her, can't you see? There has to be something there. We can't trust her, Mallory. She's dangerous."

Mallory looked skeptical. "You're saying Sheva used these women as models and then did something to them? What? You're not saying she hurt them, are you?"

"That's exactly what I'm saying. She's the one thing that ties them together. We have to tell the police. I need you to help me. We need pictures of the sculptures so we can get them to take us seriously. I couldn't live with myself if I knew this information and didn't do anything with it."

"Kadence, slow down. You're making a big leap. Put yourself in her place for a minute. If you used models for your work, this could easily be you. And even if you're right, it doesn't excuse your attacking her."

"If I used models for my work, and they'd then disappeared, I'd want to know, and I'd want to help. I wouldn't deny knowing them at all." Kadence felt defeated. *She doesn't believe me.* It was so obvious to her, she couldn't understand why Mallory couldn't see it. "But you're right. I shouldn't have gone after her the way I did. It's not something I've ever done before, but I was completely out of control. It was like I couldn't stop once I started. I feel horrible about it. I've already seen a therapist, but it doesn't make it any less shocking."

"No, it doesn't, but hearing your story helps me understand far better than I did. I can't rescind the ban from the gallery, not yet, but Sheva's show ends on Friday. Once she's moved out, I think we can go back to the way things were before."

Kadence's gut twisted. Sheva's show was leaving Friday. She had to get into the gallery before the sculptures were moved. *Play it cool. Don't say anything stupid.* "Thank you. I miss seeing you."

"I've missed you, too. One thing I have to thank you for, she hasn't come by the gallery since your outburst. There was some unresolved tension between us, so it's been a pleasant few days."

"I'm glad for that. Why did you have such a volatile relationship?"

"Ugh. You know we were seeing each other, and things went sour. She didn't take it well when I told her I didn't want to see her anymore. Her reaction was asinine. She basically wouldn't accept it from me because she had to be the one to break it off. The thing is, I have a hard time separating the personal from the professional."

"Seriously? She broke up with you?" Kadence felt a niggle of fear starting in her gut. Sheva had broken up with Carlyle, too.

"It was more me breaking up with her, I think. She did tell me I was an inspiration. She wants me to model for her."

Kadence's anxiety went off the tracks. Her hands shook. "Don't do it, please don't."

"There's no question about it. I'm not going to model for her. I've had her up to here." She raised a hand above her head.

"Good." Kadence wasn't relieved yet, but she was glad Mallory wasn't walking into this blindly.

"But she said it was no big deal, that she had the memory of me and it would be enough."

She would need more than a memory. Kadence knew for a fact she'd need something more physical to re-create the little idiosyncrasies of the body, like Carlyle's mole and the other woman's scar. "You can't let her. You can't, Mallory. I'm serious. Don't let her turn you into a bronze."

Mallory looked exasperated. "I have no control over what she creates, Kadence. You know that. As an artist, she has the right to create what she will. I'd rather not be a part of her collection, but I don't see what I can do to stop her."

"You have to try. Please, don't be alone with her anymore." Kadence knew she was being irrational, but the instinctual part of her knew Sheva was behind the missing women, and she couldn't bear the thought of losing Mallory.

"You're scaring me. Are you going to lose it again?"

"Not a chance. But, Mallory, if she intends to make you into a sculpture, then you're in serious danger. I really wasn't kidding about those three women disappearing."

"I'm not a college student, and I'm not going to live my life in fear. She doesn't scare me, she just annoys me."

"She scares me."

"You need to let that go. It's not helping you get past this. Sheva isn't dangerous. She's egotistical, narcissistic, and rude, but not dangerous. If those missing girls have some connection to her, I'm sure it's not her that was the catalyst."

Kadence couldn't let it go. Something inside her knew that Sheva was dangerous. Why couldn't she make Mallory see that? She needed to do something to protect Mallory from Sheva, she just had to figure out what.

She slid her hand across the table and gripped Mallory's. "Please don't let her use you as a model. Promise me."

"Listen, I'm not going to model for her, okay? If she uses me, it will only be from memory."

She was starting to sound irritated. Kadence sat back in her seat, desperate not to lose Mallory again. "It's not enough. You're still in danger if she wants to make you into a sculpture. I don't know how or why. I just know it's true."

"Kadence, you're not being rational. You need to stop this. Sheva isn't going to hurt me. I won't let her."

She couldn't convince her, and arguing the point was going to fracture the fragile truce they'd reached. She had to stop. Pushing down the rising panic, Kadence swallowed.

"You're right, I'm sorry. I don't know why it makes me so crazy thinking about this stuff. I'm going to stop."

"Good, that's what you need to do. Let's talk about something else. What did you do with your day today? Any new paintings?"

Kadence let the topic change, even though she still felt ill. "I have one in the works, but I didn't add to it today. Maybe when I get home. I did get more color on my tattoo yesterday."

"Really? I want to see! When are you going to show me that dragon?"

"I can't show you in person, but I did get Jake to take a picture yesterday. Here."

She handed over her phone and watched Mallory's expression as she took in Jake's amazing work.

"Wow, that's fantastic. How does he make it look so alive?"

"He's good, that's how. Jake is the best."

"Is your shoulder sore?"

Kadence shrugged. The disappointment she felt at not convincing Mallory was a hard knot in her stomach, and her fear for her was real. But she had to be present and calm, or she'd scare her off, probably for good. She forced herself to focus. "Not too much. It stings a little, but you get used to it."

"I'm not sure I could do it. I've thought about it, but I'm a wuss when it comes to pain."

"You'd be surprised. There's pain, but since you know what it's creating, it makes it easier to bear."

"What made you choose a dragon?"

Mallory was trying, she could tell. She wanted their relationship as much as Kadence did. "Oh, dragons have lots of meanings. I like to think my dragon represents power and wisdom. I love books with dragons." *And it proves I overcame my destruction. My dragon makes me stronger.*

Mallory nodded. "Power and wisdom, admirable qualities."

"Qualities I'm still trying to find myself, obviously." She smiled and was glad when Mallory smiled back. Kadence watched Mallory take her last sip of coffee, and wished she could think of something to extend their evening. She wanted more time with her. She had to figure out how to get into the gallery. She could pull photos from the website of the sculptures, but the resolution wouldn't be that great. She needed close-ups of the imperfections. She couldn't ask anyone to take those pictures without having to explain why. If she got those details, she could send them to the families of the missing women and confirm whether or not they'd modeled for Sheva.

"Do you want more coffee?"

"I'd better not. I need to get some sleep tonight."

"Hm. Okay, well, they're having a comedy show at the Café Bookstore. You want to go check it out?"

"Oh yeah? That sounds fun, I'd like that."

Kadence smiled. "Great, let's go."

They walked the twelve or so blocks from Ink to the Café Bookstore and lined up with other patrons for the show. When they were able to get inside, they found a small table in the back. They ordered drinks from the wait staff, sparkling water for Mallory and a chocolate stout for Kadence.

The comedienne was hilarious. They laughed so hard it hurt. Kadence watched Mallory; she was so beautiful when she was unguarded. Her laughter was unrestrained, her whole body involved in the action. Kadence's heart twisted a bit, seeing this side of her. *I must protect her from Sheva. I can't let her disappear, too.*

After the show, she and Mallory walked to the station. Kadence was determined to take Mallory home and to her door. If she did that there would be no opportunity for Sheva to interfere with her.

"I'll ride with you back to your place and see you to your door."

"Oh, that's not necessary. I'll be fine. It's not even that late, and you've got a much longer ride back to your place."

"I'd like to, though, just to make sure you get home safely."

"Kadence, I'm going to be fine. I told you, you've got to let go of this paranoia about Sheva. She's been a part of my life for the past two and a half months. Don't you think I'd know if she was a danger to me?"

"But you can't be sure. I'd really like to walk you to your door."

"Stop. You said you weren't going to do this anymore. You're going off the deep end again. I've lived in the city for ten years, believe me, I can take care of myself."

"Okay, okay, but can I please just take you to your door?"

"No. On principle alone, you can't. I'll be fine. You go home and stop worrying."

Kadence nodded and said good-bye after they went through the gate. Her train was on a different platform from the one Mallory would take back to Chelsea. Once she had lost sight of her, she doubled back and made her way to the train Mallory would take. She couldn't help herself. She had to make sure she got home safely.

When she reached the train, she made sure she was far from Mallory and out of her line of sight. She boarded in the final car and found a seat. The ride was a short one, and she waited until the last possible second to exit. She caught sight of Mallory on the up escalator and followed.

When she reached the street, she hung back until she knew Mallory was well ahead of her. Alarms bells rang in her head, knowing that if Mallory spotted her, she'd be upset. *You're acting like a stalker. Turn around and go back to the train.*

She wanted to, but she couldn't. She watched Mallory walk briskly down the street to her building and enter. After what she thought was enough time for her to get to the second floor, she followed. Kadence reached the steps of the building and suddenly, Mallory jumped out and confronted her.

"What do you think you're doing? Are you so crazy you think I wouldn't notice you following me? This is sick, Kadence. You need help. Go home. I mean it. If you ever follow me again, I'll call the police. This isn't how sane people behave."

"I'm sorry, I just wanted to be sure—"

"That I made it home safely, I know. That wasn't what we agreed. You don't get to decide to ignore what I say. I'm telling you for the last time. Go home."

Kadence flinched like she'd been struck. It felt that way. Mallory was furious, with every right to be. Her mouth turned to cotton and her heartbeat was like a bass drum in her ears. She'd made a fool of herself and alienated Mallory at the worst time. How could she protect her if she didn't want to see her? What if Sheva made her move tonight? Or in the morning?

"What if she'd been here waiting for you?"

"I'd have told her where to get off, just like I'm telling you. Go home."

Without waiting for a response, she whirled and entered her building. Kadence stood on the stoop, feeling a huge emptiness fill her. It was a free country. She could stay around here if she wanted, but she knew that would be a mistake. She reluctantly turned and headed back to the train. The hollow feeling grew, encompassing her every step. She could hear the echo of her footsteps in her head. She had taken half a dozen steps before she realized she'd ruined things, again. This time Mallory wouldn't call her for an explanation. This time, she'd lost her for real.

CHAPTER FOURTEEN

Mallory walked up the stairs. *Why can't Kadence stop with the crazy paranoia over Sheva? Is she mentally unstable?* It was starting to seem so. The night had been so much fun, until she let her fears ruin it. There was no way Mallory was going to believe Sheva could hurt anyone. She was mean, petty, and disingenuous, sure, but not psychotic. It was Kadence who reacted unpredictably. She was the aggressor in the chaos at the gallery. She was glad the Sheva show was ending, and maybe her departure would help Kadence get a grip. She wondered if she should lift the ban on Kadence at the gallery after all. It might be a better idea to leave that in place. Hopefully, Kadence would continue to get therapy for her issues.

Mallory was so disappointed. Her heart twisted with regret, thinking about what might have been. She believed Kadence was a good person, someone she could build something with, but the erratic behavior was too much. Why did the ones she connected with best always have something that threw up a red flag?

She unlocked her door and went in, bolting it behind her. *Too much craziness.* Tomorrow, she'd arrange the shipping of Sheva's sculptures. The two sold would go to Connecticut, the others would be picked up by the shipping company to move to Sheva's Geneva exhibition. She'd personally help with placement of the sculptures they'd sold to the gallery's best patrons. It was a courtesy the gallery provided to collectors.

She also needed to arrange the creation of twenty or so lithographs of Kadence's paintings. The gallery would purchase them, have them signed, and make them available for sale. She'd get Tarin to handle that. A little distance from Kadence would be a good idea. She shot him an email detailing what she needed, then called the freighter they used and left a message about moving the sculptures. At last she could try to wind down. Directing her agitation over Kadence into work helped her let it go. She poured herself a glass of wine and sat on the couch. A feeling of melancholy filled her. She'd been foolish to get involved with Sheva, and the way that had ended left a bitter taste in her mouth. Now she was regretting the connection with Kadence, wishing she'd kept things on the professional level. The next three months could end up being a challenge. The relationship between gallery and artist was necessarily close, often crossing boundaries other businesses didn't. It was part of working with creative people. If she didn't bond in some fashion with the artists she represented, it would be harder to promote their work and would result in less sales.

She'd always been good at knowing the balance, giving the right amount of attention without crossing into personal relationships. Sheva had blown that all to pieces, and obviously, she'd lost her footing when bonding with Kadence. This was the result, this limbo she found herself in. Not knowing how much was too much.

Later, after a second glass of wine, she thought about the things Kadence had said, about the missing women and the sculptures. Sheva did have some weird behavior of her own; the biting, her taciturn attitude, and her dismissive way with Mallory. And of course, there was the situation with her breaking into her apartment, key or not. She thought about the information card on *Torrid Heat*. It *had* been completed at CAA. There was a chance Kadence's ex-girlfriend was the model.

Thinking about it was making her skin crawl. There was no way Sheva would have hurt anyone, was there? She remembered her terrible, terrifying dream, and the way Sheva had acted when she'd broken into the apartment. She thought about their confrontation in the gallery, and how cold Sheva had been. Maybe Kadence had a point. She didn't think Sheva had made anyone disappear, but she was a little too aggressive, a little too…off. She'd be careful to keep a distance from her until her show ended. Better to be safe than sorry. If she thought there could be any truth at all to what Kadence had said, and thinking about Sheva's behavior made her allegations seem a little less crazy, then how would she go about her friendship with Kadence?

❖

Sheva flipped the face mask down. She was dressed in a heavy leather jumpsuit, steel toe boots, and heavy stick gloves. Her assistants were dressed the same. It was time for the pour. She and one of her assistants loaded the silicon bronze ingots into the crucible and moved it into the furnace. She turned on the blower, increasing the internal heat dynamically. The other two assistants heated the molds to the required 1500 degrees in the kiln. Timing was of utmost importance. The ingots took about forty-five minutes to reach twenty-two hundred degrees, the right temperature for pouring. The heated molds were carefully placed into a large kettle to hold them upright for the pouring and to catch any spills of molten bronze. Each kettle was filled with silica sand and the kettle was moved into the central area, where a deep layer of sand would protect them if anything unexpected happened. A single drop of molten bronze on concrete would cause the concrete to explode.

As they finished placing the molds, Sheva called over a second assistant. She used the lifting bar to raise the crucible and they gripped its sides with long-handled steel tongs. Carefully, she moved the lifting bar along its track to the pouring area. The assistants guided and kept the crucible from tipping. When they reached the kettle, Sheva locked the lifting bar, then used her own tongs to hold the rear of the crucible. As she tipped the molten bronze into the molds, the third assistant signaled when each was full. The leftover metal was poured into heated ingot trays to reuse.

Now the final cooling stage before divesting and despruing began. She dismissed the assistants and asked them to return in the morning to help with breaking the ceramic molds. They were all exhausted, but glad to have reached the final stage in the sculpture's production.

Sheva pulled off her gloves and skimmed out of the jumpsuit. The pour was the most critical part of the foundry. If things went awry, it was almost impossible to salvage the original work. She hated that it took so many hands to bring her girls to life, but it couldn't be helped.

The one time she tried a pour without help, she'd lost her molds and nearly lost an eye. It was worth it to have good people to help. They were hands, nothing more. The process, the creation, was all hers.

Now she wanted food and company. Too bad she was in the final stages with Mallory. It had been fun to run out to a bodega and grab things to eat in the middle of the night. Mallory's apartment was in the perfect location for that kind of thing. Here, there were no places open after ten, and none within walking distance. This was English Kills, not an area known for late night dining. She would have to take a train over to Bushwick to find something that suited her mood.

She looked down at her jeans and T-shirt. *Not too bad.* She grabbed her jacket and made it to Yours Sincerely on Wilson a little after ten. They had great burgers and that was what she was craving. The place was half full, lots of twenty-somethings dressed in too tight pants and cashmere pullovers. She sat at a table and waited for the server to bring her order. The window beside her showed the increasing foot traffic in this once quiet area. She watched couples and small groups stroll along Wilson. It amused her, thinking about young people today. They had no taste for life. Everything they did was prescribed by what others had done before them. *No originality.* As she watched, she made up scenarios for each little group. First date, never had sex. High school friends, reconnecting after the first semester at college. Then someone strikingly different walked by. Tall and gaunt, dressed much as she was, with tight ringlets of hair cascading wildly to the top of her collar. She was familiar in some way. Did she know her? The woman turned and Sheva recognized her. *The abstractionist.* Who'd have guessed they'd cross paths in Bushwick?

She watched her turn into a doorway beside a hardware store. *She must live in one of the apartments above. Interesting.* Sheva watched the windows and sure enough, a light flicked on in one of the front apartments. So this was where the troublemaker who attacked her at the gallery lived. Only a short train ride from her own abode.

How had the abstractionist connected her to the Goodwin woman? What else did she know? She could watch her now and figure out how much of a threat she was. No one was going to stop her work. If this lanky painter wanted to try, let her. Sheva knew just how to deal with troublemakers.

Her burger arrived and she ate with gusto, energized by the sudden idea of capturing the painter. Maybe she would start a whole new group of sculptures; maybe that's where Mallory would lead her. No more trying for the perfect moment of submission, maybe the perfect moment of torment would be better. How amazing would that be? *Pride*, *Malice*, and *Angst*. Perfection in emotion. She could expand on the theme once she reached Europe. It would be fantastic. Her six virtues, her original six bronzes, then her seven vices, starting with those three. *Perfection*. Her work would balance and her legacy would be absolute perfection.

Once she finished with *Pride*, she could split her time between watching this one and Mallory, capturing whichever left themselves most vulnerable. Satisfaction was like honey, thick and sweet on her tongue. She would be unmatched when her work was complete.

She paid for her meal and crossed the street to look over the hardware store and the entry to the apartments. The door opened onto a stairwell. She could see four postal boxes inside. *So, four apartments. All occupied?* Or was there a vacancy? Perhaps she could rent out a unit and make this whole experience that much more delicious. She would come back when the store was open and inquire.

Every nerve in her body fired with excitement at the new direction her mind was taking. That painter had attacked her, and it would be pleasurable to make her scream, to watch as her pain was overcome by terror and her life was extinguished. She would have that. *It's destiny*. She caught the train back to English Kills and her studio. The anticipation of creating a maquette of the painter made her fingers twitch and her pulse race.

She went straight to her table and grabbed her wire to build the framework for the maquette. She was long and lean, the abstractionist, so Sheva made the form match. How to position her? What would give her the greatest pleasure as an artist? Put her on her knees? Head thrown back? Or spread-eagle on a wooden frame? Lashed to it?

There were infinite possibilities, all of them allowing for the added bonus of finding out what she knew and who she'd told. She bent the wire at the half length of legs and made the wire effigy kneel. Yes, that fit. *She made me drop to the ground when she came after me.* She bent the head back, almost ninety degrees, a painful tilt. *Just wait. Just you wait.* Her arms she pulled out to the sides, away from her body as if she'd been struck and was flailing from the impact. This was going to be her seminal work. She pulled out her clay and began forming the lines and curves of the figure. Her face was a blank, unknown. Until the moment Sheva saw her expression, she wouldn't mar the clean surface of the clay. She worked tight coils of clay in her fingers to re-create the ringlets that surrounded the painter's face in wild waves. *Yes.* This was perfect.

When she stepped away from her table, the small figure knelt in supplication, the fear palatable in her imagination, the taste of it, pleasurable. She hadn't felt this good since the beginning. Since Carlyle Goodwin had helped her create her first bronze figure. More satisfied than she would've been with a good night's sex, she dragged herself to her bed and fell into a deep and dreamless sleep.

CHAPTER FIFTEEN

K adence slept fitfully, tossing and turning most of the night. She was worried something would happen to Mallory, that she wouldn't be there to stop it. She woke in a sweat and stumbled to the shower. When she'd dressed she pulled out her laptop, trying to find something more she could use to convince Mallory that the threat Sheva presented was real. She felt the threat in her soul, and she couldn't simply let it go.

She searched for all information she could about the sculptor. Where had she been in the two years since Carlyle? Could she track her movements? Find more missing women? Would that even help? Mallory was so certain she was harmless. She had to do it, though, had to know it wasn't her imagination. She hit enter and watched the page populate with links to Sheva.

She'd moved from CAA to a show in San Francisco the autumn after Kadence graduated. This was a show of her abstract sculptures. It ran for the requisite three months, and then she moved to a show in Chicago for the debut of her figures. She was well received, but the show closed early, after only a month. She searched for more, trying to find why that had happened. The only information she found was a note of a contract dispute between the gallery and the artist over the sale of one of the pieces.

So, she hadn't wanted to sell then, either. It was resolved by Sheva authorizing reproductions of her sculptures for the gallery to purchase to sell. That was an accepted practice, but usually reserved for patrons who were unable to afford the original piece. The entire show moved on to Miami, all originals included. In Miami, her show had run for an extended six months, rounding out the first year. Sheva had never authorized a sale of one of her original figures, only reproductions. Surprisingly, the refusal to sell made her show even more sought after, as galleries clamored to host her and be the first to make an original sale.

She left Miami for Mexico City, where she spent nine months at Galería Alegría. Again, all original pieces remained unsold. How had Mallory managed to get her to agree to sell? Would she balk in the final moments and leave the patrons with reproductions? It seemed likely.

After Mexico City, she was on hiatus until the show opened at ARA. Now Kadence had an idea of her travel pattern. It was easy enough to note when the show went from three to six figures, adding one in Chicago, one in Miami and one in Mexico City.

She made a note on all of this before she cleared her search bar and looked for missing women in San Francisco, Chicago, Miami, and Mexico City in the correct time frames. That was a mistake. The sheer number of women missing was overwhelming. She had to figure out a filter or two to narrow her search. First, she searched for college students missing, then more specifically, art students. This narrowed the results somewhat in San Francisco, but she would have to devote hours to reading accounts to see if they were applicable. It didn't help at all in the other cities. It was useless. There was no way she'd be able to sift through all these accounts and find anything to help before Friday. She needed to go at this a different way.

She paced, apprehension making her chew her lip. If she called the individual galleries involved, they might remember something helpful, but they'd think she was crazy. *Am I crazy?* How could she word her requests and keep from sounding like a lunatic? She needed to know which sculptures were in each show, to have an idea of where they were forged and when. She'd ask about Sheva's shows and see where that led.

She worked on a script to use making the calls. She'd play a student working on a research paper. If that went over on the first call, she'd try it again. If not, she'd become a blogger working on a piece about Sheva. Something untraceable, but believable.

She started with San Francisco. She found the number for the gallery online and called. As the line rang on the other end, her mouth became so dry she was afraid she wouldn't get a word out.

"Curren Gallery, how may I help you?"

"Hi, My name's Ashley Munroe. I'm writing a paper about art gallery shows. Is there anyone who could be interviewed? I'd really appreciate the help."

"Let me see if the director is available. Can you hold?"

"Sure."

"Okay." The line switched to classical music. The wait seemed long, but Kadence didn't give up.

Finally, the line clicked. "Hello? Are you still there?"

"Yes, I'm here."

"The director isn't available right now, but if you leave your name and number, he'll return your call."

She left her number and the name she'd used, then moved on to Chicago. This time she tried being a blogger. The director came on the line after only a minute or two.

"How can I help you, Ms. Munroe?"

"I'm writing a blog about a sculptor who showed at your gallery a year and a half ago."

"Wait. You mean Sheva, don't you?"

"Yes, I was hoping you could give me some insight into her, as a person? You know, what she was like, who she was friendly with, that sort of thing?"

"I have to apologize. If I'd known the subject of your blog, I'd have had my receptionist let you know, but I'm not legally allowed to comment on Sheva. That was part of our legal settlement with her."

Wow, not able to talk about her at all, as part of a legal agreement? *That must have been some conflict.*

"Okay, could you tell me if there were any people close to her that would be able to talk to me?"

"I don't know…"

"I promise, I won't reveal you as the source. I'm just trying to get a personal account of her. She's so mysterious. Her show is closing this week in New York and moving to Geneva. I'd like to get something out before Friday."

"Well, I guess giving you a name doesn't technically break the agreement. There was one woman, she was a patron and captivated by Sheva. Her name is Alyssa Shern."

"Do you have contact information for her?"

"Not anything current. She hasn't come to the gallery since the incident with Sheva. But I have her old information. I don't know how much help it will be. We've sent invitations and announcements and they've all come back as no longer at the address."

"What incident? I'm a little lost, sorry."

"Oh, I assumed you were writing about Sheva's show because of what happened. The gallery had firm sales on three of her pieces, but she refused to sell them. She's known for that."

"I knew she didn't like to part with her work, but nothing specific."

"It all started here. Look it up, you'll get more information than you want, I promise."

"Great, thanks. I'll do that."

Kadence waited while he found the information, then wrote it down in her notebook. At least she'd have a place to start. She ran a search on the name, but nothing came up beyond articles linked back to the gallery. She tried the address and found a link to property records. They listed Alyssa Shern as a previous owner, but the property had been sold over a year ago.

Where are you, Alyssa? Finally, she pulled up her Facebook and searched her name there. This gave her six names, but two were Alyssa Shernihans. She clicked on the others, one at a time. The third one showed a smiling young woman with long red hair, and in her background picture was a photo of *Love's Birth. This must be her.*

Naturally, her page was private, but she could see two posts, dated January of a year ago. It was a post to Alyssa's page from a friend. The words chilled Kadence to the bone.

Alyssa, where are you?

There were over two hundred comments on the post, all asking the same question and making suggestions as to where Alyssa might have gone, but no one knew for certain. Dread settled in Kadence's heart. Had she disappeared? She closed Facebook and ran a search for missing person, Chicago, Alyssa Shern.

The articles filled her browser page, all from April of this year. The headlines were made to grab the reader's attention.

Heartbroken art patron feared dead after car found in suburban forest preserve. Alyssa Shern, 29, missing since January 28, is now feared dead after her car was recovered from the bottom of a ravine in Barrington Hills. Police suspect she was injured in the crash and wandered into the densely-forested area. Searchers have been active since Thursday, using scent hounds and horses to cover more terrain, but have yet to turn up any sign of the woman.

The article went on to describe Alyssa as the only child of a wealthy businessman who collected art for his company. Had Sheva done something to her? This was the fourth person associated with her who disappeared. Again, there was nothing definite, but it was becoming more implausible that Sheva was innocent. She printed the photograph of Alyssa, and pinned it with that of Trini, Jackie, and Carlyle, to her wall. Four faces gone, but three of them were immortalized in bronze. Maybe Alyssa was as well.

Four. That left two women. Where had Sheva found them? Was one from San Francisco? Miami? Mexico City? Who were the other two women?

She called the gallery in Miami, but it was after hours and she only got a recording. She looked at the time. She'd spent a whole day looking for Alyssa. She hadn't had a bite to eat, either. She grabbed her jacket and ran up the street to the little Thai place. It was takeout only, which suited her. When her tom kha gai was ready, she paid and went back to the apartment. Mallory had to believe her now; she couldn't deny the evidence that was piling up. Sheva had a problem with disappearing women. Women she made into statues. She had to convince her, for her own safety.

❖

The breakout process was one of Sheva's favorite parts of lost wax casting. Using a hammer, she carefully tapped the ceramic mold and watched the cracks form. She gently flipped them away from her bronze. Every piece of ceramic had to be painstakingly removed, using a chisel when necessary. Slowly, *Pride* emerged, still in pieces, but fully realized in the bronze that would hold her eternally. She lovingly ran her hands along the lines of the torso, neck, the lift of her chin, her lips in that perfect grimace. The carved flames that emerged from the top of the figure, where the rest of her face would have been. She would smooth these some but leave the impression of roughness.

She looked at the work of her assistants on the lower extremities, where matching flames climbed the length of her legs, obscuring their form until mid-thigh. One hand extended toward the viewer.

Perfect. She was going to be perfect. She grabbed her angle grinder and began removing the sprues, loving the fierce shriek of the bronze, *Pride's* final scream. The chasing of the metal would take considerable time, and that was for her alone. The bulk of the work complete, she dismissed her assistants. She used her grinder to bring the bronze to life, starting with a coarse Roloc pad and moving to very fine as the process advanced. Her pencil grinder helped in the tighter places. The singing of the bronze was music that filled her with the same power the act of wax casting had, in the final moments before the dancer had been captured. *What was her name?* Remembering the women by their given names had been so important to her when this all began; how could she not know the dancer's name? It must be the evolution of her work, the move from light to dark, that made it so easy to forget.

She wondered if she'd forget Mallory's name. Her pursuit of her had been more like the early work, the virtues. She'd thought of Mallory as a virtue until the inspiration of the dancer. The dancer had been the catalyst for the new series, the way she had been set there for Sheva to collect. She'd realized Mallory was too coldhearted to be a virtue. Mallory had shifted then, from Virtue to Vice. She'd be surprised if she remembered her name by the time she finished her sculpture. *Pride* had no name, *Angst*, the painter, would have no name, and *Malice* should be unnamed as well, though she thought she'd probably always remember Mallory's name.

She went on with her work, content that she had found her way. She was excited to move on to *Malice* as soon as possible.

CHAPTER SIXTEEN

Mallory's heart was heavy as she walked into the gallery. It was going to be a busy day, but she couldn't shake the sadness that swamped her after Kadence's stalker-like behavior last night. She'd had such hopes for their relationship, whatever form it might have taken. The possibility that it could be real and lasting had been exciting. Now that was impossible. Her obsession with Sheva had gone over the edge of weird into scary when she followed her home. To top it off, she had to spend today meeting with Sheva about the end of her show. She had to get her signature on the paperwork for the sale and find out who was moving her work and when.

Tarin was already working in the office. He had drawn up the release for lithographs and was on the phone with Kadence arranging a meeting time. She waved a hand to get his attention, and when he looked up, she mouthed, "Not here." He nodded and continued his conversation.

She dropped her bag in her chair, then went to the kitchen to pour some coffee. She sat at the table and called Sheva, but only got her voice mail.

"Hey, it's Mallory. I need you to come by today and sign the papers on the sale. I can cut you a check once that's complete. I've got movers coming to take the two statues to the buyers on Friday morning. What about the remaining figures? Call me."

Hopefully, she'd call back before long. It would throw a kink in her schedule if she didn't get this taken care of early. Mallory's fear was that Sheva would back out of the sale in the last moment. She'd never sold an original, only the strength of her pieces kept her in the gallery circuit. If this went through, the gallery would be lauded in all the industry magazines and blogs. It wouldn't hurt Mallory's reputation, either. She wanted everything in place so she wouldn't be here late. She would be on site for the removal of the sculptures, which should happen between five and seven tomorrow morning, so they could begin making the international move. She sipped her coffee, then called Christina Lorde to check on that end of the delivery. She was going out there this afternoon to look at their proposed site. The movers would build a foundation pad, but it was her job to be sure every nuance was considered in placement. She planned to meet Chas at four at the property.

Tarin came in to tell her he was leaving to meet Kadence, so she moved into her office to make the rest of her calls. She called the Pelegrini Brothers Movers and double-checked their arrival time of five a.m.

The main room of the gallery would be taken over by a Japanese wood sculptor. Her pieces were large and dynamic, but not as challenging to move. They would start the move on Saturday morning. Her morning tasks complete, Mallory could stop and breathe. She wandered out to the loft and walked through Kadence's exhibit. Her work was full of emotion, so powerful. She walked through the spiral of *Colder than Blue,* her own heart a related shade of blue. She touched her lips, remembering the kiss they'd shared, the velvet softness of Kadence's mouth. How she'd moved to take it from a simple kiss to one of fire and passion. *Too bad that flame had to be put out.*

Her chest constricted, and her eyes felt wet. *Don't cry over this. It was a kiss, nothing more.* Kadence was broken in a way Mallory couldn't understand. Was it the abuse she'd suffered as a child? The beatings she'd taken that threw her off kilter, that made her emotions volatile? She got that it had been hard to lose her first love, but taking it to this extreme wasn't healthy. Better to find that out before getting involved. If only it hadn't felt so good being with her.

She sucked in a deep breath and walked downstairs to the main room. She didn't see pain in these figures, but rather, adoration. Sheva worshipped women's forms and she re-created them flawlessly. The emotion in these figures wasn't sinister or fear inspiring. It was passionate and deeply moving. *This isn't the work of someone evil.* Yes, Sheva was narcissistic and over-the-top, and not good with boundaries, but she wasn't crazy.

Thinking of Sheva, she looked at her watch. *Why hasn't she called yet?* It was almost noon, and she needed to leave for Greenwich by two thirty. She called again but was only able to leave another voice mail. This was going to complicate things tomorrow. If she didn't have Sheva's signature on the final bill of sale, she wasn't sure she could ethically take the statues to Connecticut. And who was coming to move the other four figures?

Worse come to worst, she had the address of Sheva's studio. She could try tracking her down, but it would have to wait until she returned from the Lorde/Drummer house. *She'd better not screw up this sale.* It would be like her to drop the ball on the sale at the last minute. But she'd been so cooperative the other day.

Tarin arrived with the signed releases from Kadence. He looked worn out. Hopefully, she hadn't given him trouble. Her show was nearly sold out, and the lithographs would be big sellers.

"Hey there, how'd it go?" she said.

"Oh, not too bad. She was just so down. I've never seen that side of her. Kadence is usually so upbeat. Any idea what's going on with her?"

"She's upset. I talked with her yesterday. She has some past connection with Sheva and it kind of made her lose control. She *really* doesn't like her. Some of the things she said were unsettling. I have to keep the ban in place until Sheva's gone."

"I know. That was a frightening scene. Still, she was so sad. Too bad we can't bring her here to cheer her up."

"Yeah, that would be nice, but no. She's got to stay away for now. Maybe next week we can invite her back."

"I hope so. What's next on our agenda?"

Mallory felt a twinge of guilt not telling Tarin everything, but there wasn't any proof and the accusations were extreme. She needed to understand what was going through Kadence's mind before she said anything more about it. And once Sheva was gone, it could be that Kadence went back to…well, maybe not normal, but her usual sweet self.

"We need Sheva to let us know about moving her work. Have you heard from her?"

"Not a word. Want me to call her?"

"I've done that, twice. I left a voice mail. We need that information before the end of the day, and I'm scheduled to go to Connecticut this afternoon. Would you go out to her studio and get her signature on the final bill of sale and find out her plan for the morning?"

"I can do that. You have the address?"

"Yes. I'll get that and the paperwork for you. Make sure you let me know when you've got everything handled."

"Okay. I'll go now."

Mallory went to the office and gathered the papers and Sheva's address. She was grateful not to have to take that trip herself. Things were too strange between her and Sheva, and in truth, she wasn't comfortable around her. *Just not to the extent Kadence is.* She handed everything to Tarin and saw him to the door.

She hoped everything went well with Sheva. She didn't need any more complications. She took the lithograph release papers to the office and dropped into her chair.

I'll never get to see that dragon, now. She missed Kadence's easygoing attitude, her smile that lit her eyes, and she felt the weight of her loss. How had that happened? How did she come to mean so much to her? *I hardly know her.* All she knew was that the absence of Kadence was painful. She wanted more than anything to undo the last two days and bring them back to where they were. Her stomach tightened and her mouth thinned as the tears started. Giving in, she laid her head on her arms and cried over what could have been.

Her phone rang, making her sit up and get a grip. She cleaned her face and blew her nose before grabbing the phone and answering.

"Mallory Tucker, ARA Gallery. How may I help you?"

"Mal, it's Tarin. I'm at the studio, but there's no one here. The place looks empty."

"You're kidding. Come back here, then. I've got to leave soon. We'll figure out what to do about Sheva later."

"Right. I'll be back shortly."

Damn her. What was Sheva's game? Hopefully, she'd hear from her before too long. She grabbed her bag and called for a car to drive her to Connecticut. Chas Drummer would be expecting her. She made a note for Tarin on things he could try to locate Sheva, then left.

The Drummer and Chase estate was lovely. The wide hedge-lined driveway opened to a large Cape Cod style home. She had the driver stop three-quarters of the way up the drive. She wanted to walk to the door and take in the green space out front.

When she reached the door, Chas was waiting.

"I see you found us. I hope it wasn't too much trouble."

"Oh, not at all. The house is lovely, and the front lawn, seriously impressive."

"Wait until you see the back. We want to put the girls on either side of the pool. Come on."

She led the way around the house. They walked through an arbor gate into a large gazebo that looked out on the pool and the terraced lawn. The pool was stepped, with a water-wall feature at the south end. On either side were what had been flower beds, but clearly had recently been cleaned out. Clean white sand filled them. This was where the statues would find their home.

"This is perfect. You have up-lighting in place, and the sand beds look great."

"Yes, I spoke with the mover you use and he recommended this as substrata. He'll move in a granite base for each and get them firmly set."

"Fantastic. I think you've done well in your selection of location. Did Pelegrini mention access to the yard? It seems a little tricky." She eyed the sloping lawn and the high fence.

"Oh, yes, I've made arrangements with my neighbor. We are going to take down a section of the fence and move in the statues."

"Good. So, let's talk about which statue, where. And how the gallery can help you."

"I was thinking *Torrid Heat* on this side." She indicated the west side bed. "And *Love's Birth* here."

Mallory closed her eyes and imagined the statues in those locations. *Torrid Heat* was a front facing piece, but *Love's Birth* held her arms out to one side. She imagined the impact of the statues as Chas wanted them placed.

"I think you'll be happier with them on the opposite sides. You remember *Love's Birth* is holding her arms to the left side. If she's on the east, she'll be focusing the viewer to the left, away from *Torrid Heat* and your home."

Chas looked puzzled. "Hm, I didn't remember that. So, switch them?"

"I think you'll like that better. Here, look." She brought out her tablet and pulled up photographs of the work. The leaning to the left was clear in the image.

"Wow, you're right. I'm glad you remembered that. Do you think the scope of the area is enough for their size? I don't want them to look jammed together."

"I think they'll be perfect here. When you have the water-wall going and everything lit, they'll be stellar."

Chas smiled at the compliment. The pool features were shut down for the coming winter season. Mallory had been able to predict what the yard must feel like when it was open and flowing. The statues would be a centerpiece of the entertainment area.

"You'll invite me up to see them when you've got the pool running, won't you?"

"Of course, you know we will. I'm so excited to show them off. We're having a party the first weekend in December, maybe you'll come up for that?"

"I'd love to."

"Well, be sure and bring a guest. I'll send you a formal invitation."

"Thank you."

"Thank you, Mallory. You've influenced Christina and me so much. Our collection is the talk of our friends and we credit you for that."

"You're too kind."

"I'm serious. You've got a gift for sensing what appeals to people. Believe me when I say, I never thought I'd be an art collector. You've done that."

Mallory took the compliment to heart. It made her feel validated in a way nothing else could. Her father's dismissive attitude toward anything she'd done made moments like this even more meaningful.

"Thank you. I look forward to adding to your collection over the next many years."

"As do we. Can I offer you a bite to eat before you head back into the city?"

Mallory considered the invitation. She needed to finish the details of this sale, so getting back to town was a priority.

"I appreciate the offer, but I've got things to finish up at the gallery. I'll see you tomorrow."

"Okay, thanks again."

They said good-bye and Mallory went back to the car. The driver was in no hurry to get stuck in traffic, so he found some creative ways to negotiate the trip back. She made it back to the gallery just at six. Tarin would be getting ready to lock up.

She went in and noticed a few people were still in the textile room. Tarin was upstairs with others in the loft. Not wanting to disturb either group, she went into her office. The release for lithographs was on her desk, but no final bill of sale from Sheva. *Darn.* She tried calling her again, but had no luck. Where in the world was she?

She slammed the phone down, taking her frustration out on it. Tarin walked in, and gave her a smirk.

"What are you smiling about?"

"Oh, nothing, I just sold another Munroe original, that's all."

"Really? That's great. How many originals are unsold now?"

"Of the sixteen pieces, five remain unsold. Our new assistant, Grace, sold three lithographs today as well."

"How could she sell lithographs when we haven't produced them yet?"

"She sold them on word. The buyers will pick them up as soon as they're ready. They're hoping Kadence will sign them."

"I can't see why not. That's great news, but what about Sheva? Any luck tracking her down?"

"Not really. I did run into a fellow who works for her at her foundry. He said they finished the metal casting of a new sculpture yesterday. She's probably busy chasing it. I thought I'd go over to the foundry on my way home."

"That's a good idea. Okay, tomorrow at five, Pelegrini will be here to pick up *Torrid Heat* and *Love's Birth*. I don't have a clue what we're going to do with the others. I suppose we could send them to the warehouse."

"Ugh. That just makes things more difficult when we have to move them again."

"I know, but she's given us no direction, so what choice do we have? I know her next show is in Geneva, but the shipping arrangements were made between Sheva and the gallery there. I'm not even sure which gallery she's in." She sighed, tired of this game Sheva was playing. "I'm not going to delay the move because she chose to vanish. Akiro Ueda has the floor starting Sunday. We're going to press forward."

"But what about the final bill of sale? Technically, shipping those statues to Connecticut is stealing if we lack her signature."

"She agreed to the sale and the price in front of a board member. We'll move forward with the sale according to that verbal contract as well as her written one. If she has a problem with that, she can take it up with our legal team."

Tarin looked worried, his lips pressed tightly into a line. "I get that, but what I'm saying is that she's putting you in the position of defense if she challenges the sale. You need to look out for yourself, Mallory. Get her to sign the papers."

She felt her anger rise. "You know I've been trying to get that accomplished all day."

"I do, and the fact that she's been missing in action tells me you need to watch your back. I'm worried."

She felt herself deflate at his words. He really cared about her and was looking out for her. "I know, thanks, Tarin. I guess I'll have to see what happens between now and tomorrow morning. Hopefully, her work on the new sculpture has distracted her from her responsibilities, and she's not just playing some kind of weird game."

"Let me go by the foundry now."

She hesitated. He'd already done so much to help seal this deal, but having him take this on would be a relief. She nodded, and he smiled.

"Great. I'll head over there now. See you in the morning?"

"I'll be here at four thirty."

He winced. "Is it okay if I come at five?"

"Sure." She smiled, knowing how much he hated the early morning setups.

After Tarin left she finished up the end of day tasks and locked the gallery. She was craving Ink's chocolate cinnamon coffee, but the thought of running into Kadence worried her. She wasn't ready to see her, yet. She settled for a mocha latte from the shop by her apartment on the way home.

Sheva watched as Mallory locked the gallery doors and left. Her perfect Mallory was in exactly the right place. She knew it must be driving her crazy that Sheva wasn't available. Her precious bill of sale and all. There was no way she was selling her beauties. Especially not now that she had a whole new series of work to build on them. No way. Her girls were all going with her to Geneva. And tomorrow morning would bring the perfect time to capture Mallory. She'd be exasperated and upset, easy to manipulate. Sheva would be in and out of the gallery with no one the wiser, and Mallory would be hers.

She savored the fear she would see in those clear brown eyes as she covered her immobilized body with alginate. In that moment, Sheva's true power would come alive again. Only by her hand could the soul of the corporeal body leave its home and be captured for eternity, the model's expression captured forever by the viscous alginate before the model's soul left the body, only to be contained in the wax mold. Sheva alone had that power. It was her gift. Anyone looking at one of her beauties could see the life essence radiating out from their bronze forms.

The panic would make Mallory's face a mask of horror and anger, but that would be for Sheva alone. No face would be on the sculpture. Her emotional essence would be transferred into the mold and her soul captured for the world to see. Her soul, once such a pure joy, was filled with malice toward Sheva, and that would show in the work, she would make sure of it. She followed her, being careful to stay hidden. She wanted to know where Mallory would spend this last night. What she would do with her final hours. *She has no clue what's ahead.*

When she realized Mallory was going home, she found a quiet table at the coffee shop Mallory had left moments before. She could stay there for the next several hours. She slid a hand into her jacket pocket and felt the leather case inside, its smooth surface hiding the first tool of her work. *Soon, Mallory.*

She sipped her coffee and watched the apartment windows. So much to capture in her, so much she had to share with the world. Sheva would make her a lasting testament to the modern woman. She epitomized the working woman, successful, driven, soft, and beautiful with a spine of steel. She would be *Malice*, to go with *Pride*, because the love of the modern woman came with a price. Their hearts were made of steel as well, and Sheva had brought that steel nature to Mallory's surface. It was a gift.

Her phone buzzed annoyingly in her pocket. She should turn the stupid thing off, but she knew it would be Mallory, searching for her. The panic must be setting in now. The realization that she wouldn't have Sheva's signature on the bill of sale would throw her off-balance, make her irritation rise and her malice that much stronger. What could she do? Sheva would let her stew in that sea of tension, let it drag her under, swirl her around and spit her out, shaken and lost. That would be the finishing touch she would need. She laughed out loud, startling the nearby diners. So what? They couldn't know how delicious this night was for her, and the ending she had planned would be well worth their baleful glances.

She watched from her table until the shop closed at one. Looking up at Mallory's apartment, she decided nothing more was going to happen tonight. She could safely go to the gallery at four and finish things. She left and headed to her studio for a few hours' sleep.

CHAPTER SEVENTEEN

K adence felt like she'd been run over by a truck. The fact that Mallory was blind to the connection between Sheva and the disappearances was hard to take. She knew it was all conjecture, that she had no proof, but the parallels were there. Two facts were unshakeable: these women had a connection to Sheva, and all these women had disappeared. The jump was easy for her, because she'd never trusted Sheva, but for Mallory, that wasn't true. She had a connection to Sheva, an intimate one, so she had a level of trust Kadence didn't.

What will convince her? Her own disappearance? Did she take anything I said to heart? Probably not. She probably wrote it off to my mental instability. If she'd only kept her cool when she met Sheva, all of this could've been avoided. She could have given Mallory the information in a way that didn't implode their relationship. Something like, *Hey, isn't it weird that all these women disappeared? You know they all knew Sheva. She's the one thing they all had in common.* That would've been more effective than her raging at Sheva and then dumping the whole idea on her like it was proof positive.

Now, Mallory had not only shut her out, she was in even more danger, at least until Sheva left the country for her next show. But Kadence had made it less likely that she would guard against anything happening to her, if only because Mallory would willfully refuse to entertain the idea. *I must make sure she's safe. I don't care if it makes me look even crazier. I can't let anything happen to her. I'd never forgive myself, and it would be my fault.* She couldn't save her grandma. When her mother had accidently knocked her down the stairs when she was in a rage, Kadence had been too small to stop her. By the time she'd gotten past her mom and made it to her side, her grandma's battered body was too shattered to help. She'd held her in her thirteen-year-old arms as she died. She couldn't let that happen to Mallory.

She threw the book she'd been telling herself to read across her apartment. She had to do something. *The best way to keep her safe is to watch over her, but I've got to do it without her knowing about it.* She pulled on her jacket and left the apartment, ignoring the definite stalker issue involved. It was eleven thirty at night, so rather than take the train she caught a ride share to Chelsea. Everything was quiet on the street outside Mallory's place. She found a sheltered spot out of the pool of light from the streetlamp. She wouldn't fail her. She watched the window she knew was Mallory's. It had a light on when she arrived, but it had gone out around midnight. There was a coffee bar near her that was still open, and the occasional passerby would stop in. She heard the mellow music coming out the open door.

Around one, the shop closed for the night, with the last of the patrons wandering out into the street. As she watched them, one stood out. She couldn't be sure, but she thought it might be Sheva. Was she watching Mallory too? She watched the woman carefully, and when she stepped into the light beneath the streetlamp, Kadence's stomach turned. Sheva had been in the coffee shop right across from Mallory's place. *Shit. I knew it, she's dangerous. Mallory, why wouldn't you believe me?*

Torn between following Sheva and guarding over Mallory, Kadence didn't know what to do. If she followed and then lost Sheva, would she have time to get back here before her? No, the best thing was to stay put and make sure no harm came to Mallory. But then again, what if Sheva knew another way into the building? What good would it do to sit out here and watch a window if she was inside doing who knew what to Mallory?

Resigned, she got up and began following Sheva, careful not to be seen. She went as far as following her to the train station, then was torn. If she followed her to her home, maybe she could get something concrete that would prove she wasn't crazy, but she'd risk leaving

Mallory unguarded. Uncertainty filled her, keeping her motionless. The train was boarding, so she had to choose. At the last second, she boarded and did her best to keep Sheva in view. The train was the same one she would take to her place, so she relaxed a bit. If she was spotted, she could honestly say she was going home. When they reached Brooklyn, she moved a car closer, not wanting to miss Sheva's exit. Sheva got off at the Grand Street station, one exit before her own. They lived this close to each other? The thought made her feel ill. She followed her to the bus stop. Sheva boarded the 59 bus up Grand. Kadence fell in with a group of hipsters, lingering at the edge of their group. She couldn't get on that bus. There was no way Sheva wouldn't notice her. She flagged a cab and slid in, asking him to follow the bus, saying a woman had left the train without her wallet and would need it. She held up her own as proof.

The driver looked at her in the mirror, gave a skeptical nod, then followed the bus. Sheva left the bus at Grand and Varick, the heart of the warehouse district. Kadence had her driver pull over and paid her fare. She slid out and tried to figure out a way to follow her in this open, deserted area. Fear and adrenaline pumped through her. She jumped into the bus stop's Plexiglas booth and peered over the advertisements plastered to its side. She watched Sheva walk three or four blocks then turn right. She bolted from her hiding place, hurrying along the route to reach the corner before Sheva vanished. At the corner, she stopped and peeked around the building edge. Sheva was unlocking a door about two blocks down. Once she entered, Kadence moved down the block after her.

As she neared Sheva's building, she slowed, pressing herself to the wall to avoid discovery. The building was a nondescript warehouse from the outside, but when she pressed her eye to a crack in the metal siding, she could see it was a studio space. The vaulted ceiling was strung with lights, making the interior bright. There was a large kiln to one side and a huge table covered with a draping cloth. *Probably where she builds her maquettes.* There was a door on the far side that hung open, showing a living space. *So, she lives in her studio.* Kadence watched as Sheva undraped the maquette table. It looked like there were eight or nine figures on the table. She only had six original sculptures on display. *These others must be current or future works.* Sheva walked along the table, her hands stroking the maquettes. When she reached the end, she went back again, repeating her touching of the small models. This time, Kadence could see her face. Her expression was compelling and frightening at the same time. Each stroke made her lips curl farther back, and Kadence could see she was getting some kind of weird high from the ritual. She felt her skin crawl at the strangeness of the scene. Whatever motivated this bizarre behavior in Sheva, it made Kadence distinctly uncomfortable.

After a third pass down the table, Sheva covered the maquettes and slipped into the living space. Was it possible for Kadence to get inside without drawing Sheva to her? She wasn't sure, she really *wanted* to get in there, but she'd come too far to turn back. She had to know. When the light under the door went out, she set her watch and waited. After an hour, she crept to the large door Sheva had entered. It was locked, of course, but Kadence had some experience with warehouse locks. The shows she'd been in were all in warehouses like this. She'd had to jimmy locks open on many occasions when the warehouse owner had failed to show up at opening time. She hadn't been about to let a hungover gallery owner mess up her little show. If Sheva's door hadn't been upgraded, she'd be able to open it with a thin card. She pulled her credit card out of her pocket and slid it between the mortise and the door frame. She found the latch mechanism and deftly slid it between the mechanism and the door, popping it open. She cracked the door a bit, listening for any sound in the still room. She could hear the faint sounds of snoring from the sleeping area.

Treading as lightly as possible, she approached the draped table. She lifted the cloth from one end and peered at the first maquette. Her breath caught and bile rose in her throat. *Carlyle.* Her beautiful face was a mask of calm, but her eyes were wide with fear. This tiny image of her one-time lover, so perfectly her, brought back a flood of memories. Naked, hands wrapping around her sides, caressing her breasts. The passion of the pose should show in her face, but there was pure terror instead. She looked at the other maquettes, and all of them showed the face of the figure, all of them reflected terror in their eyes, though their expressions were strangely blank. The last three were the most chilling. Gone was the pretense of passion found in the poses, replaced instead by poses of pain and torture. The first, a woman wrapped in flames, was clearly beseeching the viewer for help. She wasn't familiar.

Bile rose in her throat when she looked at the next one. It was her own image, her body bent, on her knees, pleading. The face was blank, empty of expression as though Sheva waited to fill that in until...until what? Kadence's reaction was visceral, and she jerked back and dropped the cloth as if stung. *Shit, I've become one of her weird obsessions.* She needed to get out of this room. First, she had to look at the last figure. She picked up the cloth again and looked beneath it. It was Mallory, reclined, but not in any way peaceful. Her body was arched in pain, the face, emotionless. *She's going to hurt her. I know she is.* She grabbed the maquette and moved as quietly as she could to the door. She would show this to Mallory. Hopefully, it would be enough to convince her. She eased out the door, and heard the latch click behind her. She hurried down the street toward the bus station. No chance for a cab out here.

She tucked the figure into her hoodie pouch as she boarded the bus. She wanted to get back to Mallory's as soon as possible. She wouldn't disturb her at home, but when she left for the gallery, she'd meet her outside. She left the bus for the train station and headed back to Chelsea. It was later than she liked being on the train, but her adrenaline helped keep her alert. It was after three when she made it back to Mallory's building. She was surprised to see lights in her apartment window. Why was she awake at this hour?

She sat on a bench across from the building, fingering the creepy maquette. She should call her, warn her, but she knew Mallory wouldn't take her call. Not now.

Something was off. Sheva had a strange feeling as she walked into the studio from her room. *What's bothering me?* She walked to the door and checked it. Locked, so the sense that someone had been there had to be false. No one could get in with the door locked. She'd chosen this warehouse specifically because it had no windows. *Why am I so jumpy?* She moved back into her room and went to wash her face. Maybe it was lack of sleep making her uncomfortable. Her studio was empty. She pushed the disquiet down and prepared for Mallory's arrival. Her pulse raced and waves of arousal flooded her. She would capture her in that perfect moment, make her a lasting monument to the experience they would share.

She checked her leather case and everything was there, so all she needed now was to isolate Mallory. If things worked as she'd planned, Mallory would be furious with her and anxious about today. She would be at the gallery well before she was needed, trying to find her. Sheva was counting on it.

She went through a door to the back of her building, to an older black van parked in the bay. She climbed in and hit the remote to open the warehouse bay door. No train today, she needed the vehicle. She backed out and headed for Manhattan.

She made good time, using the midtown tunnel, and was parked in the alley behind the gallery by two forty. Mallory would probably get here around three thirty to begin preparations for the removal of her show and the start of the next one. She slid out of the van and checked the buildings nearby for any sign of activity. All was quiet. By the time the movers arrived to take her sculptures to storage, everything would be complete.

Mallory's anger simmered as she dressed for her early morning. She slammed the closet door, and yanked on her pants. *Damn her.* If she saw Sheva right now she'd shake her. How could she be so irresponsible? Her hands ached with unreleased tension as she struggled to button her jacket. Of all the mean-spirited, awful things a person could do, to leave this sale hanging really sucked. Not even the courtesy to call back? *What the hell?* She stalked across the room to grab her shoes and stubbed her foot on the bed frame. She fell back on the bed and grabbed her foot.

"Shit. God dammit. That hurt." Her vision blurred as tears obscured her room. *Don't cry. You just did your makeup, God dammit.* But she couldn't pull the tears back in once the dam had broken, and she let rage flow out of her through her tears. Stupid Sheva and her asinine attitude. *You just wait, you can't undo me so easily. I'm better*

than that. Pull yourself together and get this fucking day over with.
All the unreleased rage from her father's rejection and never being
good enough for her mother welled up and mingled with the rage
at Sheva, only to be made worse by the complicated situation with
Kadence. She let it all out in her tears. After a few minutes, she took a
deep breath and made herself stop crying. Hobbling on her wounded
foot, she went to the mirror to assess the damage.

Crap. I look like shit. She grabbed a wipe and cleaned her face
of the blotchy makeup. Deliberately, she reapplied her morning face,
slid her feet into her shoes and left the apartment. The stubbed toe
throbbed, but nothing would stop her from snatching success from the
jaws of defeat today. Nothing. She'd send those wretched sculptures
to the gallery storage unit and pass the cost on to Sheva. It wasn't her
fault that Sheva refused to contact them.

The two pieces she'd sold would be sent to Connecticut as
planned. Sheva would have to take legal action if she wanted
to interfere. Mallory was acting in good faith, and Millie was her
witness. That mind-warped, selfish asshole would have to suck it up.
She locked the apartment and headed down to meet her car.

She had the driver stop for coffee at the 24-hour chain store on
the corner. She sipped her espresso and tried to calm down. When
they reached the gallery, it was half past three. Way too early to be
working, but she couldn't sleep anyway. She entered the building and
went to the office, holding on to a slim hope that Sheva might have
called and left her a voice mail. No such luck. The only voice mail
was a confirmation call from Pelegrini that the truck would arrive at
five a.m. While she finished her coffee, she emailed the board about
the situation. It would be better to have them informed now, rather
than at the start of legal proceedings.

Her anger was down to a simmer and she could focus on what
she needed to do. She walked downstairs to the main exhibit room.
The back wall acted as a hidden door to the loading bay to make large
work transfer easier. She opened the control box and hit the button to
lift the internal wall. The grinding of the motor was the only sound in
the still gallery.

When the door was fully open she walked into the bay and
turned on the lights. Everything gleamed in the bright fluorescents.

She walked to the back door and punched in the sequence to unlock the outer doors. Pelegrini would only have to drive up to the bay and trip the sensor to open them. She'd done this so many times that it was mechanical, and she was on autopilot, not really focusing.

She went back to her office to finish her coffee. She was going over the contract for Ueda when she heard the rumble of the bay doors opening. Was Pelegrini here already? *That's odd.* It was only four thirty, and they weren't known for being early. She walked downstairs, expecting to see Sal or Michael Pelegrini coming in from the bay, but she saw no one. She walked into the bay. Instead of the Pelegrini truck, there was an older model plain black panel van in the bay. What? She looked at the windshield, but couldn't tell if anyone was inside. The bay door had been closed behind the vehicle. *What the hell?*

She started to approach the van when she heard a noise behind her. She whirled around and found Sheva standing in the doorway.

"Mallory, I was looking for you."

Mallory's skin prickled as a chill washed through her. This wasn't right. Why had she driven a van in? Her sculptures would require a professional moving crew. And her eyes looked odd, the pupils too wide for the lighting. She stepped back, wanting distance between them.

"Stop, don't back away. I know you've been trying to reach me. Here I am."

"What is this about? Why don't you have a moving crew?"

"Oh, I do. They'll be here at eight. I figured that would be early enough to accommodate your new artist."

Mallory wanted to feel relieved, but there was something off. Her stomach was a tangle of nerves. She took another step back. "I've got a mover coming. You'll have to make arrangements to pick things up elsewhere." She hoped it would be enough to get Sheva to go away. Instead, she moved closer.

"Really, don't back away. I'm not going to hurt you. I'm going to honor you. You're going to be one of the most beautiful souls in my collection. Just stay where you are."

That was enough. Mallory turned and ran toward the bay doors, wanting to be as far from Sheva as she could get. She could hear her running after her. She reached the doors, but they were closed and the access panel was back at the main door. She slipped around the van, hoping to keep its bulk between them, but Sheva had predicted her path and stepped out from the front of the van.

"Get away from me," she screamed, backtracking. She darted around the other end of the van, blocking their sight of each other.

"You're only making this harder on yourself. I'm not going to hurt you, I promise. You won't feel a thing."

Mallory reached the far side on the van and dropped to the ground, shimmying under the vehicle. She could see Sheva's booted feet moving slowly around the other side.

Shit. She's going to figure out where I am any second. She tried to breathe as quietly as possible, wracking her brain for some escape.

"Come out, come out, wherever you are," Sheva said, moving to the far side. When she reached the back of the van, Mallory scooted as far forward as possible.

She could see the open doors into the gallery only feet from her position. If she could distract Sheva, she might be able to make a run for it. If she reached her office, she could lock herself in and press the panic button under her desk.

She looked for Sheva's feet, but saw nothing. *Where was she? Don't move. She's listening.* Sheva was invisible now, and absolutely quiet. Saliva filled Mallory's mouth, making her feel sick. *Where are you?* She was tempted to make a break and take her chances, but knew that was what Sheva was waiting for. *Why didn't I listen to Kadence? She was right.*

She looked at the rest of the bay. It was basically empty, a clean space for transporting large artwork. The only thing other than the van was a set of car ramps and a stack of moving blankets. Nothing that would help her. She heard something behind her. The tiniest scuffing sound and realized Sheva was on the ground and knew where she was. She glanced back and saw her, her grin malevolent, just as she stretched a hand out to grab Mallory's ankle.

Mallory pulled her leg up and smashed her foot backward, into her face. She scrambled out and raced for the gallery. She made it through the bay doors and raced up the stairs to her office. Just as she was closing the door behind her, she felt the impact of Sheva's body against it. She desperately pushed at the door, her hand on the deadbolt, trying to engage it, but Sheva was too strong. She pushed through the door, causing Mallory to fall back against her desk. The blow to her head sent white flashes in front of her eyes. *Get up, get up and run.* She tried, but her spinning head made her fall again and a sick feeling overwhelmed her.

Sheva fell on top of her, pinning her to the rough carpet. She put her face against Mallory's, whispering in her ear.

"You can't get away, little deer. You are meant to be mine. I told you not to back away from me. Now you've gone and cut your head. That's not my fault. I didn't want you hurt. Now be still."

The flare of heat and pain from her head was unbearable, but the weight of Sheva against her was much worse. She struggled to dislodge her, hitting her with her fists, but Sheva laughed and pinned her arms.

"You silly thing. You can't get away, I already told you that. If you'd calm down, things would be so much easier for you."

She pulled Mallory's arms against her sides and held them there with her strong thighs. She levered herself up and stared down at Mallory.

"You see? You're making this so hard. I've got the perfect thing for you, right in my pocket. In a few minutes, it will all be over." She reached into her jacket and pulled out a small leather case.

Mallory's heart was hammering in her chest. Whatever was in that case was nothing she wanted. She bucked her hips and squirmed, trying to get free, but Sheva's legs tightened. Her arms felt like they were breaking under the intense pressure.

"Stop it. Why are you doing this? Let me go, Sheva." Mallory screamed the words out, trying to make her stop. Sheva acted as if she'd said nothing.

She opened the case and withdrew a syringe full of amber liquid. She smiled down at Mallory, then forced her head to the side, immobilizing her from her waist up.

"This will only take a second. Just hold still, now."

Mallory felt the prick of the needle as it entered her neck on the right side, just above her collarbone. The cold flood of liquid was pushed into her vein, and she felt heat from her tears trickling down her face.

Sheva sat back, withdrawing the syringe and stowing it in its case.

"There. You should feel much better in a few minutes."

She imagined she could feel the poison running through her, traveling the length of her body and meeting its beginning in her neck. Sound became muffled and the room wavered in her vision. She struggled to keep her eyes open, but it was no use. Her eyelids weighed more than she could lift, and as the blackness swallowed her she could only think of Kadence. If she'd only listened. *Kadence.*

CHAPTER EIGHTEEN

Icy fingers of dread gripped Kadence's stomach. She'd lost her nerve when Mallory exited her building. She'd seemed stressed, even angry, when she'd flung open the door of her cab. It had been a cop-out to stand back and let her drive away, but she knew the car was heading for the gallery, so she hopped on the train. Mallory would probably get there twenty or so minutes before her, but she figured that'd give her time to calm down. *She won't be happy to see me, but I've got to do this.*

She arrived at the gallery at four forty-five and stood at the main entrance, gathering her courage. When Mallory saw the maquette, she'd understand. She'd know Kadence wasn't crazy. She walked to the door and was about to press the off hours button when movement inside caught her attention. Flickering shadows rolled across the walls, indistinguishable. Something was happening, but what? She moved off to one side so she could get a better look. The shadows were no more distinguishable here, but the size distortion made her realize they couldn't be coming from the main room.

Maybe this was the crew getting ready to move Sheva's sculptures? She was trying to decide what to do when she saw Mallory race through the main room and up the stairs, Sheva following behind her.

Shit, shit, shit. I'm too late. She shook the doors, but there was no way to force them open. She raced to the side of the building, looking for some way inside, but there was nothing. In the back she found the big roll-up door for the loading bay, but had no idea how to open it. She tried shoving, but it didn't move. Her chest tightened and her jaw ached with the stress, but she ignored it. She had to figure a way into the building. She searched the alley for something heavy to throw at the front window. Maybe if she couldn't break the glass, at least she could set off the alarm. *Shit.* She grabbed her phone and dialed 911. *Stupid not to think of that first.* The dispatcher asked the pertinent questions, but Kadence didn't have many answers to give. She just knew something bad was happening. She told the operator that a woman was being attacked in the gallery and gave the address. They asked her to stay on the line, but she needed to act. Mallory might not have much time. She cut the call and raced to the front, looking for anything heavy. She found a crate across the street and threw it with all her strength, but it bounced harmlessly off the glass. *If only I had a car, I'd drive through this window.*

She finally found a loose brick in the street and threw it at the stubborn window. She could see a crack in the glass where it hit, but nothing like what she'd hoped. *It's that stuff that doesn't shatter. Great.* She pulled the maquette from her pouch, set it on the sidewalk, and yanked off her hoodie. She tied the brick inside, grabbed it by the sleeves and peppered the window with blows, each causing more crazing to the glass. Finally, she could see the center of the area she was hitting begin to bow inward. She kicked the glass, forcing it down, and shimmied through. She felt the broken chunks of safety glass scrape against her side as she wiggled and fell, face first, onto the floor.

She scrambled up and raced to the stairs. From her left she caught movement and turned in time to duck the missile aimed at her head. Sheva was behind her, Mallory hanging limp over her shoulder. She'd thrown something at her that clattered to the ground against the stairs.

Sheva was rushing through to the main room, so Kadence ran after her.

"Stop. You'll never get away with this."

Sheva ignored her, continuing across the room. Kadence dove at her feet, needing to stop her. If Mallory fell now, she might get injured, but at least she'd have a chance. If Sheva got away with her, Kadence knew she'd never be heard from again. She caught one of Sheva's boots, causing her to kick savagely at Kadence with the other.

Thanks to her childhood, Kadence knew how to protect herself, and she curled around the trapped boot and shielded her face by moving to the outside of Sheva's leg. She quickly grabbed the other boot and held her in place.

"Dammit, let me go."

"Put her down."

Sheva twisted her legs, struggling to break Kadence's hold, but she knew if she let go, Mallory would be lost.

Sheva dropped Mallory's limp body to the side with a terrible thud and reached for Kadence, but she'd been waiting for this. As soon as Mallory was down, Kadence reared up, sweeping Sheva from her feet. She should've hit the floor hard, but she managed to keep her head up and catch the weight of her fall on her arms. Kadence was on her knees, still holding Sheva's feet, when she pivoted and yanked one foot free.

Kadence felt the crack as the cartilage in her nose broke loose. She tasted the bitter copper of her own blood as it washed into her mouth and spilled down her shirt. Instinctively, she grabbed her nose with both hands, freeing Sheva. Realizing what she'd done, she stood and kicked out at her, hovering over Mallory. Sheva belted her with a stone-hard fist to the gut. The pain was fiery hot and swelled out like a wave, doubling her over and making her grunt. Sheva moved to grab Mallory, but Kadence was no stranger to pain. If there was one thing she knew how to take, it was a punch. She let fly with her own fist, taking Sheva in the ribs. She woofed out air and crumpled, but quickly heaved herself to a standing position.

They were in the middle of the room of statues, between *Love's Birth* and *Broken Wave*. Sheva moved close to *Broken Wave* as Kadence rushed her. Just before she closed the distance between them, Sheva stepped back and pulled the sculpture down on her. Kadence had no time to adjust and was knocked to the ground. Pain flared everywhere and light exploded in her vision before everything washed into blackness.

Sheva watched the fall of her first masterpiece, savoring the sound of hard metal meeting soft flesh. She would take them both. She'd load Mallory into the van, then come back for this ignorant, meddling woman. It would be obvious that something had happened in the gallery, but she would be long gone before her movers arrived at eight. No one would be able to connect her to this mess. *And I'll have both my models at the same time. I can finish them both and show them to the world as a pair.* Maybe it wasn't such a bad thing the abstractionist had showed up after all.

She clutched at her aching ribs, wishing she'd been able to avoid that punch. Nothing broken, just sore. That would wear off soon. She tried lifting Mallory to her shoulder, but her ribs screamed at the effort, so she dragged her toward the loading bay. She was about to pull her down the steps when the grinding of the motor signaled the arrival of a vehicle outside.

Shit, what now? She couldn't be discovered here, with the painter crushed under her statue and Mallory obviously unconscious. She dropped her and ran to the front of the building. Using the same access the painter had, she slid out into the night and away, remembering only as she rushed down the stairs to the train that her van was still in the bay. *Nothing I can do about that. I can get another.* She punched her thigh as she settled into a seat, angry that things had fallen apart. *Damn that painter.* She made her body a mask of calm, no sign of the rage and panic pumping inside to alert others there was something going on. She had to get to her studio, grab her money and passport, and leave. Time was her enemy and she had to overcome it. It struck her then the real cost of her failure, her beauties were lost to her. There would be no way to retrieve them. She would never trace their smooth forms and feel the souls inside again. Fresh pain ripped at her, but this time at her heart. Her girls weren't hers any longer.

Kadence's first awareness was blinding pain. She couldn't move. Every heartbeat was a throb of excruciating pain, focused mainly in her right hand. She struggled to open her eyes, to move, but it was useless. She groaned and heard someone's sharp intake of breath. *Was that me?*

Warm hands were running up and down her left arm, and she could hear someone, faintly. *Mallory?*

"Just be still, okay? We're bringin' in the lift and we'll have this off of you in a second."

Not Mallory. Who? She tried to ask, but her mouth wouldn't move, and she could only moan.

Soon she heard the sound of an engine getting closer, then hands again on her arm.

"I'm going to slip this belt between you and the sculpture, okay? Don't worry, we'll go real slow lifting. We don't want to add new injures. The paramedics are right here. They've taken Ms. Tucker to the hospital and will help you as soon as we get you free. Hang in there, okay?"

Hospital. Mallory's safe. Sheva didn't get her. The resulting relief was replaced with excruciating pain, making her breathless and nauseous. She grunted, wishing he'd stop talking and take the pain away. She felt the hands trying to maneuver the rough nylon belt across her stomach, the pressure and pain making her gag. She was going to die choking on her own puke, but death would be a welcome relief.

They must have gotten the thing secured because the motor whined with effort and she felt the weight above her shift. It felt like they were forcing stone through her palm, grinding it into the granite floor. As she screamed out her pain, the wall of darkness moved over her again and she sank back into unconsciousness.

When Mallory finally, slowly, moved back toward consciousness, humming and beeping filled her aching head. She tried to sit up, but was held fast to the bed by the array of tubes and wires around her.

"Try not to move, Ms. Tucker. You'll only hurt yourself. You're at Presbyterian Hospital, in the ICU. The doctor will be here in a moment to talk to you about your situation. Just be still and try to relax." A nurse fiddled with the tubes and machines next to Mallory's bed.

She tried to force the fog from her memory. *How did I end up here?* The throbbing pain in her head made it a challenge. It felt like a ripe melon, and her stomach roiled with nausea. She made herself take inventory of her body. Had she been in an accident? Everything seemed fine except for her head and stomach. Images flashed through her mind; the gallery, the loading bay, what? An uneasiness rose inside, making her shake. Her mouth went bone dry, and she hoped someone would come soon. She needed to know what had happened.

As if he heard, a young doctor walked in, smiling encouragingly. "Ms. Tucker, good morning. I'm glad to see you're awake."

"What—" She cleared her throat and tried again. "What happened?"

"Don't try to talk. I'm sure your head is killing you. You were attacked at the gallery. Looks like whoever did it knows a bit about sedation. They injected you with a powerful sedative. Right here." He pointed to a spot low on his neck. "They managed to get it directly into your jugular, so its effects were quick. You're one lucky lady. All you'll have to deal with is the headache, but things could have been much worse. It should start to fade later today. For now, you need to rest."

His words jolted her memory, and it came flooding back in waves, and sour acid filled her mouth. Sheva, the eerie grin on her face, hiding under the van, all of it. She needed to vomit.

The panic must have shown, because the doctor rushed to put a small tray under her mouth. It was like she was being turned inside out, the force of the heaving was so intense. Her head exploded in fresh waves of pain, and she was grateful for the cool hand of the doctor on her forehead. He pressed the call button, said something, and a nurse rushed in. She had a syringe in her hand, which she passed to the doctor. He injected it into her IV, and she felt the nausea ease.

"There now, you'll be okay. Get her some oral swabs. Nothing to eat or drink for at least two hours, then ice chips. I'll stop back later today. Don't worry, Ms. Tucker. You're in good hands."

Questions filled her mind, but she knew she wasn't going to get answers right now. She let herself relax, and soon sleep claimed her. When she next awoke, there were two strangers in her room. They were obviously law enforcement, probably here to get a statement. She tried to shake the fog again so she could answer their questions.

"Ms. Tucker, I'm Detective Morris, and this is Detective Simms. We have some questions if you feel up to answering."

She nodded, not trusting her voice.

"Okay, good. What do you remember about what happened yesterday morning?"

Yesterday? Her confusion must have shown, because their expressions softened and Morris moved closer to her.

"It's okay, you've been here since Friday morning. It's now Saturday afternoon. You were found unconscious in your gallery, and it was obvious that you'd been attacked. There was one other person found on the premises, and at this point we aren't considering her a suspect, given her own injuries. What we need from you is anything you can remember to help us find whoever did this."

Mallory did her best to tell them what she knew. What Sheva had done, what she'd said. The way she'd attacked her, held her down, and injected her. But she knew nothing about someone else in the gallery. Anxiety gnawed at her, making it hard to focus on their questions.

"Do you know why this Sheva attacked you?"

"The sculptures."

"Excuse me? Did you say she attacked you because of the sculptures? Was there a dispute of some kind?"

Mallory couldn't make them understand. Her head was splitting and she couldn't focus. "Yes, the missing women."

"I don't understand. Could you give me a little more detail?"

"Ask her. You have to ask her. She was right." She had too many questions of her own. The headache was roaring, filling every space in her head. She wanted, needed, to close her eyes, to shut out any thought of what had happened, but she had to know. "Who? Who else was in the gallery?"

"Kadence Munroe. One of the artists you're showing, right? She was found pinned under a statue, also unconscious. Do you know how she was involved in the attack on you, or why she was there?"

Mallory went to shake her head but couldn't because of the pain. "Kadence? Is she okay?"

"I don't have the answer to that, ma'am. What I know is that she is also here, and hasn't been questioned yet."

"She tried to tell me."

"Ma'am? Who tried to tell you what?"

"Kadence. She tried to warn me that Sheva was dangerous. You have to ask her, get her to tell you about the sculptures, the missing women."

The detectives exchanged a glance. "We'll ask her as soon as she's able to be questioned."

Her head forgotten, pain pierced her heart. Kadence was hurt and it was her fault. She felt the sting of tears and wanted more than anything to beg her forgiveness. She'd been right all along, her paranoia justified. *It's not paranoia if she was right.*

"Ms. Tucker, are you okay?"

She nodded weakly. She wasn't okay, but there was nothing he could do to help her. *Why didn't I trust her?*

"I can see that you're upset. We'll let you get some rest. We may have follow-up questions, in which case, we'll contact you. Take care of yourself."

They left her alone and the grief of what might have happened surged through her. Aching emptiness, like a chasm, filled her. She curled around herself as best she could and gave in to it.

She woke when the door opened and someone entered. She didn't want to see anyone, so she kept her body turned away.

"Mal? Can I come in?" Tarin called softly.

Go away. She wanted no company, not even his, but she couldn't make her mouth speak the words. She heard him slip quietly in and move toward the bed. His warm hand stroked her hair. Tears came without warning, snaking down her cheeks and wetting her pillow.

"I can tell you're awake, kiddo. I'm here for me, so don't worry. I'll be here, but you can ignore me."

Her sobs increased as she realized she was shutting out the one person in her life she could count on. She rolled over and let him hold her while she cried. He made gentle shushing noises as he patted her back, but said nothing more. It was just what she needed. She cried herself out, moving from soul-deep weeping to little hitches of sobs as her emotions exhausted her. Finally, she lay quietly against his shoulder, feeling bad for ruining his jacket.

"There now," he said, "that's better. I'm here and you don't have to worry. I'm not going anywhere. If you need to talk, I'm listening. If you need answers, I'll find them. If you need solitude, I'll sit outside your door in a chair. Whatever you need."

"Water?"

He poured some water into the cup on her table and held a straw to her lips.

Mallory drank greedily. Water had never tasted so good. Its cool fingers massaged the strained lining of her throat.

"Here." He held out a tissue box, and she grabbed a few to blow her nose.

"Thank you." She hoped he knew how much his being here meant to her. He was her rock.

"Don't mention it. Is there anything I can do for you, hon?"

She wanted to know how Kadence had ended up in the gallery, how she was doing, but didn't know how to ask. The weight of her guilt over her denial held her tongue. How could she ask that? What right did she have?

As if he could see into her, read what was written on her heart, Tarin began talking.

"I checked on Kadence earlier, when the police were with you. I'm not sure if you know what happened. When Mike Pelegrini arrived for the sculptures, there was a van in the loading bay. He and his guys jumped down and went in the gallery to see what was up. They found you lying on the floor, unconscious, and Kadence pinned under *Torrid Heat*, injured and unconscious. The cops pulled up about that time and started investigating. There was no one else around, but the front window had been busted, so they figured whoever did this probably got out that way."

"How is she?" Mallory had to ask.

"Not good. Mild concussion, some bruising and such inside, but the worst, most devastating part? Her right hand was crushed. When Pelegrini lifted the statue off her, he said her hand looked like ground meat. That's going to be hard to come back from. I called your mom, and let her know you were okay. I told her you'd call her as soon as you were up to it. I couldn't find anyone to call for Kadence. I figured we'd ask her when she's awake."

Mallory felt the words like shards of glass going through her. Kadence would be shattered. Her hand was her tool for communicating her passion and emotion to canvas. If she couldn't paint, she'd be crushed. *And why? Why was she at the gallery? Was she still trying to protect me? Is this my fault?* She felt the blackness well up inside as she struggled to understand, and the tears fell again, this time for Kadence.

She held Tarin's hand as she told him everything. From her relationship with Sheva, to the end of it, to Kadence's warnings about the women who had gone missing after being involved with Sheva. After being attacked, she couldn't believe she'd been so dismissive of Kadence's warnings. She was overwhelmed with guilt. Kadence would've never been hurt if not for her. *She was trying to keep me safe. I don't deserve her.*

Sheva arrived back at her studio to find everything in order. She'd waited nearby for more than a day, watching her studio to make sure the cops hadn't shown up. *Maybe the painter is dead. Maybe Mallory hasn't told them anything yet.* Too many unanswered questions were making her crazy. Finally, she took a chance and ran to the studio. She knew she didn't have much time. She had to get what she needed and get out of there. She had a plan, a place to run. She never expected to be found out, but she'd always taken precautions when moving to a new location. She had found a small foundry in rural New Jersey and bought it through an intermediary. She could be there in a couple of hours. She grabbed what clothes would fit in her bag and looked longingly at her maquettes, still shrouded on the table. Maybe she could fit one or two in? She pulled the shroud back and immediately noticed Mallory's maquette was missing. How could that be? Had she put it somewhere else? No, she always put them back on the table. Had someone been in the studio?

She struggled to remember her actions before leaving. She was struck by the memory of something being off when she'd awoken, and the feeling had been hard to shake. Now she knew why. Someone had been there and had taken the maquette. *Who?*

There was only one possible answer. It had to be that meddling painter. Who else would be stalking her? That was why she'd shown up at the gallery, ruining everything. The image of that woman pinned under her beautiful artwork was the only satisfying thing about the whole night. *Stupid pig, she should've minded her own business.* Now she'd have to run. Her whole career was destroyed because of that woman. Her name would be poison, her work, in an instant, gone from wonder to macabre.

Damn. Europe was out of the question. There was no way she could continue with her plans once the police were involved. If the movers hadn't chosen that moment to arrive, she'd have been out of there with Mallory in moments. But it was no use dwelling on what might have been. They'd come and she'd barely gotten away.

She had a sizable bank account under a false name, thanks to sales of her reproductions. All she needed was a destination. Somewhere she could reincarnate herself, become a completely different person.

She grabbed a hammer from her tool shelf and began smashing the maquettes. Each blow hurt, a gouge to her heart, but keeping them intact was too dangerous. She could leave none of her past behind. The police would be looking for her because of Mallory, but if they talked to the painter and found the maquettes, they'd want her for even more.

When nothing remained of the clay figures but lumps and dust, she threw the hammer as far away as possible. Her stomach roiled and threatened to lose its contents as she ran her hand through the dust of her creations. Her precious souls, caught forever in the grip of gleaming bronze, now they were out of her reach. She'd never again commune with them, asking for inspiration. She was on her own. Even these small keepsakes of them were gone. Rage filled her, gripping her with fiery hands and burning its message on her heart.

How can I let them go? How can I simply walk away and pretend like I didn't love them? She couldn't. Her only hope was to finish the job she'd begun. Finish *Malice* and *Angst*. When the two women who'd destroyed her were themselves destroyed, she would be free to reinvent herself.

She would wait for the right moment. No buildup this time. She'd snatch them out of their lives the way they'd taken her from hers. She grabbed her bag and walked out into the predawn light.

CHAPTER NINETEEN

K adence stared at the insulated tiles on the ceiling, counting divots, anything to keep from thinking about the pain radiating up her right arm. She wouldn't look at it, had to cut the idea of it out of her mind. When they came in to dress the wound, she turned her head as far away as she could.

They'd been in again to ask her questions, but she ignored them. Her world had been destroyed, so why should she try to get back into their world? They were blobs of flesh moving in and out of her perception and she couldn't connect to them. She'd woken up yesterday, head filled with fog, and found her hand swathed in layers of gauze. Surgery, they'd said. *Crushing injury, compartment syndrome,* and *future reconstruction.* It was all too much for her to handle. They were words, horrible, terrifying words, that made no sense. The thing at the end of her arm was nothing more than searing pain. She couldn't move it, bend it, anything. It was separate from her.

That which had been her lifeline, her safety valve, was gone. She counted divots in the ceiling tile, forty-nine, fifty, fifty-one. They were there again, swooping around her, moving this, checking that.

"Are you hungry?"

"Can you drink this?"

"I'm going to change your dressing."

The litany of *I don't care* ran through her head, making her lose her count and have to start over. Then new faces, different in their countenance, stern, serious faces, in suits.

"Ms. Munroe? You're going to have to talk to us. The doctor assures me that you're conscious and able to respond. If you continue this silence, I'll have no choice but to assume you're responsible for the break-in and attack at ARA Gallery."

Something flickered in her awareness, something she needed to remember. ARA Gallery, attack, Mallory? It flooded into her mind, the images so real and disturbing she had to close her eyes. Her heart raced and her breathing became labored. *Mallory.*

"No!" She'd been so shocked by the pain and loss, so caught up in what she could never do again, she hadn't stopped to really think about what, or who, had taken it all away from her.

"Ms. Munroe? Should I call someone?" The suit was panicked.

"Where is she? Is she okay?" Kadence struggled to get out of the bed, tugged at wires, tangled in sheets.

"Ms. Munroe, calm down. You're going to hurt yourself. Be still."

The suit was holding her by the shoulders, keeping her pressed to the bed. *Mallory. Unconscious on the floor. Sheva and that evil look in her eyes. The paramedic said hospital.* "Please, tell me, please. Is she okay?"

"If you calm down, I'll answer any questions I can. Your hand shouldn't be shaken around like this. Please calm down."

She sucked in a breath and willed herself to be quiet. She needed to know, and he could help her. She breathed in through her nose and out through her mouth, imagining that she could see her heart slowing its frantic pace. The pressure on her shoulders relaxed and he stood back. She knew it was working. She could feel the pinpricks of electricity calming along her arms and legs. She was ready.

"Okay, then. I presume you're asking about Mallory Tucker, the gallery director, right?"

She nodded.

"Well, she's here, in a private room. She's in good condition and will probably go home later today."

"No, she can't. Don't let her go home. She knows where she lives."

"Who would that be? What can you tell me about yesterday at the gallery?"

"It was Sheva, the sculptor. She did something to her. I saw Mallory run up the stairs, then Sheva run after her. I knew Mallory was in danger, so I tried to get in. I couldn't open the doors, so I took a brick and broke the window. By the time I got in, she had her over her shoulder. I had to stop her. She was going to do something to her, like the others."

"What do you mean, like the others?"

"The other women, the statues. They're all missing, well, I mean, all but one, but I don't know who that is. She did something with them, and she was going to do it to Mallory."

"Hold on, wait. You need to start at the beginning and tell me everything you know."

She told him all she knew, beginning with Carlyle and ending with the maquettes she'd found of Mallory and her.

"I followed her from Mallory's apartment. She has a studio in a warehouse in English Kill. She had the maquettes there. But there were nine of them. She only has six sculptures, so nine wasn't right. But they were us, me and Mallory. She was going to kill us. Did you find it? The maquette at the gallery? I left in on the sidewalk outside when I put the brick in my hoodie to break the window. You had to find it."

"Maquette? Like a model of a statue? Yes, they found something like that."

Kadence was relieved. She had proof, not that she needed it now. "That's Mallory. Look at it. It's her. And the information on the other girls is in my apartment, on the wall."

"We will. I think it's time for you to get some rest. We'll be back later. Don't worry, we're going to find Sheva."

She was exhausted and wanted nothing more than to sleep, but she had to make sure Mallory was protected.

"Please, don't let her go home alone. Keep her safe."

"Rest easy, Ms. Munroe. She's going to her mother's home when she's released. We'll make sure nothing happens. I'm going to let you sleep, now. Thank you for all the information."

Relief was a warm blanket of comfort, soothing her, letting her know Mallory would be okay. Fatigue weighed heavy and her eyelids fell before they even left her room.

❖

The ache in her head was down to almost nothing. Mallory fiddled with the call button, considering pushing it again, but there was no point. The nurse would be here as soon as possible, and she'd be released. Waiting made her crazy. All she wanted was to be home in her own bed. Tarin had left a few hours ago and was coming back to pick her up. The police expected her to go to Monhegan. Recuperating there would be relaxing, but it would be on Tarin to make sure the gallery was running smoothly while she was gone. *I'd rather be here. I'm not going to Maine, I'm going home. Maybe to work tomorrow. Life doesn't end because this happened. I need to get back into my life.*

She needed to check on Kadence before she left, but her guilt weighed her down. She was afraid Kadence wouldn't want to see her. She'd discounted her warnings, and because of that, Kadence's hand had been crushed. How could she face her? Part of her knew if she didn't see her she was being a coward, and Kadence deserved better. But the other part of her really believed she'd be the last person on earth Kadence would want to see. She was conflicted, as she had been since the moment they'd met. She had to do it. She wouldn't be able to leave without seeing her and knowing she was safe.

The door swung open and Tarin came in.

"You look great. Are you ready to get out of here?"

"More than ready, but I haven't been discharged yet. We have to wait for the paperwork."

"Okay. Want me to see if I can hurry that along?"

"I doubt it'll do any good, but there is something you can do for me."

"Yes?"

"Would you go ask Kadence if she will see me? I asked yesterday, but they said she was drugged and sleeping. I'm so worried about her—"

"Why don't we go together? I'm sure you'll feel better seeing her with your own eyes."

"I'm not sure she'll want to see me. This is all my fault. She probably hates me."

He scoffed at the idea. "Don't be so melodramatic. You didn't pull a statue down on her, did you?"

"No."

"And she threw herself in the path of that monster. She can't blame you. That's on her."

"No, you don't understand. She tried to warn me about Sheva, more than once. But I wouldn't listen. I just made her feel like she was crazy and banned her from the gallery."

"I do understand, but truthfully? She attacked Sheva before this. You didn't have a choice. Again, not on you. This is on Sheva, all of it."

"Dammit, it *is* on me. When she was pleading with me to be careful, I was brushing her concerns aside. I didn't even look into the things she was telling me. I just wrote her off. How can I not feel responsible when she got hurt saving me?"

"I get it, but I think you're being unfair to yourself. You were operating on what you knew. That's human nature. She won't hold that against you, I'm sure."

"I'm not. I just hope she can forgive me. Would you just go ask her if she will see me? Please?"

He obviously wasn't finished with the argument, but he conceded and left to find Kadence. She felt sick to her stomach thinking about it. If only she could go back and change things, so Kadence wouldn't be hurt. She had to be okay. Her hand had to heal so she could paint again. She remembered the incredible softness of Kadence's lips on hers and the passion she aroused in her when they'd kissed. What if none of this had happened? What if she and Kadence had been able to nurture and kindle the flame that had sparked between them? Where would they be now without Sheva coming between them?

She sank onto the bed, wishing she could erase the past and bring them back to that kiss, that energy, the day before Kadence's opening. An overwhelming sense of loneliness filled her like an endless vacuum. *I'm so sorry.*

The nurse came in and said something that didn't register. Mallory numbly signed the papers set in front of her. She was brought to focus by the nurse standing in front of her, unmoving.

"Did you ask me something?"

"I asked if you're feeling okay. You seem distracted."

"I'm fine, but, yes, distracted. Am I free?"

"Yes, you're free to go. You have your discharge instructions there. Make sure and check in with your personal doctor no later than next week for a follow-up."

Mallory nodded. She wondered how long Tarin would be, because now that she could go, she couldn't wait to leave. She sat on the bed and tried to push back the waves of depression rolling over her.

Tarin walked in a short time later, looking sad. Mallory wasn't sure she wanted to hear, but she had to know.

"How is she? Can I see her"

He looked down, avoiding her gaze. "Not good. She's had one surgery and will have to have more. They're leaving the wound open so they can keep infection risk down. Poor thing. She's pretty despondent, but she doesn't want to see anyone. I'm sorry, Mal."

Mallory took in the words, physically aching for Kadence, and knowing it was her fault. She never would have been there if Mallory had listened to her.

Hiding how much the words hurt, Mallory stood. "Let's get out of here. This place is making me sick."

"Sure. But we have to wait for transportation, right?"

"What?"

"You know, the wheelchair ride to the door. They have to do that."

"Would you find out when they're coming?"

"I'll be right back." As he slid out the door, it was opened wider to admit the two detectives from earlier. *What now?*

"Ms. Tucker, I hear you're leaving?"

"As soon as I can."

"We have a few more questions we'd like to ask you."

"Can it wait? I'm so sick of being here."

"It really can't. I understand you're leaving for Monhegan, Maine, from here, is that correct?"

"No, I'm going to my apartment."

"Are you sure that's a smart decision? We haven't apprehended Sheva, so that puts you at risk."

"I don't think she'll come after me again. She has to know you're after her. Why would she risk coming back?" Even as she said the words, her chest tightened and she forced herself to breathe. Would she be coming back? Her legs went weak and she was glad the bed was behind her. She sat, trying to block the images of Sheva's face as she pressed down on her. Her heart raced and the headache she'd managed to conquer flared. *I won't let her win.*

"In my experience, people like her have motivations we can't comprehend. I believe the risk to you is too high to ignore. Isn't there someone you could stay with? Until we have her in custody?"

"She can stay with me. There's plenty of room and I'll keep her safe." Tarin was followed into the room by the wheelchair orderly.

Mallory's eyes were suddenly wet with tears. The relief, knowing she wouldn't be alone, was indescribable. Her body felt rubbery and disconnected. *Thank God for Tarin.*

"Is that acceptable, Ms. Tucker? That way we don't have to talk today."

She nodded, overcome with emotion.

"We'll need an address and contact information so we can arrange a time to talk."

Tarin gave them the information and they agreed to call her in the morning. Mallory was so glad to sit in the chair and be rolled out of the room. She needed to breathe, and the hospital was stifling. She understood why Kadence wouldn't see her, but it hurt. It was like a white-hot knife of pain in her heart. She was the reason Kadence was here, why her hand had been crushed, but to leave without seeing her was agony. Tarin walked beside her carrying her small bag and chatting innocuously.

When they reached the main door, he led the way to a waiting taxi and held the door for her. They were soon on the way to his apartment, and spent most of the drive in silence. Mallory was at a loss for anything else to say, and Tarin seemed to respect her desire for quiet. Tarin's husband, Jack, was an investment banker, and they lived on the Upper West Side. Mallory had enjoyed the view from their balcony many times, and this wouldn't be the first time she availed herself of the guest room.

When he settled her on the couch, Tarin had her write out a list of things she would need from her place. He was going to the gallery, but would grab her items before returning home. When he'd gone, she slid open the balcony door and walked out into the sunshine. She tilted her face to the sun and let its heat warm her. Tarin's cat, Ziggy, wandered out and rubbed against her legs. She scooped him up and sat in the deck chair with him, his gentle purring a soothing counterpoint to the emptiness inside.

She needed to see Kadence. It was necessary to know and confront the damage she'd caused. The thought of her crushed hand, the potential loss of her work, was so overwhelming it made her sick to her stomach. She had to take responsibility, to show Kadence how sorry she was that she hadn't trusted her.

She'd discovered Kadence, fallen in love with the raw emotion in her work, and done everything she could to bring her the attention she deserved. But because she couldn't accept the crazy idea that Sheva was truly dangerous, she'd pushed Kadence away, and now this had happened. If Kadence never painted again, it would be on Mallory.

Every inch of her felt beaten, as if a huge fist had grabbed her and squeezed every good thing out of her. She was gutted and empty, but knew it had to be so much worse for Kadence.

❖

Kadence watched the drip of the IV line, trying to think of anything but the pile of meat that had been her hand. She couldn't look at it. The physical therapist had just left. She was nice enough, but Kadence didn't understand why she was there. She'd told her it was important to move the two uninjured fingers on her hand, to keep the blood flowing and prevent stiffness.

Her hand was disconnected from her. She felt the pain, but couldn't accept that it was hers. Her hand had been the price of saving Mallory, and she'd pay it again, gladly, but the thought of not being able to paint hurt worse than the hand. It was easier not to think about it. She regretted pushing Tarin away when he'd come by. He only wanted to show he cared. And Mallory, she'd wanted to come, too, but Kadence couldn't face her yet. It was still too raw. She didn't want her to see this side of her. The pain was one thing, but the blackness that engulfed her spirit was something else. No one should have to see that. It was a part of her she wanted to excise. It was better to be alone right now. When she'd pushed the black wall back into her subconscious, she'd be able to be around people.

She hadn't felt so depressed since Carlyle had dumped her and shredded her work. Mallory had been the one to bring back her belief in her painting. She couldn't let her see the mess she'd become.

The doctor entered the room. He was trying to be warm and positive, but Kadence wasn't playing along. Nothing about this was encouraging. She wanted to curl around herself and shut out the rest of the world.

"Ms. Munroe, how are you feeling?"

What a stupid question. Her whole world ended when her hand was crushed. She'd never paint again. How could she possibly feel? "How do you think?"

"Come on, now, you have to try and stay positive. You're the biggest part of your recovery. If you can stay motivated to heal, the end result will be better, I promise."

She looked at him without answering. She couldn't be positive right now. There wasn't a silver lining to this, other than Mallory being safe. Why didn't they get that?

"If you were me, would you be positive?" She watched his face drop slightly in response. As a surgeon, he understood how intimately self-identity was tied to skill of the hand.

"You're right, of course. A devastating injury to the hand is hard to come to terms with. Would you like me to have a therapist come and talk with you?"

She considered that. It wasn't a bad idea to talk to a professional about her feelings, but she wasn't ready. "No."

"Okay. I'll tell you, I have seen remarkable recoveries from injuries even worse than yours. It takes time, persistence, and a positive attitude. Work on that."

"I'll try."

"So, I wanted to update you on the plan for your reconstruction. The first surgery was to debride the wound and assess what damage we're dealing with. I've got good news and less good news."

She waited, her stomach tight with dread, to hear what they found.

"Your injury caused severe damage to the muscles, vessels, and nerves in your hand. We harvested superficial veins in your upper arm to restore good vascularity to your hand. You seem to be responding well to this. Three of your fingers have crush injury to the bone. We were able to reattach the major tendons, but we'll need to take you back into surgery to wire the bones so they can heal."

"Is this the good news or the not so good news?"

He smiled. "The good news, of course. I think you have the potential for an almost full recovery."

The hope contained in those words almost too much to bear, when she'd convinced herself her art career was over. "What's the not so good news?"

"When we close your wound, probably three days from now, we'll have to take a skin graft from your thigh. We want the swelling to go down as much as possible before we close. The infection risk seems to be lessening, but you can't be too careful."

It was too much to think about. Take skin from her leg? How would that work? "Why is it taking so long to close the wound?"

"There are many factors in reconstructing your hand. We have to be sure infection is no longer a risk. We'll repair the minor tendons after we're sure we've stabilized the skeletal structure. You have to keep in mind the amount of physical movement your hand will need during recovery. Again, we can't be too careful. I want you to have good use of your hand, to feel things with your fingers. This requires diligence and time. The other good news is that your concussion was minor and the headache should be about gone. We'll keep doing the protocol for a couple of days, but I'm sure you're out of the woods."

Kadence made herself look at the wreck that had been her hand. It was swathed in gauze, her purple fingertips poking out. She couldn't move them or feel any sensation in her hand. Thinking about recovery was too weird when it felt like the hand wasn't a part of her.

"Do you have any questions?" he asked.

She dreaded the answer, but had to ask the question. "How long before I know if I can paint again?"

"Well, that's hard to say. The damage to your nerves is the determining factor. That could take up to a year to fully assess. Now, it might take only a few months, but we just can't put a time on it. As

I said, I think you have the potential for a near full recovery, but a lot of that is on you. Your dedication to therapy is critical. Some people with this type of injury never regain use of their hand. It's up to you. Do the work and you'll get the results."

She didn't have much to say, and the doctor looked pained. She shook her head, needing time to digest what he said. Warm tears snaked down her cheeks, puddling in her ears. She made no effort to stop them or wipe them away. This was reality and it was more crushing than the stupid statue that caused it.

"Okay, I'll let you rest. Your PT should be by again in an hour. Try to think positive. We're going to do our best for you, and I really believe we're going to be successful."

She didn't acknowledge his effort to reach her, just watched as he patted her leg and walked out. If she could turn on her side, she'd curl up into a ball and sink into the uncertainty that remained. *Stupid brace.* Her arm was strapped down to a wedge brace to keep her from moving it, but it restricted all her movement. She closed her eyes, the memory of Mallory slung over Sheva's shoulder hit her. *Sheva, this was all her fault.* She thought about Mallory's smile, the way she tilted her head when Kadence wouldn't show her the dragon. Her velvety soft lips, in the loft, when they'd finished setting up her show.

She wouldn't let herself think about the other times. It wasn't Mallory's fault that she couldn't see the connections Kadence had tried to show her. It was a hard story to swallow, but it had been the truth. She knew that now, and so did Mallory. Now she just had to figure out what the next step would be when she got out of the hospital. She had no friends and no family, and now, no way to paint. Not for a year, at least, and maybe not ever. She let the tears fall. *What am I going to do?*

CHAPTER TWENTY

Mallory woke the next morning and sat on the balcony with her coffee. Ziggy curled up in her lap, and she stroked him until he fell asleep. She wondered if Kadence was awake. Would she be willing to see her today? *God, I hope so.* She needed to see her, to touch her and know that she was okay. She had to tell her how sorry she was for not listening, and thank her for saving her life.

She closed her eyes and remembered each touch they'd shared, the kiss on her hand, the playful bumping of shoulders over lunch. She wanted to see that dragon tattoo and hold Kadence and let her know she wasn't alone. No one should be alone. *I have to see her.*

She showered and was dressing to go to the hospital when the phone rang. It was Detective Simms, reminding her they would be there in an hour. *Damn, I forgot about them.* She looked at her watch. Eleven. She would grab a sandwich and wait for them, but as soon as they left she was going to see Kadence.

She padded across the living room in her socks and went to the kitchen. There were plenty of options for a bite to eat, but she settled on comforting peanut butter and jelly with a glass of milk. She took her lunch to the table and grabbed her phone on the way. Three missed calls. One was from Chas Drummer and the others were from Tarin. She called him back in case it was something that need handling at the gallery.

He sounded harried but assured her he'd just called to check on her. She called Chas next, knowing the delay with the sculptures must be on her mind.

"Hello?"

She put on her best gallery manager voice. "Hi, Chas. It's Mallory Tucker."

"Oh, Mallory, how are you doing? Tarin told us you'd been hospitalized. Christina and I have been so concerned."

How much did he tell you? She played it cool, not wanting to upset the ladies. They might not want to keep the bronzes when they knew the whole story. *Hell, will I still be allowed to sell them? Or will they be evidence at this point?* She had no idea, and she'd have to find out. For now, she'd simply go on as planned. She would tell them, but first she needed to know what Tarin said. She didn't want to give them a different story. "I'm doing well. They released me from the hospital, so I think I can start sorting out the problem with the sculptures today."

"Oh, didn't Tarin tell you? They've been delivered. He took care of it yesterday. We were lucky that the sculpture from the crime wasn't one of the two we'd purchased."

That was a relief. They knew about Sheva. She had to be clear and let them know the suspected provenance of the work. She had to prepare for the fact that they might want to forfeit the sale at a later date. Keeping her clients happy was a huge responsibility. She knew she would never want to lay eyes on those bronzes again. She'd have to thank Tarin for handling the situation tactfully. Which sculpture had been toppled onto Kadence? She needed to check with him. It felt important.

"I'm so glad to hear that. You're happy with their placement?"

"Oh, yes. They're fabulous, even more stunning than we expected. You'll have to come out and see them when you're up to it."

Mallory got a queasy feeling thinking about it. They were remarkably beautiful sculptures, but she'd never get over the fact that women died to make them happen. "I look forward to that. So, was there anything else I could help you with?"

"No, dear. We just wanted to check on you."

"Well, thank you."

They chatted a bit more before saying good-bye, and Mallory felt more like herself than she had since the attack. She needed to work; it gave her purpose and anchored her. Tomorrow she would go in and see how things went. Today, she needed to see Kadence. She wouldn't take no for an answer, either. After she met with the police she'd call her mother and let her know she wouldn't be coming to the island this week. She wanted to be close to the hospital. She needed to be there for Kadence.

She was finishing her lunch when the doorbell sounded. Certain it must be the police, she walked to the door. She checked her instinct to yank the door open. What if it was Sheva? She hesitated, then snatched her hand back. She leaned toward the bolted door.

"Yes?"

"Ms. Tucker? It's Detectives Morris and Simms. May we come in?"

She squinted out the peephole, just to be doubly certain. When she saw the two men, she relaxed.

"Sure, hold on." She let them in and they sat at the table. Her nerves were jangled. Was everything she did from here forward going to be predicated by Sheva? Would she hesitate to take the train, or open the gallery solo? Probably, at least for a while. She couldn't undo what Sheva had done, and yes, it would affect her day-to-day routines, but Sheva wouldn't win. She'd put her in the past, someday.

"What can I do for you?" *Dumb question.*

"We have some questions about the sculptor involved in the case. What can you tell us about this Sheva?"

"You mean the crazy snake who almost killed me and destroyed the career of a promising artist? That Sheva? What do you want to know? She's vile and vindictive. She likes to play mind games and enjoys rough sex. What else? Maybe she's a serial killer, but if not she's definitely a psycho." She was losing it. She had to calm down. These were the people who would get Sheva off the streets. She needed to help them, if she could.

"Calm down, calm down. I know this is upsetting, but you know her better than anyone else we can talk to. Please help us help you. Can you do that?"

"I'm sorry. I guess it's all too much. I was terrified to open the door just now. It's not your fault, and I know you want to catch her as much as I want her caught. Seriously, what can I tell you?"

"Okay, Kadence Munroe gave us a statement yesterday. The implication is that Sheva caused several women who modeled for her to disappear. Do you know anything about that? What's your feeling about Ms. Munroe's state of mind and how reliable do you think her statement is?"

"I'd believe anything Kadence said from now on. She saved my life. I nearly lost it because I didn't credit her theory. I won't make that mistake again. Clearly, Sheva planned to make me disappear. If Kadence says she made others disappear, I believe it."

"Now that you're feeling better, have you remembered anything more about the attack?"

"No, not really. I told you everything yesterday."

"We've been checking out Ms. Munroe's story, and the connections are definitely there. She's already done some great legwork, and I have a hunch we'll be able to prove Sheva is connected with at least three of the disappearances. The key now is to catch her. Any ideas on where she might have gone? Did she ever mention anywhere she particularly liked?"

"If you didn't find her at her studio or foundry, I have no idea where she could be." *And that scares me to death.* "Her next show is scheduled in Geneva, in January. You should probably be watching the airports."

"That's being handled. What about her last name? Any idea on that? We've taken her prints from the gallery and the van she left at the scene, but so far, we haven't had a match. If we had a last name, we might be able to lay hands on her sooner."

Mallory thought about that. Sheva was her pseudonym, but she thought she had a record of her legal name. She wracked her memory, going back to the signing of Sheva's contract.

"She told me her legal name a few months back. It was Martha something. Martha Gray? Martha Graham? Martha Graves! That was it. Her legal name is Martha Graves."

"Excellent. How certain are you that it's Graves? Ninety percent? Fifty percent?"

"One hundred percent. I remember it clearly. Tarin will have a copy of her contract at the gallery, if you want to pick it up."

"Thank you. Is there anything you can tell us about Ms. Graves that might give us insight into her?"

"She's very charismatic. She has no trouble convincing people to trust her. She had me fooled. I knew she was volatile, but I just thought she was a crazy artist. She found the key to my apartment once, and broke in, kind of. I threw her out." She didn't tell them about the weird, small fights. There were far bigger things on the table now. "Kadence knew. I guess I refused to see." The thought made her insides knot up again.

"Okay, well, thank you for your time."

Mallory started to show them out when she remembered Sheva's strange reluctance to sell her sculptures. That might be something they should know.

"Wait, there's one more thing. She has an unnatural attraction to her work. I mean, most artists have a hard time parting with favorite pieces, but Sheva flatly refused to sell any of her sculptures. Not just with me, she's known for it. She did agree to sell two of them this week, but if she'd succeeded in her plan to take me, the sale would probably have been challenged. I don't know if that helps, but it was very unusual."

"So, if she didn't sell anything, how did she make a living?"

"Oh, she sold, just not the original pieces. She commissioned reproductions. They're great sellers, so I'm sure she has a more than comfortable income. She may have money coming in from somewhere else, but I wouldn't know that." Mallory felt bad for not telling Chas about the sculptures. She needed to call her again. What if Sheva tried to get them back? *Are they in danger?* "The ladies who bought the sculptures, do you think they'll be safe? You should watch their home, too. She's crazy enough to try and steal them back."

"Who bought the sculptures?"

Mallory wrote down the contact information for Chas and Christina.

"Thanks, we'll contact the state police in Connecticut to be on the safe side. Well, we better be going. You take care, Ms. Tucker. Remember, as long as she's out there, you're at risk. Don't take unnecessary chances."

Like she needed a reminder. She wasn't taking any chances. "I won't, thank you."

She closed the door behind them and went back to the table to clean up the remnants of her lunch. She had to call Chas, and more importantly, she had to get to the hospital.

Her phone rang, making her jump. She had left it on the couch, so she dropped down to take the call. Sanford Tucker. Damn, she'd forgotten to call her.

"Hello, Mother."

"Darling, are you okay? I heard about what happened. You're coming out to the island, right?"

Her mother's normally commanding voice had a waver in it today. Mallory felt her heart warm knowing her mother was worried about her. "Yes, I'm fine. Shaken, but okay. I think I'm going to stay in the city. I need to get back to work." *And I want to be close to Kadence.*

"Mallory, you've been attacked and drugged. You need to take some time to deal with this. I understand Sheva is still out there. Don't you think you'd be safer here with me?"

"I know, but I can't leave, Mother, I need to be here, in case—"

"In case what? You need to take time to heal, honey. Trauma induces fear, and if you don't come to grips with it, it ends up doing more harm than the event itself. You need to be in a peaceful quiet place to confront your fears. Believe me, you won't be sorry in the end."

"In case my friend Kadence needs me. She's all alone, Mother. I can't abandon her."

"How is she? I heard she was injured when she rescued you."

"Not good." Mallory's guilt flooded her and she couldn't help but open up. "Oh, Mother, her hand was crushed. Tarin said she's despondent. It's all my fault. What if she can never paint again?"

"Nonsense, you didn't cause the injury, and Tarin said it was one hand that was crushed, yes? She has another hand. We won't let her wallow in this. I'll get the best therapist possible to work with her, but here, on Monhegan. You both need to heal. Wait, you say Tarin said? Does that mean you haven't seen her yourself?"

"She didn't want to see me. She must blame me, and I think seeing me will just upset her."

"Oh, my goodness. You are my daughter, right? You don't have the sense God gave a goose. Her hand was crushed saving you. She obviously thought it was worth the risk to fight off that sculptor. You're compounding her injury by staying away, don't you see that?

My God, Mallory, it's plain cruelty not to go thank her, at the very least. Tell me you'll do that, right away."

"Yes, Mother. I was about to go to the hospital when you called." Her mother's words reassured her that she was doing the right thing by going back to the hospital, even if Kadence didn't want to see her.

"Good. And be ready to leave for the island in the morning. I'm coming to pick you up. When she's well enough, I'll bring Ms. Munroe out, too."

"Yes, Mother." Mallory felt the familiar smothering sensation of Sanford's maternal instincts. She fell back into the pattern of her childhood, answering with simple compliance, but the feelings of reluctance and resistance were strangely absent. She'd gotten so good at redirecting her mother's overbearing need to make every decision for her, but now she appreciated it. She wanted to be smothered, protected, loved. It *would* be good to be on the island, to take time to deal with the emotions the attack brought up. The knot of fear unwound in her stomach. *I could use a little mothering and so could Kadence.*

"I'll see you in the morning."

"Yes, Mother."

"Good, I love you, my dear."

"I love you, too."

She hung up and called Chas to warn her about Sheva, then Tarin. She let him know she'd decided to go to Maine after all and would only be staying one more night. Then she called for a car to take her to the hospital. She needed to see Kadence. It was beyond time.

The room was quiet when she arrived. It looked like Kadence was asleep. She turned, looking for a chair when Kadence spoke.

"Aren't you going to say hello?"

Startled, Mallory jumped. "Oh, I thought you were sleeping."

"No, just counting divots in the ceiling."

She sounded so down. "Huh?"

"The little chinks in the ceiling tiles. That's how I spend my time. Counting."

Mallory walked to the bedside, her stomach tensing as she took in the huge wrap on her hand. She felt like everything inside her was being compacted into a tense ball of energy. She wanted to touch

Kadence, to give her some physical assurance that she was there, but Kadence was so distant. Like a wall had come between her and the world, one that nothing could breach.

How could she break that wall down? What would it take? "I want to thank you for saving me."

"Okay." Kadence's reply was monotone and her eyes never left the ceiling, but after a second, Mallory saw light hitting the tears sliding down her cheek.

She reached out and put her hand on her cheek, wiping the tears away. "Kadence, look at me. Please?"

She turned her head, and finally, Mallory could see her pain and fear breaking through her shell.

"Oh, Kadence." She leaned down and wrapped her arms around her, holding on tightly, hoping to feel something in return. It was slow, but eventually Mallory felt Kadence shaking and heard her crying. Her heart broke at the sound, so like the cry of a child it melted her.

"I'm here, you're not alone. It's going to be okay."

Kadence didn't answer, but her sobs became more pronounced and she pulled Mallory to her with her good arm.

"No matter what happened, you're not alone, Kadence. I'll always be here for you. Let it all out."

With Kadence pressed against her, she felt her own emotions swell and tip over, and soon she was crying as well. They held each other and cried themselves out. Finally, Kadence pushed Mallory up and asked for a tissue. She got the box so they could share. When they were cleaned up, Mallory sat beside her and held Kadence's good hand.

"I asked if I could see you while I was here, but they said you were sleeping. Then I tried to see you yesterday, but Tarin said you didn't want to see anyone. I should have come anyway. I'm so sorry about your hand. That's my fault. It wouldn't have happened if I'd believed you. I'm so, so sorry."

"It's not your fault. I sounded crazy, I know that. You were only doing what you thought was right."

"But it wasn't the right thing. You were right, and your hand..." She trailed off, not knowing what to say. How could she ever make it up to Kadence? She'd made this happen.

"My hand was the price for saving you. It was worth it, no matter what. I stopped her from taking you, and that's what counts."

Mallory noticed the way she avoided looking at her hand. *She's given up already. I have to change that.* "What do the doctors say about your recovery?"

"Sheesh, you don't want to know."

Kadence's already pale face blanched, and Mallory dreaded what would come, but she had to know. "Yes, I do." She not only wanted to know, she *needed* to know. She had to have some sense of what Kadence was dealing with so she could help her.

Looking at Kadence, so helpless, so lost, she felt an aching sense of rightness. She needed to know so she could heal with Kadence. She pulled Kadence's hand to her cheek, and willed the feeling to flow from her and into Kadence. It was as if warm chocolate was flowing through her instead of blood. Sweet and rich, it nourished her soul and made the hard, rough places that had dominated her smooth over and soften. She knew it was working when Kadence uncurled her fingers and brushed gently at her cheek.

Mallory stood and leaned over her, kissing her like the first time, but with so much more. The kiss became a bond, almost holy, between them as they explored the depth of each other. Finally, Kadence broke the spell by pulling back to catch her breath. Her eyes never left Mallory's and they spoke, without words, the feelings they shared.

"Tell me," Mallory said into the perfect silence.

"I love you."

"I love you, too."

They kissed again, so deep that the emotions inside became too big and they were crying again. This time, the tears were completely different, tears of joy.

"I love you," Mallory said again, "but I still need to know what the doctors are saying."

"I know. It's not good. They completed the second surgery today, and reattached the tendons. The ulnar nerve was in bad shape. They're not sure how much feeling I'll get back. One more surgery tomorrow to close. The doctor said we should know about nerve response in the next forty-eight hours, but it could be a year before we know the full extent of the damage. He said it's possible I'll have full functionality back, but they can't be sure."

Mallory knew that had to be devastating news. Her hand was her outlet, her way of expressing her emotions. "Hm. Well, we'll do everything they tell us to do to make sure you get back as much as you can."

Kadence looked up and almost smiled. "We will, huh?"

The feelings that welled up inside her were powerful. Whatever happened, she wouldn't take a chance on losing Kadence. "Yes. You saved my life, but more importantly, you saved my heart. I'm not letting you go again, Kadence Munroe."

Mallory watched the color come back into Kadence's face. Was she blushing? "Lucky me. I feel better than I have all week. No matter what, with you beside me, everything else will come together."

"Mother wants me to bring you out to Monhegan to recuperate. What do you say?"

"I say, I'll go where you go. If you're going to Maine, so am I."

She smiled and Mallory felt her heart turn over. *I'd do anything for that smile.* "Good answer."

"What about Sheva? Have they caught her yet?"

"Not so far as I know. They were at Tarin's asking me questions before I came here. It's only a matter of time, though. She can't hide for long." Mallory kept her fear from creeping into her voice. She needed to be strong for Kadence. She wasn't going to let anything happen to her.

"I suppose you're right. I'm sleepy. Will you stay while I rest? Please?"

"You can't get rid of me. I'll be here. Sleep, love."

Mallory watched as Kadence's eyelids dipped and dipped then closed. She held her hand fast as she slept, knowing the connection made her feel better and hoping it did the same for Kadence.

CHAPTER TWENTY-ONE

Sheva fired the furnace, testing to see that it came up to the proper temperature. Satisfied that it was adequate, she checked her molding supplies. She had several large containers of Alja-Safe alginate on hand. She loved the roll-on product because it captured the minutest detail. It also had a short curing time, and that mattered. It was crucial that the curing process was complete before any of the body's fluids escaped. That would ruin the molding process, and she only had one chance. She knew precisely what she needed after doing it so many times.

It would be a challenge to complete the final two stages on her own, but she always did the silicon mold alone anyway. Maybe she could find some likely assistants in one of the nearby towns. Working with molten metal generally appealed to teenagers. She regretted the loss of her well trained assistants, but there was no helping that. They were in New York, and she was in the ass-end of New Jersey.

The slurry vat was ready, as was the silica bath, so all she needed now was her model. *Mallory.* She had to go back into the city and find a way to capture her. It would be dangerous, but she had to do it. She was *Malice*; she'd proved it by wrecking everything Sheva had made. Her soul would replace the ones she'd had to leave behind. *When I've got you, and your soul is captured, it will correct the balance and my life will be mine again.*

She'd purchased another old panel van from the nearby car lot, so she had her transportation, now she just needed her transformation. She took a last look at herself before beginning. She cut at her thick dark hair with the razor-sharp edge of the fifteen-inch Bowie knife she'd bought at the hunting store. Wisps of hair tumbled down her shirt to pile around her feet.

When she looked back into the mirror, a cloud of black wafted across her face, cut jaggedly, just below her ears. *Nice.* She trimmed the ends with shears and smoothed the jagged bits as best she could. The bleaching came next. Her eyes burned as the chemicals did their work, turning her ebony hair to silver white. She'd pay the price for this later when the hair started breaking off, but for now, it was perfect.

Her pale complexion was suited to the white hair, so now she only need rid herself of the dark brows. A quick job with the bleach and a new outfit finished her off. She looked like a throwback to the early eighties punk scene. No one who'd ever met her would recognize her. It was time.

She loaded up her newly minted grab box, a plywood box lined with foam rubber acoustic tiles to mask sound, and headed back to New York. Mallory would be able to make as much noise as she liked and no one would be the wiser. She just had to find the moment to snatch her.

She decided it was risky sleeping in the van, so she parked it at the airport long term parking and took the train into Chelsea. There was a hostel there with cheap nondescript rooms, and she was lucky enough to book one. Only three city blocks from the gallery, it was the perfect place to watch for an opportunity.

When it was close to closing time at the gallery, she dressed in the multicolored leggings with cat faces all over them, and an oversized white sweatshirt she'd bought in New Jersey, so she could look more like a tourist and less like the master sculptor people knew. She tugged a hair band over her white head and walked toward the gallery. She knew Mallory always took the train to and from work, unless she had to be there after dark, so she felt certain she would see her on the street. A convenient street vendor made waiting near the entrance fairly easy.

As the gallery began its closing, she watched the people leaving, first the patrons, then the support staff, and finally, the lighting changed from day to night, and she saw Tarin exit the building. He was alone, though, so that meant Mallory was either staying late, doubtful after the attack, or she wasn't working. The large plywood sheet covering the broken window kept her from seeing as much as she'd like. Were her sculptures still there or had they been moved? She watched Tarin walk down the street and wondered if following him would be worth her time. She decided against it when she noticed the police car sitting in the alleyway beside the building. No sense arousing suspicion. She bought a hot dog from a street vendor and went back to her room. Sooner or later, Mallory would return to the gallery. She would be ready.

❖

Mallory waited anxiously to hear how the final surgery went. They had taken Kadence to the operating room at seven that morning. The doctor hadn't yet come out to talk to her, so she was worried. *Why is it taking so long? It's been five hours.* Her stomach churned, and she felt panic building. When she'd finally decided she couldn't wait any more, the door opened and the doctor came in. She couldn't tell by looking if it was good news or bad. He looked exhausted.

"Ms. Tucker, we're finished. Things went about as well as expected. We had some trouble, but we finally got the wound closed. From here out it's going to be all about the therapy."

"So, she's okay? Will she be able to use her hand?"

"Only time will tell. As I said, her physical therapy is key to regaining use of her hand. We won't know about the nerve function for a while. The median and ulnar nerves were compressed badly. It may be that she regains full sensation and use of the hand, or she may have only partial nerve recovery. It's pointless to speculate until we reach a point in healing that we can assess these things. That could take several weeks. Try to stay positive. As I told Kadence, I've seen full recoveries, but a lot of it has to do with the physical therapy and effort the patient puts in after. For now, what's going to trouble her most is the donor site for the skin graft. That's going to be painful and require daily attention by a skilled nurse. We'll want that somewhat healed before we discharge her."

"I don't understand why you had to take skin from her leg. Why couldn't you use the skin that was there?"

"There had been partial degloving. That means the skin was separated from the fascia and went without proper blood flow. Basically, it died. This happens in crush injuries. Luckily, there was no compartment syndrome, so her muscle and tendon recovery should be good."

Mallory felt sick to her stomach. It was so much worse than she'd imagined. Degloving? She drank a sip of water to wash the bile down. "Okay, thank you for talking to me."

"No problem. When you see her, you'll notice she's in a splint. We've superglued some bands to her nail beds for therapy. She needs to keep from overusing those tendons, but she does need to stretch them. Will you be with her at home?"

I'll be with her as long as forever. It made her feel warm inside, thinking about being with Kadence. "Yes, actually, we'll be traveling to Maine as soon as you think it's okay."

"Well, as I said, we'll keep her here until we reach a stage in healing that she can manage on her own. I'm guessing about two weeks."

Mallory was stunned. She'd thought they'd be able to leave later today or tomorrow at the latest, but if Kadence needed to be hospitalized for an additional two weeks, she would handle it. It brought home, again, just how seriously injured Kadence was, all thanks to saving Mallory's life. She thanked the doctor and called her mother. After explaining the situation with Kadence and her need to be close by, they agreed that she and Kadence would wait until she was released before traveling to Monhegan. Her mother insisted on coming to New York until then, so Mallory would have to go home to tidy up before her arrival. She'd get Tarin's housecleaner to meet her there. She'd appreciate the extra work, and Mallory wouldn't be alone. First, she would have to wait until Kadence was awake and she could spend some time with her.

Kadence was back in her room a half hour later, and Mallory sat beside her, watching the gentle rise and fall of her breathing. She'd wrapped Kadence's good hand in her own and was content to wait for her to wake.

When her eyelids began to flutter, she squeezed her hand to let her know she wasn't alone. Kadence turned her head and smiled at her. Heat rushed through her at that smile, making her choke up. She cleared her throat.

"Hey, sleepy. How're you feeling?"

"Like I'm drugged. How're you feeling?"

Mallory laughed. *Leave it to Kadence to think of my feelings at a time like this.* "I'm good. The doctor said things went well."

"Yeah?"

"Mm-hmm. You've got a splint now, and there are some bands on your fingernails." She touched the long rubber bands glued on each of Kadence's nails. "He said the therapist would show you how to use those."

"Cool. Did he say when I can get out of here?"

Mallory knew this would be disappointing news, so she took Kadence's good hand in both of hers. "About that, yeah. It's going to be a couple of weeks."

"What? Why?"

"You had a skin graft, and the donor site has to be cared for here. It should be healed enough for home care in two weeks."

"But, that's…"

Mallory watched Kadence's face fall. She looked so sad. She knew it would be hard. She didn't want to be separated from her either, not now, not ever.

"It's okay, we'll get through this. I'll be here every day with you. I promise."

"But how can you? You're going to Maine today."

Mallory shook her head. "I was going to Maine. This changes my plans. I'm not going until you can come with me." *No matter what, I'm not leaving you.*

Panic rose in Kadence's eyes. "Mal, you have to go. You need to be safe. Sheva is still out there and you're at risk."

She crossed her arms over her chest, signaling that the decision was made. "I'm not going to let fear rule my life. My mother will stay with me. She'll be thrilled, and I won't be alone, okay?"

That should be reassuring, but Kadence still looked worried.

"You'll be careful, right?"

"Of course I will. I've got lots of things to look forward to. I'm not going to do anything that risks that." She ran her hand through Kadence's hair to ease her worries.

"Promise?"

Mallory leaned forward and kissed her, their lips melding and making them one.

"I promise. Now you should try and sleep some more. I'm going to go get ready for Mother. I'll be back as soon as she arrives. Be prepared. She's going to insist on coming in here to see you."

Mallory kissed her again and watched as sleep drew her down. She looked so beautiful, it made her heart ache. She ran a hand over her tangle of curls. *My sweet Kadence, I won't ever let you down.* The wave of emotion that swept through her nearly overwhelmed her. She'd nearly lost this. She'd never risk losing it again.

When she was sure Kadence was deeply asleep, she left to buy a few groceries and meet the cleaning person at her apartment.

Sheva watched her walk to the door of her building. She was as beautiful today as she'd been the first time she'd seen her, the moment she'd known she had to enshroud her in bronze and capture her soul. It was time. She moved quickly across the street and entered the building after her. It was too simple. In moments, she'd caught up to her, and when she opened her door, she forced her way in behind her, syringe of GHB already in hand.

Mallory never knew what happened, never even saw her. She crumpled to the floor, spilling groceries across the smooth hardwood.

She had to act fast to find a place to stash her until she could return with her grab box. She checked the back stair, going down to each level and locking the inner locks on the doors behind her. That would keep anyone from stumbling in on her. She carried Mallory over her shoulder into the stairwell, pulling her door closed behind her. When she reached the ground level, she continued into the basement. There were storage lockers for the apartments here. It took her only a few minutes to find an empty one. She dumped Mallory in and closed the door.

She'd be out for a while, hopefully long enough for her to get back with the van and grab box. If not, she'd risk getting caught, but everything felt so perfect. She'd moved the van to a lot a few blocks away this morning. It had felt right, and now she knew why. She had to make it back before Mallory woke. It had to happen. This was her calling, her gift, to create works of beauty infused with the souls of beautiful women. If it wasn't endowed from above, how had she stayed free all this time?

Traffic was light for midday, another sign. She was back at Mallory's apartment within ten minutes. She should still be soundly asleep. Sheva asked the first likely homeless man if she could pay him to help carry her box to her storage area. At first, he waved her off, but when she showed him the twenty, he smiled and helped her pull the box out and carry it down to the basement.

She'd made the box like a trunk, making it easier to disguise what it held. She handed him the money after they placed the trunk on the basement floor. She walked him back up to the street before returning to the basement. In moments, she had Mallory tucked inside the box, her lithe body bent at the knees, her arms wrapped around them. She was like a sleeping angel. *An angel who ruined my life.*

Sheva closed the lid, latched and padlocked the hasps. When she went back up to the street, she found a high school kid walking by and asked him for his help. He was happy to give her a hand and it cost her nothing.

She waved good-bye after giving him her thanks, then climbed into the van and drove away.

CHAPTER TWENTY-TWO

Kadence woke, fuzzy-headed from the anesthesia. She looked for Mallory, but she was alone in the room. *How long was I asleep?* The ache in her arm was ramping up as the painkiller wore off. She thumbed the morphine drip and waited for relief.

There was a tapping on the door and Sanford Tucker peeked around its edge.

"Hello, sleepyhead. May I come in?"

"Please."

"How are you feeling? Has my daughter been taking good care of you?"

Awful, that's how she felt. Depressed and miserable, except for Mallory. How could she say that, though? Sanford didn't really want the answer to her question, it was just what was supposed to be said. She gave the perfunctory answer.

"Come now, I mean it. How are you feeling? You've had quite a shock, not to mention injury. Are you staying positive? Or are you letting that sculptress beat you?"

Kadence smiled. Leave it to Sanford. "I'm doing okay, I guess. It's kind of hard knowing how I really feel, since they keep taking me in and out of surgery."

"I'm sure that's disorienting. And Mallory? Is she taking care of things for you?"

"She is. She's been wonderful."

"Good, I'm glad to hear that. Where is she?"

"She said something about getting ready for you. I figured she went to the lobby to meet you. You didn't see her?" Kadence felt panic rising. Had she misunderstood?

"No. But I wasn't looking. I'll go back down and see if I can find her. She probably curled up in a chair and didn't see me come in. Don't worry, I'm sure she's here somewhere. I'll find her."

But she didn't. After thoroughly checking the lobby Sanford returned. "I tried calling her, but she's not picking up her cell or her home phone."

Kadence looked up and saw her panic mirrored in Sanford's eyes. Fear was like a tidal wave washing over her. Where was Mallory? Her heart was a storm of misery, and frustration at her trapped position made her powerless to do anything to find her.

Sanford took control, helping Kadence shake off her fear. "We have to stay calm. We need to focus on finding her. We'll call the police and security, then the gallery. Someone must have heard from her."

"Call Tarin, maybe he's heard from her. Or maybe the detectives have asked her to come to the station." It could be something simple. *Don't panic.*

Sanford called security first, then the detectives who'd been working on the case. Neither had heard from Mallory. Tarin was no help either. The last he'd heard she was leaving for Maine. The detectives were sending uniformed officers to her apartment, in case she'd gone there, and more to the hospital to check security footage.

"She couldn't have gone home. She knows it's not safe," Kadence said, "She promised me she'd stay safe. They'll find her. They have to."

When the phone rang ten minutes later, it was Kadence who answered.

"Hello?"

"Ms. Munroe? It's Detective Simms. I've got some news about Ms. Tucker. Is her mother still with you?"

"Yes, she's here."

"Good, now, I don't want you to panic, but it looks like something has happened to Ms. Tucker."

Kadence felt her body turn to jelly and nearly lost her grip on the phone "What do you mean something's happened to her?"

"It's obvious from her apartment that someone interfered with her."

"What? What happened in her apartment?"

"The door was ajar and there were groceries spilled across the room, and her purse was left behind as well. Her car is there, but she definitely isn't in her apartment. That's all we know. We have to presume she was the one who opened the door, and therefore, she was assaulted and is now missing."

Kadence lost it. The phone tumbled out of her hand to clatter to the floor. *She's missing.* It had all been for nothing. Sheva had gotten her anyway. She closed her eyes and tried to shut out the sound of Sanford retrieving the phone and talking to Simms. She just wanted to die, to close everything out and be gone. If Mallory was gone, she wanted to go, too.

The hum of Sanford's voice was all she was aware of. As it rose and fell, she wondered if there was a way to override the pump on her morphine. If she could open the line and let the bag drip freely into her arm, oblivion would be a gentle sleep.

She was studying the mechanism when she subconsciously recognized a change in Sanford's voice. She was excited about something. Curiosity and hope drew her back from the edge.

"What? What's happening?"

"It's good news. Just wait, I'll tell you in a minute."

She watched as Sanford visibly brightened, almost hopping with excitement. Good news, it was good news. *They must have found her. She must be safe.*

Sanford disconnected the call and grasped Kadence's hand. She could feel her shaking through her intense grip.

"Please tell me what it is. I have to know if she's safe."

"Okay, I'm going to tell you, but promise me you'll not overreact. You have to try to keep from jarring your hand."

"I promise, just tell me, for God's sake."

"They haven't found her, that's not it, but they have found a property in New Jersey that belongs to Sheva. It's under her real name, a small foundry in Lambertville, west of Trenton. They're cooperating with the New Jersey State Police and the feds to get a team out there. If she has her, that must be where she's taking her. They said the operation should be underway in less than an hour."

"What if Mallory doesn't have an hour? Why is this happening?" Sobs tore from her, as her inability to keep Mallory safe ripped her apart. She'd never forgive herself if something happened to her, never.

"Hush, now." Sanford held her, stroking her hair and comforting her. "This isn't your fault. Just calm down. They're going to rescue her, I'm sure of it. And this time, Sheva won't get away, so you and Mallory can relax."

Kadence wanted to believe that, but it was hard. The rock of fear wouldn't be easily moved. Until she knew for certain that Mallory was safe, she couldn't believe it.

The next few hours were torture, not knowing what was happening, or if they were off the mark. Tarin joined them after an hour, lending his support to Kadence and Sanford. Kadence briefly considered escaping from the hospital, but she wasn't supposed to move her arm, and the skin graft on her leg meant she could barely walk. She'd never felt so helpless.

Every time the phone rang, Kadence jumped, hoping for news, but it usually turned out to be nothing. They needed something to assure them that things were going well, but silence was all they received.

❖

Sheva drove north from the city, not wanting her van to be photographed in toll plazas along the way. She knew if she went through White Plains and Peekskill it would be a much longer drive, but she didn't want to take any chances. She would be back at her foundry in a little over five hours, plenty of time to plan her next step.

She couldn't believe how easily she had claimed Mallory. It had been so smooth she'd had to pinch herself when she got back out of the city. Someone was looking out for her, that's for certain. When she cast Mallory, her final figure, the world would see why she was driven to do these things. She'd given up the idea of casting the painter. She had no real connection to her, and adding her would have perverted her work, taking it from beauty to repulsiveness with a single pouring of molten bronze. No, she had to finish her work in the vein it had begun, beauty and purity of soul. Mallory wouldn't be *Malice*, she'd be *Patience*, because that's what it took to capture her.

She settled in for the long drive north, then south. By the time they reached Bridgewater, she felt her excitement rising. Her foundry was so isolated she would have all the time she needed to help Mallory show the best part of her soul. She would take that time to relish the experiences she had enjoyed in following her calling. She would have time, when *Patience* was complete, to assess what she should do next, where she should go. The satisfaction she'd garnered from capturing women's souls would be hard to top, but she knew she would be given a new calling, a higher calling. She felt weak with anticipation of her new direction.

All that was required of her was to complete this path and the next would be revealed. Her near failure of four days ago had been bitter, but in hindsight, she realized it had been her own fault. She'd known from the first that her job was to capture souls in the perfect moment of release. Turning from that and toward darker ideas had led to the fiasco. Now she was clear and wouldn't be deterred.

She practically bounced with excitement as she crossed into Mercer County and neared Lambertville. She was nearly there.

The turn-in for her property was somewhat obscured by the deep woods in and around it. She slid the van into the drive and pulled up toward the foundry. She parked the vehicle and jumped out, stretching her back and anticipating the thrill of applying the Alja-Safe. She would use her hands instead of a roller. She wanted the contact with Mallory's skin. But first, she'd have to remove her clothes and pose her.

Breathing deeply and shivering with anticipation at the thought of the next few hours, she opened the back doors of the van and tugged the grab box. It moved sluggishly, not wanting to exit the vehicle, but she pulled and tugged until it hit the smooth rollers on the ramp and slid down and into her foundry.

As she closed the van doors and moved to follow the box inside, light exploded around her. Her yard was lit by high-power light beams from all directions, and a booming voice echoed through some sound system.

"Martha Graves, stop where you are and put your hands in the air. This is the New Jersey State Police and we have a warrant for your arrest."

Sheva froze. How could this be? She'd been so careful. No one had known about this property. Worse, if they knew who she was, they must know where she'd come from, and who she had in the box. She dove for the roller ramp, sliding on her belly into the foundry right behind the box. They couldn't stop her; it was meant for her to complete this.

She heard the shouting and running as they reacted to her quick escape. It would take them time to get through the doors. She slammed the iron door closed and locked the ramp well. Nice thing about a foundry, there were plenty of metal doors around to secure the premises.

The clanging on the iron doors had begun, deafening her, but she didn't need to hear to create. She unlocked the box and pulled Mallory out and hefted her onto a table. Using a razor, she quickly cut away her clothes. She no longer had the maquette to show her how she'd meant to pose her, but it didn't matter. That maquette had been corrupted. She'd made it when she was at the whim of darkness, but now she was back in the hands of light. The light would guide her, and Mallory would be captured as she was meant to be.

Closing her eyes, she let her hands roam over her unconscious body, moving this joint, folding that hand. When done, she opened her eyes and saw perfection. There was no time to waste in appreciating this part of the process, though, as she heard the wail and whine of power grinders working to open the doors.

She pulled out four five-gallon buckets of Alja-Safe and filled a vat with the viscous stuff. Taking a smaller bucket, she scooped some up and poured it over the reclining figure. *Faster, must be faster.* She dipped and poured and dipped and poured, until gradually, Mallory's body was covered in a layer of rubberized silicone. It would harden in twelve minutes, so she needed to cover her entire figure, fast. Like the others, Mallory would suffocate under the alginate, and once in the kiln, her body would turn to ash, cremated, leaving behind only the beautiful bronze that had captured her soul.

The head and shoulders were all she had left when the whine ended sharply with a chink, and she knew they'd broken the lock. She heard, rather than saw, the men and women surround her. She didn't slow her movements. One more pour and it would be done. She dipped the final bucket and lifted it high.

"Freeze! Drop the bucket and back away from her, or we will shoot."

Let them. She was a god, and she had to finish this. She tilted the bucket forward, and the slow river of pink liquid sloshed forward, falling toward Mallory's upturned face.

The noise was greater than anything she'd ever heard, and the punch of the bullet sliding into her middle rocketed her body away from Mallory, the bucket flying harmlessly away to a far corner. The fire inside her was so painful she could do nothing but scream. *This must be what it feels like, to be filled with molten bronze.* Part of her cherished the feeling, a last connection to her beautiful models. She tumbled to the ground in a heap, her breath rattling. The pain faded, as did the sounds around her, until only her own breath filled her ears. She continued to stare at Mallory, her soul uncaptured, Sheva's final masterpiece ruined. She closed her eyes as the darkness claimed her.

Mallory walked behind the wheelchair toward reception. It was finally release day and her mother was waiting out front with the car. They would be on their way to Monhegan in a few minutes. Sanford had spent the past two weeks helping Kadence adjust to the idea of her injured hand. She was much more positive and looking forward to the daily therapy Sanford had arranged.

The shock of being drugged senseless and nearly being killed by that lunatic for the second time was slowly shifting, letting the future dominate her thinking. She still woke screaming from nightmares of being kidnapped, but she always woke to the warmth of Kadence's hand in hers.

She'd spent every night since being rescued on a rollaway bed in Kadence's room. Nothing else gave her the security she needed to feel safe. Only Kadence could give her that.

Sanford had arranged for private counseling for both of them, something she knew she'd be thankful for at some point, but couldn't think about right now. Right now, she could only think about the next breath, the next step, the next touch of Kadence's good hand. They were going to come out on the other side of this, together.

The memory of waking in the foundry, the echo of the shot ringing in her ears, pink goo running all over her naked body, made her shiver. The State Police had been quick to get help, and she'd been moved outside and hosed off, but it'd felt like an invasion. All those eyes on her, trying to reassure her, but only adding to her discomfort.

The two female officers had stood in front of her holding a drape to offer her some privacy, but she'd needed someone to wash the goo off, and she wasn't strong enough to stand. So they'd handed the drape to male officers and come to her aid. Once she was clean, they'd wrapped her in a blanket and stayed with her until the ambulance arrived.

As the grogginess lifted from the drugs, she'd seen Sheva's lifeless body lying in a heap where she'd fallen. It took a moment for it to all sink in. She'd come after her and this time had succeeded in carrying her off. If not for good police work, she'd be dead, covered in alginate, waiting to be demolded. She'd have suffocated under the silicon without ever having woken up. She wondered if the other women Sheva had killed had been awake, and she knew deep down they had. That knowledge had been part of her nightmares every night.

She'd lost her mind a little when she realized how close it had been, sobbing uncontrollably and rocking back and forth. Thank God for the detectives back in New York and for the police officers here. The EMTs had checked her over when she refused to go to the hospital. They'd been reluctant, but when she told them she would be going straight to Presbyterian Hospital in New York, they relented. Simms and Morris arrived soon after and Simms immediately loaded her into the car for the trip back to the city. Morris stayed to tie up loose ends with the New Jersey police.

Her relief at pulling up in front of Presbyterian was like cool water on a hot day. Her mother and Tarin met her outside and went with her to the emergency room. A few hours later, she was by Kadence's side, and there she remained.

Now, they were going to Monhegan. Her mother had arranged a flight to Bangor on a private jet, then they would take the ferry. Tarin would manage the gallery in Mallory's absence and they would have time to heal. As the cool morning air hit her, Mallory inhaled and let herself be in the moment. The monsters were gone now, and she felt something inside give. Warmth flowed through her, and she pulled Kadence's hand to her lips and kissed it.

Kadence smiled up at her. The dark shadows of depression were gone from her face, but it was still too pale and too thin. Mallory was going to make sure and change that, starting today.

CHAPTER TWENTY-THREE

Kadence poured her happiness into the painting as her left hand flew across the canvas. Sharp waves of yellow and pink fought with each other in the boundaries of the painting. It was going to be phenomenal when she finished it. Her heart was in this painting, the pure joy of the past six months with Mallory.

There had been plenty of pain, too, but it was healing pain. Sanford had hired Bertram Black, a fantastic physical therapist, and put him up in her sea cottage so he could work with Kadence several times a day. It was paying off. Her right hand was showing improvement almost daily now. They'd had a scare when the sensation didn't return to the left side of her hand, but a minor surgery had fixed that. Scar tissue had been impinging on the nerve in her palm. She wasn't ready to use the hand full-time, but she'd moved to a light brace and was able to go several hours with nothing on it twice a week.

She stepped back to look at her painting from a distance when she heard Mallory's laughter from the terrace. Her smile widened as she thought about how far she'd come. How far they'd come *together*. When she met Mallory, she'd been so shutdown. She'd had little confidence in her work, no close friends or family, and had not expected that to change.

Now, her life was full of people—Mallory, Sanford, and the friends on Monhegan who'd adopted Kadence and Mallory into their hearts. And Chas and Christina Lorde, that had been a surprise. When the two women heard the story behind the sculptures they'd purchased, they had them melted down and reformed into a memorial for all Sheva's victims. Sheva's death meant they couldn't question her about the women she'd killed, and because she'd moved around there was no way to get to the previous kilns she might have used to check for DNA. But they'd used Kadence's work as a base, and had quickly worked out who all the victims were. They'd notified the families, who got an awful kind of closure.

Now they were regular visitors to Monhegan and had asked Kadence and Mallory to join them on a trip to Europe later that year to expand their art collection.

And Mallory, her heart. She'd been so determined to prove her father's assumptions about her wrong, that she'd lost sight of what she really wanted. She'd given up her directorship to found a nonprofit dedicated to developing young artists in low income areas. She was vibrant and alive in a way Kadence had never seen before.

"Hey there, cutie, it's your turn with Dr. Parker. She's waiting on the terrace." Mallory had snuck up behind her and slid one arm around her waist. The other traced the dragon's neck across her shoulder. Kadence smiled thinking about when she'd finally shown Mallory the dragon. She'd traced its form over and over, making Kadence break out in gooseflesh. It was Mallory's touchstone, now, her dragon. The destruction and creation it symbolized held power for them both. Mallory's breath was hot on Kadence's neck, making all kinds of places comfortably warm.

"Okay. But don't wander off while I'm with her. I've got plans for you later."

Mallory raised her eyebrow and smiled wickedly. "Is that so?"

"It is. Bertram gave me some new exercises to work on, and I think you're going to like them." She gave the same wicked smile right back.

They'd recovered from their bouts with nightmares and not letting each other out of sight, thanks to Dr. Parker, but they'd had a hard time with intimacy. They hadn't been celibate or anything, but Kadence had a hard time having to be the pillow queen all the time. Today she'd gotten clearance from Bertram to try something different. She couldn't wait.

She washed her brushes and cleaned her palette then rushed to the terrace for her hour with Dr. Parker. When they'd finished she found Mallory sitting on a lounge chair in the garden.

"Hi, beautiful. Come with me." She held her hand, her right hand, out to Mallory and led her down to the boathouse. It was more of a clubhouse than a boathouse. Decked out with deep-seated chaise lounges and a glass wall that looked out over the Atlantic, it was way more romantic than a place to store a boat.

It was the perfect place for what Kadence had in mind. She drew Mallory to her, untying the simple shoulder ties of her sundress and letting it slip down her body. She was bare beneath the dress, and Kadence felt her body react. She ran her hands down the smooth lines of Mallory's torso and then moved them to her bottom. She pulled her toward her gently until Mallory gasped with arousal.

Kadence kissed the tender flesh of her neck and felt Mallory respond, her hands gripping Kadence's curly hair. She bent her back slightly and kissed her way down to Mallory's full breasts, sucking each nipple to a tight point.

"Oh, Kay, don't stop." Mallory was breathless, and Kadence knew she was having the desired effect on her.

She continued down until she was even with Mallory's belly. It was her favorite part of Mallory. So soft and responsive. She loved to kiss and suck at the tender flesh, watching as bumps erupted across the surface. As she kissed her, she moved her left hand to the warm cleft between Mallory's legs. So wet, so ready for her. She slid one finger along either side of Mallory's clitoris, stroking her, making her whole body writhe.

She sensed the change in Mallory's body as she got close and shifted down until her lips replaced the fingers. She slowly moved the fingers into her and built a rhythm that matched Mallory's own. Her right hand was gently cupping Mallory's bottom, stabilizing them both.

At exactly the moment Mallory crested and fell into her orgasm, Kadence sucked her clitoris with more force and felt herself explode as Mallory moaned with pleasure.

God, she felt so complete when they were together, and this time, she'd been the one leading. It made her orgasm ridiculously delicious, hearing the sounds of her love echoing through the warm room, knowing it was because of her.

Mallory slumped down, wrapping Kadence's head in her arms. Kadence felt wet warm tears on her scalp.

"What is it, baby? Did I hurt you?"

"No, love. You didn't hurt me. You released my soul and it filled this whole room. I love you so much."

Kadence felt the words like water in the desert. She beamed with joy as she kissed at Mallory's neck again.

"I love you too, my heart. I love loving you."

Kadence leaned into Mallory, loving the feel of her arms around her. This was what life was about. All her loneliness and insecurities had been made of mist and broke apart when she felt Mallory's heart beating against hers. She never felt like she wasn't enough or that she had something to prove. She had all she'd ever need.

About the Author

Laydin Michaels is a native Houstonian with deep Louisiana roots. She finds joy and happiness in the loving arms of her wife, MJ. Her life is also enriched by her son, CJ, and her four fur children. Her love of the written word started very early. She has been a voracious reader all her life.

Books Available from Bold Strokes Books

A Date to Die by Anne Laughlin. Someone is killing people close to Detective Kay Adler, who must look to her own troubled past for a suspect. There she finds more than one person seeking revenge against her. (978-1-63555-023-8)

Captured Soul by Laydin Michaels. Can Kadence Munroe save the woman she loves from a twisted killer, or will she lose her to a collector of souls? (978-1-62639-915-0)

Dawn's New Day by TJ Thomas. Can Dawn Oliver and Cam Cooper, two women who have loved and lost, open their hearts to love again? (978-1-63555-072-6)

Definite Possibility by Maggie Cummings. Sam Miller is just out for good times, but Lucy Weston makes her realize happily ever after is a definite possibility. (978-1-62639-909-9)

Eyes Like Those by Melissa Brayden. Isabel Chase and Taylor Andrews struggle between love and ambition from the writers' room on one of Hollywood's hottest TV shows. (978-1-63555-012-2)

Heart's Orders by Jaycie Morrison. Helen Tucker and Tee Owens escape hardscrabble lives to careers in the Women's Army Corps, but more than their hearts are at risk as friendship blossoms into love. (978-1-63555-073-3)

Hiding Out by Kay Bigelow. Treat Dandridge is unaware that her life is in danger from the murderer who is hunting the woman she's falling in love with, Mickey Heiden. (978-1-62639-983-9)

Omnipotence Enough by Sophia Kell Hagin. Can the tiny tool that abducted war veteran Jamie Gwynmorgan accidentally acquires help her escape an unknown enemy to reclaim her stolen life and the woman she deeply loves? (978-1-63555-037-5)

Summer's Cove by Aurora Rey. Emerson Lange moved to Provincetown to live in the moment, but when she meets Darcy Belo and her son Liam, her quest for summer romance becomes a family affair. (978-1-62639-971-6)

The Road to Wings by Julie Tizard. Lieutenant Casey Tompkins, air force student pilot, has to fly with the toughest instructor, Captain Kathryn "Hard Ass" Hardesty, fly a supersonic jet, and deal with a growing forbidden attraction. (978-1-62639-988-4)

Beauty and the Boss by Ali Vali. Ellis Renois is at the top of the fashion world, but she never expects her summer assistant Charlotte Hamner to tear her heart and her business apart like sharp scissors through cheap material. (978-1-62639-919-8)

Fury's Choice by Brey Willows. When gods walk amongst humans, can two women find a balance between love and faith? (978-1-62639-869-6)

Lessons in Desire by MJ Williamz. Can a summer love stand a four-month hiatus and still burn hot? (978-1-63555-019-1)

Lightning Chasers by Cass Sellars. For Sydney and Parker, being a couple was never what they had planned. Now they have to fight corruption, murder, and enemies hiding in plain sight just to hold on to each other. Lightning Series, Book Two. (978-1-62639-965-5)

Summer Fling by Jean Copeland. Still jaded from a breakup years earlier, Kate struggles to trust falling in love again when a summer fling with sexy young singer Jordan rocks her off her feet. (978-1-62639-981-5)

Take Me There by Julie Cannon. Adrienne and Sloan know it would be career suicide to mix business with pleasure, however tempting it is. But what's the harm? They're both consenting adults. Who would know? (978-1-62639-917-4)

The Girl Who Wasn't Dead by Samantha Boyette. A year ago, someone tried to kill Jenny Lewis. Tonight she's ready to find out who it was. (978-1-62639-950-1)

Unchained Memories by Dena Blake. Can a woman give herself completely when she's left a piece of herself behind? (978-1-62639-993-8)

Walking Through Shadows by Sheri Lewis Wohl. All Molly wanted to do was go backpacking…in her own century (978-1-62639-968-6)

A Lamentation of Swans by Valerie Bronwen. Ariel Montgomery returns to Sea Oats to try to save her broken marriage but soon finds herself also fighting to save her own life and catch a murderer. (978-1-62639-828-3)

Freedom to Love by Ronica Black. What happens when the woman who spent her lifetime worrying about caring for her family, finally finds the freedom to love without borders? (978-1-63555-001-6)

House of Fate by Barbara Ann Wright. Two women must throw off the lives they've known as a guardian and an assassin and save two rival houses before their secrets tear the galaxy apart. (978-1-62639-780-4)

Planning for Love by Erin Dutton. Could true love be the one thing that wedding coordinator Faith McKenna didn't plan for? (978-1-62639-954-9)

Sidebar by Carsen Taite. Judge Camille Avery and her clerk, attorney West Fallon, agree on little except their mutual attraction, but can their relationship and their careers survive a headline-grabbing case? (978-1-62639-752-1)

Sweet Boy and Wild One by T. L. Hayes. When Rachel Cole meets soulful singer Bobby Layton at an open mic, she is immediately in thrall. What she soon discovers will rock her world in ways she never imagined. (978-1-62639-963-1)

To Be Determined by Mardi Alexander and Laurie Eichler. Charlie Dickerson escapes her life in the US to rescue Australian wildlife with Pip Atkins, but can they save each other? (978-1-62639-946-4)

True Colors by Yolanda Wallace. Blogger Robby Rawlins plans to use First Daughter Taylor Crenshaw to get ahead, but she never planned on falling in love with her in the process. (978-1-62639-927-3)

Unexpected by Jenny Frame. When Dale McGuire falls for Rebecca Harper, the mother of the son she never knew she had, will Rebecca's troubled past stop them from making the family they both truly crave? (978-1-62639-942-6)

Canvas for Love by Charlotte Greene. When ghosts from Amelia's past threaten to undermine their relationship, Chloé must navigate the greatest romance of her life without losing sight of who she is. (978-1-62639-944-0)

Heart Stop by Radclyffe. Two women, one with a damaged body, the other a damaged spirit, challenge each other to dare to live again. (978-1-62639-899-3)

Repercussions by Jessica L. Webb. Someone planted information in Edie Black's brain and now they want it back, but with the protection of shy former soldier Skye Kenny, Edie has a chance at life and love. (978-1-62639-925-9)

Spark by Catherine Friend. Jamie's life is turned upside down when her consciousness travels back to 1560 and lands in the body of one of Queen Elizabeth I's ladies-in-waiting...or has she totally lost her grip on reality? (978-1-62639-930-3)

Taking Sides by Kathleen Knowles. When passion and politics collide, can love survive? (978-1-62639-876-4)

Thorns of the Past by Gun Brooke. Former cop Darcy Flynn's heart broke when her career on the force ended in disgrace, but perhaps saving Sabrina Hawk's life will mend it in more ways than one. (978-1-62639-857-3)

You Make Me Tremble by Karis Walsh. Seismologist Casey Radnor comes to the San Juan Islands to study an earthquake but finds her heart shaken by passion when she meets animal rescuer Iris Mallery. (978-1-62639-901-3)

Complications by MJ Williamz. Two women battle for the heart of one. (978-1-62639-769-9)

Crossing the Wide Forever by Missouri Vaun. As Cody Walsh and Lillie Ellis face the perils of the untamed West, they discover that love's uncharted frontier isn't for the weak in spirit or the faint of heart. (978-1-62639-851-1)

Fake It Till You Make It by M. Ullrich. Lies will lead to trouble, but can they lead to love? (978-1-62639-923-5)

Girls Next Door by Sandy Lowe and Stacia Seaman eds. Best-selling romance authors tell it from the heart—sexy, romantic stories of falling for the girls next door. (978-1-62639-916-7)

Pursuit by Jackie D. The pursuit of the most dangerous terrorist in America will crack the lines of friendship and love, and not everyone will make it out under the weight of duty and service. (978-1-62639-903-7)

Shameless by Brit Ryder. Confident Emery Pearson knows exactly what she's looking for in a no-strings-attached hookup, but can a spontaneous interlude open her heart to more? (978-1-63555-006-1)

The Practitioner by Ronica Black. Sometimes love comes calling whether you're ready for it or not. (978-1-62639-948-8)

Unlikely Match by Fiona Riley. When an ambitious PR exec and her super-rich coding geek-girl client fall in love, they learn that giving something up may be the only way to have everything. (978-1-62639-891-7)

Where Love Leads by Erin McKenzie. A high school counselor and the mom of her new student bond in support of the troubled girl, never expecting deeper feelings to emerge, testing the boundaries of their relationship. (978-1-62639-991-4)